5th Avenue

Whore

Val Edward Simone

A Morningside Publishing Book
Payson, Arizona

5th AVENUE WHORE

A Morningside Publishing Book

Text Copyright © 2017 by Val Edward Simone
All Rights Reserved.

Printed in the United States of America

Library of Congress Control Number: 2010905930

Printed Version
ISBN 978-1-936210-64-0

Cover Design: Val Edward Simone

For more books please visit:
www.valedwardsimone.com

Dedication:

MORNINGSIDE
PUBLISHING
PAYSON, ARIZONA

For Mickey Spillane…. You still the man!

With Special Thanks To:
Editor
Rita Samols

Musical Inspiration
Ernesto Cortazar II
Kevin Kern
Secret Garden

CHAPTER 1

She exploded into my life like a hydrogen bomb. And in the midst of that lethal blast, I knew I was a dead man and that she would be the cause of my demise.

It didn't really matter when the end came. I was going to die. There was no getting around it. Hell, the way I figured it, I was already dead. I just hadn't yet found the place to fall over and rot.

I should have known better right off. A woman like her doesn't just come drifting gently into a guy's life — at least not into *my* life. And there's rarely any good reason for it except to bring a nasty end to the poor sap who happens stupidly into her path. On that particular evening, the poor sap just happened to be me.

Bad timing, some would say. Bad luck, others would say. Simply put, it was bad. And I loved it. Yeah, I know, famous words from dead men like me.

That just sort of summed up my life, police detective Jacob Brewer — Jake to both friends and enemies alike.

I was beat. Battling with criminals can get brutal at times. Especially the kind that like to shoot back at cops. I refer to them as Darwin Award Wannabes.

It had been one of those days. It was a hell of a gun battle and even though I didn't get off a single shot myself, the surrounding gunfire left my ears ringing like a church bell for at least an hour after.

This time around the award went to a liquor store robber who had taken a hostage thinking his .45 pistol would be an even match against ten SWAT cops with automatic rifles. And it *was* an even-steven affair — for about two seconds.

By the end of the ceremony, the award winner got himself Swiss-cheesed and shipped off to the city dead shop — the morgue.

I knew the morgue well. Over the years I had spent a good deal of time there appreciating the silence of the dead. As strange as it may sound, I found it sort of peaceful there at times. It wasn't long, however, before I found that the dead have no sense of humor and they're not much fun to drink with. But that is a story for another time.

A recent case, a few months ago, involved a corporate Chief Financial Officer by the name of Arlen Cutley. It had taken me a full month to complete an investigation into his part in the case. Cutley was a well-known personality who murdered the Chairman of the Board and Chief Executive Officer of a very powerful media company after he was discovered having a very sordid affair with the CEO's wife. Cutley was about to be fired and decided that murder would prevent that from happening. His method of murder involved the use of a chain saw. Needless to say, I spent quite a bit of time working with the Medical Examiner at the morgue as he reformed the puzzle pieces of the CEO's body. I really hate morgues now.

I left the morgue and felt the dryness settling into my mouth. And now that I was finally off duty, I just wanted to drop by my favorite watering hole on the corner near my apartment and get hammered until I killed off enough brain cells to forget what I'd seen earlier that evening.

My alcoholism wasn't exactly a secret, but it wasn't exactly common knowledge either.

The department wasn't happy that I had this *alternative condition*. *Alternative Condition*. That's what the department called it. Sounded to me like some kind of alternate-state-of-existence thing. Hell, from my perspective, there was nothing *alternative* about it. I was a drunk, plain and simple. I knew it. I accepted it. It was normal to me.

In fact, that had been my typical life for the last ten years out of the twenty I had been on the force. I did my job during the day and then tried to drown away any memory of it that night. I was getting pretty good at it too.

Each and every desperate and disillusioned night, I'd destroy the recollection of each and every desperate and disillusioned day, only to repeat the horror the next morning. Yeah, it wasn't much of a life, but it was mine and there didn't seem any way of avoiding it short of opening up my veins in a warm bath, or eating a bullet — or drinking myself to death. That last option, apparently and unknowingly, had become my intended plan of escape.

Many have asked me why I don't just retire and get away from all this horror. I've asked myself that very question several times over the last few years. I still don't have a good answer, except that I'm a cop. It's not what I do, it's who I am. And *that* is the only excuse I offer to those who care to ask.

Now, normally, I don't go looking for trouble. Funny that. I mean how trouble always seems to find you when you're least looking for it. On that particular night, I sure as hell wasn't looking for it. But it found me just the same.

I was only a few steps away from slipping into the bar when she blew around the corner and detonated into my arms.

She was gorgeous — in her early thirties. Her blonde hair felt like silk as it slapped my face. Her sleek petite body was perfect. Her breasts pressed against me so hard and firm that I wanted to take her right there on the sidewalk. I didn't care if the world watched. Then it struck me. *So this is what the bringer of my death looks like.*

Little did I know just how prophetic that thought was.

She looked up at me. Her blue eyes got even bluer, but they were wide open and filled with a living terror I had seen only one other time in my twenty-year career. I had no idea what had her so spooked, but she was one scared doll.

She tried to speak. I tried to listen. But all I could concentrate on were those blood-red full lips only inches away from mine and needing to be kissed. Kissed hard.

"I saw him," she said robotically, her unfocused eyes staring through me at something horrifying only she could see.

I gathered myself. It was hard as hell to do, but I'd been on the job for centuries it seemed. I responded almost as mechanically.

"You saw who?"

"I saw *him*," she repeated.

"You look like you need a stiff one, doll."

She just continued staring through me, confused and terrified.

"A drink," I lied, knowing what I really wanted to give her.

The tortured years of being a gumshoe kicked in and took over as usual. "You look like you need a drink. I know *I* do. Join me and we can kill time with all the particulars later."

I didn't wait for her answer. I grabbed her arm and pulled her through the door and into the barely lit bar. I walked her past Bobby, the bartender, and nodded. "Two of the usual, Bobby."

He nodded.

I delivered her to the booth in the back of the bar. It was dark and alone. It was always dark and alone. And it was always available for me. It was my spot and everyone knew it. It was like it had a 'reserved' sign on it just for me, the drunk detective who had spent too much time on the force and should have retired. They knew the truth, though. I was too stupid to retire.

I sat her down and crawled in on the other side of the table. I stared at her. I think I got an erection. It was the first in almost a year. Hard drinking will do that to a man. Especially to a man who hasn't gotten laid in almost ten years.

After Jennifer, my ex-wife, finally realized there wasn't going to be a fairytale life with me, she tried to settle for stable. It didn't take her long to figure out that wasn't going to happen either. She jetted. I can't really blame her. If I was her, I would have jetted too.

I mean, a fairytale life wasn't ever in the cards for me to begin with. And any kind of stable life was a pipe dream as well, for that matter. Hell, no kinda life was in the cards for me, except this worn-out drunk-cop-at-night kinda life. If you could even call that a life.

In the years that followed my divorce, I hadn't put forth much effort toward replacing her. I used to visit a hooker named Tasty Stacy once a week, but after a while even that seemed more work than it was worth. Eventually, life for me settled into the liquored-up mundane waste of breath it was.

I saw it as safe and comfortably predictable. That is to say, I got used to it. I even grew to appreciate the solitude. And I didn't wish to muck it up with another sure-to-fail relationship. This chick, however, got me thinking old thoughts again. I hated that. The last thing I needed at that moment in my screwed-up existence was another problem. And this problem was certain to become a disaster.

She sat staring out into the surrounding darkness of the light-challenged bar, her eyes flicking left and right rapidly.

There's a good reason why bars are kept so dark. No one wants to look into the face of a fellow drunk. They're afraid they might see their own hollow, horror-filled reflection staring back at them.

What the hell was she seeing that I couldn't see, I wondered.

Bobby showed up with four short glasses of Maker's Mark, neat. He dropped them onto the table, nodded again, and left without a word.

I picked up one of the glasses filled with the exquisite bourbon and downed it in one shot, then dropped the empty glass to the table. I picked up a second glass and held it out to her.

She didn't even know I was there.

I placed the rim to her lips and tipped it up. To her credit, she slugged it down like a pro, but it had no effect on her.

"You saw who?" I asked again.

Her eyes didn't stop flickering a bit. I reached up and snapped my fingers in front of her face. Nothing changed.

I slugged my second bourbon just as Bobby appeared with four more. He knew me better than I knew myself. He scooped up the two empties and walked away as quietly as before. I love a bartender who knows how to serve drinks to drunks like me. It makes being a functional alcoholic so easy.

My new drinking partner was still lost on some other planet. I was drinking alone. I didn't mind drinking alone. I was used to it. I'd usually sat in this booth and stared out across the room and took note of all the other losers. Christ. I think we all look exactly the same. Like the world has just beat the hell out of us and we're left a bloody pulp knowing we can't change a thing about our sorry lives. So we just keep drinking.

I think we all have the same expression at the end of the night, too — the look of horror, knowing the morning of another ass-kicking day is only a few agonizing hours away. And we all ask ourselves the same question each and every night. *"When is this bullshit life going to end?"*

It's sad because we know it's never going to end until we go tits up. Then the real hell of this life sets in on us. Until the end comes to save us from all our self-inflicted misery, we'll have to live each sorry day without ever knowing when our last day will finally arrive — when the nightmare of this crap reality will finally end and we'll be liberated from the terror.

"What's your name?" I asked the hot zombie.

She didn't answer me. I fed her another bourbon. She drank it, but remained in her trance.

"Look, doll, if I'm gonna try and help you, I need to know what's going on with you. Now pull it together and tell me what you're talking about."

I lifted another glass to my lips and swallowed it straight while staring at her face. Goddamn, I wanted to kiss those lips.

I shook her a bit. "Come on, honey. Give me something."

"I saw him," she repeated.

"Saw who?"

"I saw him kill her."

Now those words *really* got my attention. I slugged another drink. "Okay. You saw a murder? Is that what you're saying?"

"I think he saw me."

Now I was *truly* intrigued.

"The murderer saw you? You mean you witnessed a murder and the murderer saw you?"

"He saw me."

"Excuse me for stealing your drink, honey," I said, reaching for hers, "but I think I might need it more than you."

I picked up the glass and downed it in one gulp.

"Where was this?" I asked. "Where did the murder take place?"

"I saw him. I saw him. I think he saw me."

"Yeah, yeah. I get it. Where? Where did you see this?"

I reached out and grabbed her shoulders and shook her hard. She turned her dazzling eyes to me. She stared at me. Then she screamed so loud, I thought my ear drums would burst. She went into a full panic attack. I covered her mouth as best as I could and shouted to Bobby to call for help.

CHAPTER 2

Black-and-whites lined the curb in front of Bobby's bar and uniforms walked in and out of the place like it was a freakin' parade. The paramedics had taken control of Miss Blue Eyes, using stethoscopes and flashlights and drugs I'd like to have flowing through my own veins.

Lieutenant Hank Grayson sat across from me staring at me like I was a drunken idiot. In fact, I *was*, right up to the gills, but that's beside the point. No matter, he'd seen me this way many times before. It wasn't anything new. He knew I was a lush.

"And then she started screaming her head off like she was seeing a monster," I said.

"Can you blame her?" asked Grayson. "Christ, I mean, she *was* looking at you."

"Goddamn, Lieutenant, you should take your standup routine on the road. You could make a fortune."

"That hurt, Jake."

"Good."

"Have the medicos gotten any more out of her?"

"Hell, they just got her to stop screaming seconds before you walked in. She's seen something and it's shook her up pretty good. I got the black-and-whites out canvasing the area. There's been a murder, I'm sure of it, but when and where is still a mystery. Miss Screw-My-Brains-Out-Please is the only one who seems to know the answers to those questions. And who knows when she'll be able to speak coherently."

"They'll get her to Bellevue," said Grayson. "Maybe *they* can get her back."

I slammed another Maker's Mark down my throat.

"Hitting the sauce harder than usual, I see," said Grayson.

"I'm off duty. It's *my* life."

"Fine. Have it your way. You want this one?" he said as he slid his drink toward me. "The case, too, I mean?"

"The case sort of fell into my arms, Lieutenant. Literally. Why not?"

I lifted the glass straight from the table to my lips. It was gone in one swig.

"Will you be able to keep your big head in the game and your little head in your pants?" asked Grayson. "This chick looks too good for you, anyway. I think she'll mess you up."

"Hell, Lieutenant, I'm certain she'll get me killed."

"Like you said, it's your life, but don't screw this up — literally. I don't need any harassment suits in my department."

"You know me, Hank. I love to look, but I don't think I can get it up for the fight anyway."

"Get off the Maker's Mark and you might."

"So what if I do? You think she'd let me use it on her? I mean, Christ, look at that. On a scale of one to ten, she's a goddamn twenty. Women like that don't have nothin' to do with drunks like me."

"I've seen stranger shit happen, Jake."

"That's true enough, I guess, but don't worry. I got this under control."

"I've heard that before. Look, Jake, you got your twenty in. Why don't you just walk away while you can and go take up golf on some tropical island? I hear it's nice on St. Croix for ex-cops."

"I ain't the kind to go chasing little white balls across the lawn. And if I did, I'd go chasing mine first."

I laughed at my own joke. Grayson just smiled agonizingly.

"Why do you continue to put yourself through this, Jake?"

"As I see it," I continued, "there's nothing else I can do with what's left of my shitty life. Being a cop is what I am."

"It's a job, Jake. It's *not* who you are."

"Hell with that. It *is* who I am. You know it and I admit it."

"You know, Jake, if you had stayed off the sauce, *I'd* be working for *you*."

"You can have all the rank and glamour, Hank. I'll take the crap. It suits me more. And at least I get off duty now and then."

"That's bullshit, Jake. You're never off duty. You dream of this shit."

"Maybe so. But I don't have to take the heat for assholes like me. That's why you get the big bucks and the fancy office."

I smiled at Hank. He said nothing. I'd won. Finally, he shook his head with resignation.

"Fine. Have it the way you want, Jake. Get on this case first thing tomorrow and wrap it up quickly. Now get your ass back home and get some sleep, for Christ's sake. You look like holy hell."

Grayson got up and walked out. That's the way he was. When he was done talking, he left. No clever departing words or even a *goodbye*. He just stopped talking and left. I wish I could do that sometimes. Hell! The truth? I'd like to be able to do that all the time, with everyone. But then, if I am being truthful, that wasn't me. I liked to go in as a smartass and go out the same way.

I decided he might be right for once. I felt like shit. I stood up and started for the door.

Miss Blue Eyes saw me get up and walk away, and she went berserk again. I stopped and turned toward her. She was reaching out for me.

I moved toward her and she grabbed my arm like she wanted to tear it off.

"He butchered her!" she shouted. "He's back!"

"*Who's* back?"

She didn't answer. She just stared through me again as if she could see something horrifying behind me. *Shit*, I thought, *maybe it's me*.

"Talk to me," I said, trying to ignore my own fears.

"Fifth Avenue. I saw him cut her up. It was horrible. He looked up and saw me. I ran away. He was cutting her up like...like..."

"Yeah? Yeah? Keep talking. He was cutting her up like...?"

"He was cutting her up like…Jack the Ripper!" she said.

"Like Jack the Ripper? You gotta be kidding me."

"I saw him."

I grabbed the arm of one of the departing uniforms and stopped him. I took hold of his radio microphone. "This is Detective Brewer. Have any black-and-whites cruising Fifth Avenue look in the alleys. You're looking for a murder victim. Get back to me." I let go of the mike and let the uniform walk away.

"I need more information, doll. Are you well enough to make a statement?"

She shook her head.

"I need a drink," she said.

My kinda girl, I thought.

"Hell, I need lots of them," I said. "Let's chat, doll."

I chased away the medicos and then looked up at Bobby. He nodded and reached for the Maker's Mark.

"So, your name is Madison Dumont, huh?

"Maddie, Detective. Everyone calls me Maddie."

"Okay. Maddie Dumont. That figures."

"What does that mean, Detective?" she asked.

"The name is as hot as its owner."

"Do I take that as a compliment?"

"You can take it any way you want."

"I can take it all kinds of ways, Detective." She fluttered her eyelashes and spoke the words the way she did, no doubt, to figuratively slap me around a bit. She was toying with me. Chicks like her usually have their fun with me and then dump me just as it gets interesting. So I was prepared for her abrupt exit at any moment. I'm an easy mark. But it was working. *Shit*, I thought, *I'm doomed.* I think I actually got another erection.

"I meant it as a compliment. Yeah, you're quite a looker."

"Thanks," she said simply and then tipped her glass up. I saw it was empty.

I signaled Bobby. He was already pouring fresh drinks.

"Don't you guys usually run in pairs?" she asked.

"Normally. My partner retired a few months ago. He was the smart one. He's living on St. Croix now, golfing every day and drinking umbrella drinks.

They haven't found me a replacement yet. Actually, they can't find anyone who's willing to work with me. To be brutally honest, they can't find another alcoholic cop who can stand to work with me."

She snickered.

"So you've got an office over on Fifth Avenue, then?" I continued. "That's high rent over there."

"The finer the sand, the nicer the box," she replied.

"Shit!" I murmured.

"What was that?" she said, twirling me around her little finger like a bobble on a piece of string.

Bobby delivered four glasses and left with a small smirk.

"Nothing. What's your business?" I asked.

"I'm a senior editor for a fashion magazine, *Le Chic Fashions*."

We both chugged one of our drinks.

"Of course you are," I murmured again.

"What did you say? You're mumbling, Detective."

"I'm dribbling, too," I shot back.

"How's that?"

"Never mind. So you left your office and walked along Fifth Avenue? Have I got that right?"

"Yes. I felt like a walk. It was a tough day."

"A tough day?" I wondered what was considered a tough day for a senior editor of a fashion magazine.

"Yeah. The stress sometimes gets to me."

Stress for an editor? I again wondered what that might look like. *Perhaps it was dealing with the pain of a particularly nasty paper cut.*

I then imagined her office staff surrounding her, all yelling their questions at the same time. If it was me, I'd pull out my piece and put a couple rounds into the ceiling. Then I'd chuckle as they all ducked for cover. That'd shut 'em the hell up, I bet. But I was pretty certain she handled her stress differently.

"How did you run across the murder, then? I mean, murders don't generally happen on Fifth Avenue. At least not along that part of Fifth Avenue."

"I saw shadows on the alley walls."

"Shadows on the alley walls?"

"Yes. So I walked into the alley."

"Wait! You saw shadows on walls and you walked into a frickin' alley alone? Are you crazy?"

"I was curious. I wanted to see what was making such odd shadows. I regret doing that now, of course."

"Hey, doll, I'm curious about what it feels like to jump out of an office window, but I'm not going to do it just to satisfy my curiosity. You walked into an alley alone? Jesus! That's something only dumbass cops like me do."

"I don't envy you."

"I don't envy me either, but that sums up my crazy, sorry life. So, what exactly did you see when you ventured into the alley?"

"He was bent over her and using a large knife of some kind. He was cutting her up. I didn't see clearly what he was doing, but I got the idea clear enough."

"That's when he saw you?"

"No. He saw me when I screamed."

"Then what?"

"I ran away."

"You're in Hell's Kitchen, doll. You know that?"

"I know it now."

"Why did you come here?"

"I have no earthly idea."

"How did you get here? Taxi?"

"I can't answer that either, Detective. The last thing I remember is running away from the murder scene."

"You just ran away and ended up here for no reason?"

"I must have blacked out and here is where I came."

"Do you know someone over here?"

"Hardly."

"Yeah. That *was* a dumb question, wasn't it?"

"I didn't mean it that way, Detective. I'm sorry. I just mean that—"

"Forget it. You don't have to explain. I understand. It makes no sense for a doll like you to know anybody over in these parts. This area is for people like me — slummers. What part of the city do you live in?"

"Just off Central Park."

"Why doesn't that surprise me?"

I slammed another bourbon. She sipped at hers.

"I've never drunk bourbon neat before. Not like this anyway," she said.

Then she giggled.

"I think I like it. It makes me feel sort of bad."

"Bad?"

"Naughty. Sitting here in this part of town, in this dark little bar, sipping bourbon with you. I'm feeling sort of naughty."

Christ! I definitely got an erection this time.

CHAPTER 3

After another hour of staring into those icy blue pools of pure sex and listening to that angelic voice talk about her job and her life in New York, I looked at my watch. It was getting late — 1:30 a.m.

"After what you've been through, I don't think you should be alone tonight," I said.

"Oh, yeah? I should spend the night with you instead, I suppose?"

"Christ. I wish."

"Be careful what you wish for, Detective."

"Yeah. I'm trying to. I mean, I'm going to send you home in a black-and-white. They'll be outside your door until later this morning. Could we finish our little chat later? If you don't mind, that is."

"I have a ten o'clock appointment at my office. I can't miss it. Can we meet there?"

"Can I pick you up earlier at your place so we can chat on the way in? I need some quality time with you."

"If you think you should."

"I know I *shouldn't*, but I have to. I just need a few minutes."

"I've heard that before."

She giggled again. I loved hearing her laugh. My manhood tingled once more.

"Sorry," I said. "I mean, I've got a few questions. It shouldn't take long at all."

"Fine. Pick me up at nine-thirty. You can drive me to my office. Will that be time enough?"

"That should be just fine. Nine-thirty it is, then."

"I'll write down the address for you."

"No need," I said. "I'll get it from the uniforms later."

"The who?"

"The uniformed cops. I'll get it from them."

"My, how devilishly efficient, Detective."

"I have my moments."

I did have my moments of lucidity, I reasoned to myself, but they tended to pass quickly. This one did, too. I knew it and didn't try to stretch it out. I would have failed in the attempt anyway.

The black-and-white pulled away from the curb just outside Bobby's with Miss Screw-Me-To-Death-Please in the backseat just as my cellphone went off. I pulled it from my pocket and stared at it, not knowing how the hell to answer the damned thing.

Earlier that morning, the department had finally *forced* me to give up my old, 'dumb' flip phone and I was handed this new 'smart' phone. They showed me the basics, which obviously didn't take. It seems a modern 'smart' phone and a dinosaur 'dumbass' detective weren't yet compatible.

I walked back inside and up to the bar.

"Bobby, how the hell do I answer this damn thing!"

Before Bobby could respond, the phone stopped ringing.

"Damn it all to Hell!" I bellowed. "I want my flip phone back. I don't need all this fancy crap."

Bobby smirked.

"Calm down, Jake," he said, pulling the phone from my hands. "Next time it rings, put your finger on the green icon and slide it toward the red. Got it?"

He handed the phone back to me. I stared at it for a few seconds. Where the hell is the green icon?"

"Wait for it to ring. You'll see it then."

"Okay. Green to the red. Jesus. What idiot designed it that way?"

Bobby smiled, shook his head, obviously entertained by the dumbass detective, and went back to washing glassware.

The phone started to ring again. I looked at the screen and saw the green icon. I looked at Bobby again, who was staring at me.

"Green toward the red."

He nodded.

I touched the green icon and slid it toward the red icon. I'll be damned. It worked. I put the phone to my ear.

"Brewer here, I think. Is it working?"

It was Hank.

"I see you finally found out how to answer the phone."

"Yeah, Hank. Bobby showed me. Can I have my old phone back, please?"

"No. Start learning how to use the new smart phone."

"This phone ain't so smart, Hank. If it was, it would have answered by itself."

"I have no time to argue with you. It's been found."

"What's been found?"

"A body. Right where your witness said it was. Get over here. I'll text you the address. And before you go bellyaching about it, ask Bobby to show you how to get your texts. Get over here right away."

Hank disconnected. I looked at Bobby.

"Uh, Bobby? What's a text?"

The uniforms had found a body and it had been ripped apart, just like Miss Dazzling Blues had told me. The morning was only getting started and it wasn't going to get any better. I was exhausted, but I responded just the same.

I started for my car, but I realized I was drunk on my ass. It probably would be better to call a black-and-white to pick me up. It wouldn't look good for me to crash my car because I was plastered. At least, at that moment, I had some unimpaired brain matter left. I dialed.

As I walked into the alley where the murder scene was, a uniform walking toward me leaned into a nearby dumpster and emptied his guts. I had, in that instant, some idea of what I was about to see. I wasn't disappointed. But I wished I had been.

She might have been a pretty girl. It's hard to look your best with your face missing, your throat sliced wide open, your belly torn apart like a slaughtered animal, and all your guts ripped out and piled next to you on the filthy, oil-stained concrete. The flesh of her face had been carved off viciously and most of her teeth were missing, as if the killer had purposely knocked them out. It was clear to me that the killer intended to cause a delay in identifying her. In my book, the destruction of her face and teeth were proof of willful intent.

I believe you've got the picture by now of what greeted me. I was certain this was not done willy-nilly, that this victim wasn't selected at random. I believed the killer and the victim were acquainted. I had no proof of that connection; it was just my gut reaction. But I was going to pursue that avenue until I hit a roadblock.

I was glad my stomach was empty to begin with. Miss Blue Eyes was right about what she had briefly described. If this were 1888 in Whitechapel, London, the scene could only have been described as a Jack the Ripper murder.

The coroner and CSI team were already on the scene doing what they do when I arrived. I was greeted by another one of the uniforms.

"Hey, Detective. You sure called this one."

"You first on the scene?"

"Yes, sir."

"Was that your partner puking into the dumpster?"

"I'm sure it was. They got me saddled with a rookie. But hell, I pretty near lost it myself."

"Why didn't you?"

"Five years next month. This ain't the worst I've seen."

"I know what you mean. So what do we got?"

"Pretty much what you see is what you got. Whoever did this tried like hell to make it look like a classic."

Just then the coroner, Doctor Christopher Harrigan, Doc to everyone, shouted out.

"We got something."

"What ya got, Doc?" I shouted back.

"Come see for yourself, Jake. That's why I yelled. I yell to get others' attention. Yelling works like that, you know?"

"Okay, okay. Jesus. I get it."

Doc Harrigan was old — years past retirement, but he couldn't manage two pennies. That's why he was still on the job. And he was ornery. He didn't like getting awakened for murders anymore. But he was like me. He was broke as a bum and didn't have anything else to do with his life. At least he had a life. He had a life and a wife, which was more than I could say for myself.

I walked over to where Doc was kneeling over the body. He held a set of large forceps and was inserting them into the belly cavity.

"This is messy, Doc."

"This is savagery. No skill required to do this damage. Just a perverse will to destroy."

"Any ID?"

"No. Jane Doe Number 1 is what I'm calling her."

Seconds later, he pulled out a piece of folded paper from where her stomach used to be.

"Put on a set of gloves, Jake, and have a look at this."

The coroner's assistant helped me into a pair of surgical gloves and I carefully took the folded piece of paper from Doc's forceps.

I studied the folded note for a minute or more. I took note of how it was folded, what kind of paper it was, what kind of ink was used, whether or not the ink had come through the paper. I think Doc Harrigan got annoyed. In fact, I'm sure of it.

"You usually unfold a note and read it, Jake," he said. "That's how you learn what's inside it."

"Didn't get enough sleep tonight, Doc?"

"Didn't get enough to drink tonight, Jake?"

"Not nearly enough, Doc."

"Same for me. Just read the damn thing, okay?"

I unfolded it touching only the edges of the paper and read the note inside.

"Oh, shit," I said.

"Are you going to make us beg?" asked Doc. "Or maybe you'd like your own mystery series on TV where you could slowly unfold the clues to the murders for the viewers?"

"Doc, maybe you shouldn't respond to these late-nighters anymore."

"And maybe you should just shut the hell up and read the damned note," he shot back with a wry grin.

"It's a note, all right."

"No kidding."

"It reads, '*Hey, Boss. I'm back. One whore done and the Fifth Avenue Whore, who saw me, will be done soon enough.*' It's signed *JTR*."

The note had been written with what I guessed was a sharp instrument, using the blood of the victim as ink. I could only assume at that moment that the initials meant Jack the Ripper.

"I don't get it," I said. "Where did the stationery come from? Does Jack the Ripper carry his own stationery around with him now?"

"Is there a letterhead? Does it say 'This murder was brought to you by Jack the Ripper' or something?" asked Doc.

Everyone around smirked. Doc's sniping wit even got a smile from me.

"I get writing a note, like the original killer," I said, "but this note, or a note in general, had to be planned. Now, this paper is common typing paper found just about anywhere. Not much help there specifically, in and of itself, but the killer had to be carrying it with him at the time of the murder."

"Good thought, Jake," said Doc. "So that would support your theory of planning, I suppose."

"I would say so."

Doc Harrigan returned his attention to the body, leaving me to ponder the varied significances of the note.

Well, there it is, I thought. Getting to bed anytime soon was out of the question. To make it worse, I was sobering up quickly. Too quickly for my liking. Yeah, that was the worst part. I was starting to think clearer.

"Jack the Ripper," Doc mused. "If this continues on track, it's going to get ugly."

"What does that mean, Doc?" I asked, awaiting a smart-ass response.

"You're telling me you've never read about the Whitechapel murders, Jake?"

"Read 'em? I studied them in detail in criminology class. But that was a long time ago. So, why did you say that?"

"Go read through them again, Jake. Then you should be able to guess what's coming next."

"Don't play twenty questions with me, Doc. I'm stressed out enough already by this stupid phone. You have something to say, just spit it out."

"Well, Jake, simply put, this is going to get very messy if it continues. I'm talking Mary Jane Kelly messy."

"What the hell does that mean?"

"I'll say it again, O'Brain-of-the-Bunch. Go read about the Whitechapel murders again. You'll understand then.

"Fine. Don't tell me. I will go look it up. Any sign of the murder weapon?"

"Not right now. But I got a clean stab wound to the heart. I should have more for you after I do an autopsy. I should be able to pattern the blade out. And since all the damage was done postmortem, it shouldn't be difficult to figure out."

"What killed her?"

"Preliminarily speaking, her neck was snapped."

"That takes some strength to do that."

"Not really. There are techniques that are quite easy and effective even for someone with little strength."

"Wonderful. Have you got a T.O.D. for me?"

"I'm guessing right now, but I'd put the time of death at about four hours ago."

"Great. Here goes another shitty night."

I got real quiet, stilled my mind, and emptied it of all other thoughts. It took a minute or two, but I got a blurred vision of the murder. That was my charm — my *thing*, my *secret*, my *mojo*, if you will. I could, on occasion, get a vision of how a crime was done. It wasn't always deadly accurate, but it usually gave me the edge I needed over the long run.

I wasn't psychic or anything like that. It was more of an intuitive thing — an empathic sense. I put myself in the mind of the murderer as I committed the crime, or at least how I imagined the crime could have been committed.

Although my visions were never accurate to a T, I gained an insight that no one else apparently got. That's why I became the go-to guy in the department when it came to solving bizarre crimes. And I had to confess, this was one at the top of my *weird-o-meter*.

I turned my attention to a young CSI forensic technician photographing the scene.

"Malcolm?"

"Yeah. I'll have the photos on your desk later this morning, Jake."

"Thanks. Bag the note for me, will ya?"

"Sure thing." Malcolm carefully took the note from my hand. "Hey, Jake, did you see it?"

"Just in my mind, Malcolm. Just in my mind. I'm outa here, guys."

"So what now?" asked Doc Harrigan.

"A triple Maker's Mark," I answered, walking away.

"Have one for me."

"Will do, Doc. You can count on it. No rest for wicked souls this night, it seems."

"There is for this wicked soul," said Doc Harrigan.

"What do you mean?"

"She was a whore."

I turned and walked away.

"Ain't we all, Doc."

CHAPTER 4

I had the black-and-white first stop by my apartment, where I pulled out my old criminology textbooks and then had them drop me off at Bobby's. I yanked a map of the city from the glove compartment of my car, still parked along the curb.

I walked into the bar. Bobby nodded and set two filled glasses down on the bartop.

"I expected you back," he said.

"If you weren't so ugly, I'd marry you," I said.

"Back at ya, you gnarly old bastard."

We chuckled.

I picked up the drinks and carried them back to my table.

I swallowed one right away. Then I laid out the map of the city across the table and plopped down into the seat and stared at it.

I recalled that Miss Blue Eyes burst into my arms about eleven-thirty. That meant she must have witnessed the murder about nine-thirty, according to Doc Harrigan's T.O.D.

From the murder scene to Bobby's was less than a mile and a half. Even I, an out-of-shape alcoholic, could make it from there to here in twenty to thirty minutes — forty-five at the most, walking at a normal pace, or, in my case, a normal stagger.

So where had she been, what had she done for the two hours after the murder? Wandering around the city before making it over here? Unlikely, I guessed, knowing how people in this town are quick to take advantage of someone in a vulnerable state. How many reports had I heard of someone taking their eyes off their possessions for a second or two and they were gone? And yet Maddie arrived in front of Bobby's intact, albeit out of her mind. It was clear to me that she had not been wandering around the city for those two hours in some bedazzled daze. But just where she was for that time, for now, would remain a mystery.

Right then, I realized I had my first difficulty with the case. I was betting it was only going to get more bizarre before I could solve it.

Bobby dropped two more filled glasses on the table. He could have combined the drinks into one glass, but he knew I liked to chug my drinks individually. Besides, the smaller portions were easier on my throat. I drank down the second drink and stared at the two others. I'd be drinking more before the night ended.

By three o'clock in the morning the bar had cleared out, leaving Bobby and me the only occupants. Bobby cleaned up everything and then brought a bottle to the table. I had been scanning the pages of my old textbook, re-familiarizing myself with the Ripper murders.

"Here you go, Jake," Bobby said. "As usual, I just put on a large pot of coffee for you for later. What you reading?"

"I'm reading about the Jack the Ripper murders in Whitechapel, England. Want to hear about them?"

"No way. I don't want nightmares."

I reached into my pocket for some cash, but Bobby put up a hand to stop me.

"I already closed out the register, Jake. We can square up later. I'm going upstairs to bed. Lock up when you leave, buddy."

"I still might marry you."

"Thanks. Now *that'll* give me nightmares."

We both grinned.

"Goodnight, Jake."

"Goodnight, Bobby."

I was soon left alone and went back to studying the map. I began the usual tracking of the events. I had been down this road so many times before, it was second nature. Having witnessed the crime scene now, I again put myself into a trance-like state and walked through what I thought the steps to the murder were. I did it several times and with each walk-through, of course, I also included Miss Blue Eyes' part in it.

Halfway through a visionary walk, I slammed the last drink down the old gullet. After twenty years on the job, I had seen just about everything humans can do to each other. I was recalling the Ripper murders in detail now. Those murders had to have torn that city apart.

Drawing on that ancient history, I studied the crime that evening with the same scrutiny. I then re-read the details about the Mary Kelly murder. The Ripper had cut her up so thoroughly that it easily became one of the most horrific murders in recorded history. The old police photographs of her mutilated body were too grainy to do justice to what the Ripper had done to the poor girl.

Now I knew what Doc Harrigan meant by his comment. There was a good chance the next murders were going to be bad — really bad. I came to a preliminary conclusion. We were dealing with a real sicko and this case wasn't going to be easy to solve. I had one more thought: it was going to get really grisly from here on out.

I walked into the station at seven-thirty and was greeted by the desk sergeant, who waved a hand in front of his nose upon my passing.

"Whew! You smell like a distillery. Try vodka. It doesn't smell."

"You drink it, you Communist!"

We shared a chuckle and I walked to the locker room, where I kept a complete change of clothes and some basic toiletries.

A hot shower and a shave and I felt great — almost human again. Of course with all the coffee I had drunk since five o'clock that morning trying to sober up, I had to piss like a racehorse. But perhaps that's more information than you really need.

I plopped down at my desk and what greeted me was a note from Doc Harrigan. It read:

"Jake, murder weapon confirmed to be a seven-inch Liston amputation blade. If you don't know what that is, Google it. You are definitely dealing with a copycat."

I stopped a rookie walking past my desk.

"Hey, Jackson. What the hell is a Google?"

"Internet, Jake. Search engine."

"Don't you dare use that kind of language around me. Go find out what a seven-inch Liston amputation blade is and bring the info back to me on some kind of paper."

As normal for me when initiating a new investigation, I pulled a sheet of paper from a stack in a box on my desk and laid it before me on the blotter pad. This paper contained several pre-printed questions that I attempt to answer during all my investigations. Questions all crime investigators are required to answer in order to develop their suspect: motive, means, and opportunity.

Of course, to successfully prosecute the suspect, the prosecution would be required, beyond a reasonable doubt, to provide convincing evidence, such as DNA, etc., and prove that the opportunity to act was actually acted upon by the defendant.

Still, these questions helped me to narrow down any list of suspects that might have existed during the commencement of my initial investigation.

The first major question was:

Why does the killer do what he/she does?

That question contained the psychology of motive, the reason the killer committed the crime.

The next major question asked:

What are the means of the killer? That goes to what provided the killer with the ability to commit the crime.

The list of sub-questions requiring answers included:

What weapon or weapons were used to commit the crime?

What is their typical availability? That is, where would they most likely be obtained?

Are the weapons unusually unique in any way?

Then there is the third major consideration. *What provided the opportunity for the killer to commit the crime?*

The sub-questions requiring answers here included:

How does the killer select his victims?

How does the killer meet his victims?

Are the victims connected to each other in some way?

Are the victims and killer in any way connected to each other?

Are there any witnesses to the murder?

Is there any connection between the witnesses and the killer?

Is there some connection between the witnesses and the victims?

Over the many years in this business, answering all of these questions soon developed a keen list of possible suspects. It could be said that by then, I was glued to the suspects and made their lives very difficult. Properly applied pressure often made the right one snap.

My ex-wife typed up the list on her computer and then printed it up. It was about the only thing she did for me near the end of our marriage that was truly helpful, except for the kindness of having me served with the divorce papers.

Considering the stack of pre-printed sheets, I thought about how I had once believed that when I reached the last sheet of paper, it would be time for me to retire.

I was real good at living in fantasies. I had photocopied the original about ten times over the last few years, making fifty copies each time after I ran short. See what I mean?

Over the years those questions had developed into a tried and true method for establishing a list of suspects. They had never let me down.

At this point in this investigation, all I had so far was a murder victim — an unidentified suspected local hooker — and a bunch of questions staring up at me from my desk.

It was much too early to begin answering any question on the paper, except one. I had an apparent witness — the blue-eyed dream of my life.

Officer Jackson walked past my desk and plopped a short stack of paper down in front of me.

"Liston blade, Jake."

"Thanks. I owe you."

"When can I expect to collect?"

"I owe you. That's the best you're going to get."

He laughed.

"Don't change, Jake. We wouldn't know who you are."

"Get lost, rookie."

He walked away chuckling.

I sorted through the printed pages. I was impressed with how fast Jackson had found the information on the murder weapon. Someday I would have to explore this Internet thing.

Oh, who was I kidding? I wouldn't be caught dead trying. As long as there were rookies to do the work, I'd always have paper to fill my hands.

Reading through the pages, memory of the kind of knife returned. I remembered studying about the blade as we tried to unfold the mysteries of the Jack the Ripper murders. Through all the floating bubbles of booze in my brain, the significance of the seven-inch Liston amputation blade returned.

And then another more insidious and compelling thought swept through my brain. How the hell did ol' Doc Harrigan know about this Google thing?

I glanced at my wristwatch. It was nearly nine o'clock.

I walked out of the station, got into my car, and headed for the address written down on the file on my desk by the uniforms who gave her a ride back home the night before. I was heading to the high-class part of town all right, and I was excited as hell for the opportunity to see Miss Blue Eyes again.

When I arrived in front of the building, I reached for my phone to give her call and let her know I had arrived. I didn't have to dial. She was waiting for me and walked to the car upon seeing me pull up to the curb. Seconds later, she was seated next to me, smelling like flowers and looking like a million bucks. Her outfit probably cost more than my entire wardrobe. I supposed that the editor of a fashion magazine had to look the part, always.

Goddamn those eyes! Goddamn those lips! Goddamn those legs! I got an erection so hard I could have pounded spikes through solid oak planks with it. It didn't last, though. It never did.

"Good morning," she cooed.

Holy Christ! Her voice sounded like a choir of angels.

"Good morning. Did you sleep well?" I said, pulling away from the curb and mixing into traffic.

"I did. I think the drinks you gave me helped me to get to sleep. Thank you, by the way. I appreciate you taking care of me last night."

"You're welcome. Are you feeling better?"

"Yes. Although it still feels surreal. Have you found—"

"Yeah. We found the body. Right in the area where you said we would."

"Did he...uh...?"

"Yes. You were right about that too. He carved her up."

"My god! How can someone do that to another human being? It makes me gag just thinking about it."

"You're not alone. More than one cop blew chunks... Geez, I'm sorry. I lack a few social graces."

"I'm not offended, Detective. Do they know who she is yet?"

"No. And there's a chance we never will know. Sometimes these are people who have come into town under less than normal circumstances. They exist, eking out whatever existence they can. They've changed their names, their looks, their lives. Some do great. Some don't do so well. We have thousands of Jane and John Does here in the city. And they might live out their lives in mystery. Besides that, the killer carved her face off."

"Oh my god."

"Sorry! Sorry!" I said. "I'm such an insensitive ass."

"No. It's fine, Jake. It just caught me off guard. Poor thing. There's the advantage of not having a memory of it all... So you don't have a motive either?"

"We know it wasn't robbery. She had almost a grand in her purse."

"Really? That's quite a bit of money to be carrying around in a purse."

"We think she was a hooker. She probably was just finishing up her night when she met Mister Wrong."

"Still, that's a lot of cash to have."

"You pull down a million a year plus. What's a grand to *you*?"

She looked at me, astonished.

"I saw the readout on you. It's in the file. Everything is in the file."

"I had no idea. I report a crime and all my personal information goes into a file?"

"It's all confidential."

"Still, it bothers me."

"Hey, we are all in some file, somewhere, on someone's desk, in some manner or another."

She smirked.

"Well, since you put it that way. By the way, do you know where my office is?"

I patted the file jammed between the seat and the console and smiled.

"Of course," she said.

She thought a moment and then her eyes dropped down to the file. "I don't suppose…"

"Sorry. No can do. For official eyes only. Besides, it has photos in there I don't think you want to see."

She shivered. "Thank you. You're right. The poor thing."

"Listen, Miss Dumont—"

"Maddie, please, Detective."

"Jake, then, Maddie. Everyone calls me Jake."

"Like Gittes?" she asked.

"What?"

"Like Jake Gittes. From the movie *Chinatown*?"

"Oh. I don't know. I've never seen the movie."

"You've never seen the movie?"

"No. Don't need to see detective movies. I see them every day for real."

"Oh. I suppose you do. So, Jake-Sort-of-Like-Gittes-in-Chinatown, what questions do you have for me?"

"All the wrong ones, I'm sure, but minus those, I do have a few pertinent to the case."

She smiled. "Let's get to those first. We can get to the others later over drinks."

"Don't jerk my chain, doll. Please. It hurts enough already."

"I would have guessed that you would like getting your *chain* jerked, so to speak." She batted her eye lashes teasingly for good measure.

"God, you're good," I said. "You do that so easily, so believingly, so matter-of-factly. Damn. You're the whole package, aren't you? Smart. Sexy. Witty. Goddamn it all. You're the whole ball of wax."

She smiled seductively. "Play your cards right and you might find out. But I'll take you someplace better suited to our needs tonight. Drinks and dinner are on me."

"Holy shit," I said, not believing the moment to be real. "I suppose it's too early to discuss marriage and making lots of babies."

She laughed. I got hard.

"Maybe a little."

I lost my erection again.

"What questions do you have for me, Jake?"

My mind didn't want to return to the case, but it knew it must.

"Initially, we can't find you."

"What?"

"You're not in the system. We don't have a birth date or a place of birth. Can you help me here?"

She giggled.

"A phantom, am I?"

"No. We run into this a lot. Our system only has information that is...what do you call it?"

"I think you're looking for the word 'digitized'."

"Yeah. That's it. Digitized. We don't have information that might still be only in written form or on microfiche. We run into this often; someone from a small town that doesn't have the funds to put their historical records online. That kind of thing."

"I see."

"So, tell me about your birth, Madison Dumont."

"Lemmingberg, Ohio. May 12. Thirty-three years ago, Jake. And if you can find Lemmingberg on any map, let me know. You'd be the first. We were small then, when I was a kid, and I don't think we've grown since. In fact, we shrank by one when I left."

She laughed.

I became more intrigued.

"You've got a fancy name for being from Smalltown, Ohio."

"My real name is Margaret Skimmer. Not exactly what you'd call a high-fashion magazine editor's name. More like a dairy farmer."

I chuckled.

"So you changed it."

"Had to. Is that a problem?"

"No. Like I said earlier, lots of people come here and change their names. It's a good place to get lost if you need to. It's a good place to start over."

"Well, there you go, then. What else?"

"This next one is a bit more of a struggle for me. I'm having a problem with the timeline. I was hoping you might be able to help me with it."

"Timeline?"

"Yeah. From the examination of the body, the coroner put the time of death at around nine-thirty last night. I met you around eleven-thirty. I can't figure why it took you so long to get to the bar. I mean it's less than a mile and half from the crime scene to the bar. Can you recall what you did after you witnessed the murder?"

"I told you, Jake. I only remember running away and then the bar. I have no memory of time or distance. I was on Fifth Avenue and then I was in the bar reaching for you."

"You don't remember running into me on the sidewalk outside the bar?"

Maddie thought for a few seconds, then shook her head. "Sorry, Jake. I have nothing."

A few minutes later I stopped the car next to the curb along Fifth Avenue in front of a swanky office tower. "I'll get the door for you," I said.

"Such a gentleman," she replied, dropping a hand onto my arm, stopping me from getting out. "I'm touched, but I can get it myself."

She thrust open the door and slid her beautiful, tight behind from the seat. I watched it go without any shame. It was perfect. She stopped, turned, and came back to the car, leaned into the car through the open window and smiled. "How about picking me up here at eight. Can you do that?"

"Yeah, sure. How should I dress?"

"In something that can be removed quickly, I should think."

She winked and walked away, leaving me stunned and blinking, and reminded of the old adage: "*I hated to see her leave, but I loved watching her walk away.*"

CHAPTER 5

I strode up to the desk of Officer James Calhoun and dropped a Post-it note in front of him.

"Jimmy, make a phone call to Lemmingberg, Ohio, and ask them if they have a birth record for the person here on the note. Put the answer on my desk when you have it."

"Sure, Jake. Wow! Don't you look all clean and shit."

"Got a hot date."

"Right. Let me guess, first name is Maker's and last name is Mark. How did I do?"

"Are you doubting that I have a screaming hot dinner date with a screaming hot chick?"

"Uh, yeah, Jake."

"Well, believe it, kid. Believe it."

I was in front of the office building, at seven-thirty. I didn't want to be late. I felt like a teenage boy, nervous as hell on his first date. Felt good. Felt strange.

A gorgeous young woman in a floral skirt and a pink blouse, with shoulder-length blonde hair, walked out of the building and toward my car. I noted her elegant gait and slim, perfect legs. I wondered if she was one of the models who gave form to their fashion.

I was intrigued and mesmerized as I rolled down the passenger window. She stuck her head in and smiled.

"Hello, Detective. My name is Ellen Benning, Ms. Dumont's personal assistant. She has asked me to show you up to the office. She's been briefly delayed. Would you mind following me, please?"

"Sure. No problem." Hell, I thought, I'd follow her into hell just for the view.

I reached under my seat and withdrew a placard that read "POLICE" and placed it on the dash.

I was overwhelmed with delight as I followed the beautiful blonde into the building, into the elevator, and toward the reception desk on the thirtieth floor. It was an experience I would never forget.

Le Chic Fashions' offices were elegantly furnished, the walls of the lobby filled with covers of back issues of the magazine. The clothes on those covers represented the highest of high fashion.

They made me think about my own clothing. It would not, in a thousand years, ever be considered chic. It was barely above what could be found on the shelves of a Goodwill store.

I was silently thankful that the magazine was dedicated strictly to women's fashion.

Then I chuckled to myself as I thought of a magazine dedicated to gumshoe fashions. They could call it *The Mister Gumshoe Quarterly*, and I envisioned all the polyester double-pleated Dockers and short- and long-sleeve rayon white dress shirts and neckties that were already ten years out of style when we detectives purchased them. There isn't much you can do with clothing like that except wear the shit out of them and then toss them into the garbage when they get too worn out or bloody.

I chuckled to myself. Yeah, I've been known to entertain myself frequently with such bizarre thoughts.

I thanked the gorgeous babe and stepped through the door. What a sight! Maddie was sitting at her desk, talking on the phone. She motioned for me to take a seat in a chair directly in front of her desk. I sat.

She was speaking with someone regarding a change in fashion layout that was to be in her magazine. I stopped listening when they started using words like environmentally friendly embroidered ergonomics and faux fur.

Jesus, I thought, women actually understand that shit. Such a discussion was completely out of my league.

My eyes wandered to the shelves behind her desk and off to the side. I was intrigued with some apparent decorative items like ancient-looking statues and photographs.

I got up from the chair and walked to the shelves to the side of her desk. I studied each item curiously. The breadth and depth of their diversity indicated a free and wanderlust spirit of adventure. Some of the photographs were of her in shorts, hiking boots, and a tank top, sitting in a pit. She had in her hands a small brush that could have been used as a dusting tool. My eyes then moved to the curious little statue next to the photo. It looked old, like one of those ancient cultures from South America. For all I knew, though, it could have been a modern art statue molded from an original piece. All that shit looked the same to me.

Just then Maddie finished her phone call and hung up.

"Jake," that angelic voice called out from behind me.

I turned and caught an out-of-this-world smile shining back at me. My knees went weak, but I was determined to be macho about it.

"Maddie. I'm impressed," I said.

"At what?"

Jesus, I didn't have a damned clue about what I had just said. I thought for a millisecond and then faked an answer.

"The photograph here of you in a dirt pit."

"Oh, thank you," she cooed. "I was only fifteen then. The photo was taken at a dig site in Piquillacta, Peru, when I was thinking of becoming an archaeologist. I volunteered for it."

Okay. With my mind blown, I took a shot at a quick recovery. "Archaeologist? I would never have guessed that about you."

"Those days are among my most favorite. I thought I could do anything then. But life has a way of bringing you back to reality. The photo reminds me of being young and free. That statue next to the photo came from that dig. To be honest, I shouldn't have it. I sort of smuggled it out of the country. But darn it all, I found it; why shouldn't I be able to keep it? I just love it."

"So there's a little larceny in your soul, huh?"

"A bit of a thief, I guess. But I have to tell you, Jake, it's not valuable as artifacts go. It's probably not worth more than fifty dollars on the black market. But to me, it's the most important thing I have. It represents the best time of my life; a time when the horrors of growing up poor were left behind and a truly wonderful future was waiting for me, if only I could capture it. I could lose everything in my life. Fancy condo, clothing, riches, fame, I could lose it all. But as long as I have this little statue near me, I'll always be happy."

"I don't blame you," I answered. "It's a great little Mayan keepsake."

Okay, I had given it my best shot to sound smarter and more knowledgeable than I was. I failed miserably.

"Actually, Jake, it's Incan."

"Of course. How silly of me to say Mayan."

She, in all her grace and refinement, smiled warmly.

"Jake, darling, just be yourself. You don't need to be anything else. I adore you just the way you are."

I felt better, but still woefully inadequate to even be in the same room as her.

"Sorry. I don't really know anything about Incan art, or whatever. I'm just a shamus. That's the best I'm probably ever going to be. And if I want to see something dead and ancient, I just have to look in a mirror."

Maddie laughed.

"You're too much, Jake. But I'll tell you this. If I weren't here, I'd surely be there. I think I was happier there in the dirt than I am here in my million-dollar condo."

"Maybe so, Maddie, but I'm happy you're here."

She stood up and came to me. She hugged my neck tightly and lovingly.

"And that, Jake, is all I ever want you to be. Just be happy. You're an amazing man, in my book."

She was great at lifting a guy's spirit. She pulled away from me. I wanted to grab her and pull her back into my arms. I wanted to disappear into her embrace and never come back out into this screwed-up world again. I resisted the urge to do so. Instead, I put on a brave front.

"You have a great life here, kid."

"Not always. Things are a bit hectic at times. Publishing a monthly magazine is not always a nine-to-five job, especially when an issue printing is just days away."

"I completely understand," I said.

I was lying. I had no idea what kind of pressures she must deal with as the publisher of a top-of-the-line fashion magazine.

I only knew that she could have any part of me she wanted and discard the rest. What part remained would have been forever grateful for the privilege to be near her.

"I'm so very sorry for the delay," she said. "I'm ready to go if you're still willing to put up with me."

Mister *Couth* rose to the challenge.

"Oh, hell yeah," I said.

I had a moment to study her as she moved back to her desk to straighten it up before we left.

It was then I noticed that she had changed her clothes as well. I wasn't questioning how she had done that. She probably kept a change of clothing at the office, the way I did. I don't know why it took me so long to notice that little fact. Goes to show you how unobservant I was around Maddie. When I was near her, I didn't really notice anything but her. But now I noticed what she wore.

She looked so freaking hot in that little black dress, I thought I was going to explode. Her legs were perfect. Those high heel, stone-studded shoes took my breath away. Her small purse was covered with shimmering stones as well.

She looked every bit the part of a fashion magazine editor. She was probably used to being chauffeured around town in a limousine. I felt suddenly bad picking her up in my shitty five-year-old black unmarked police sedan.

"Would you like for me to call for a limo?"

"Why, Jake? Did something happen to your car?"

"No. It's just an old police cruiser, though. I would think you'd prefer…"

"What? A limo? You're too much, Jake. Your car will be just fine."

I couldn't believe this woman. Her grace, her manners, her sense of being was more than I had ever known could exist.

"I just want you to be comfortable," she said. "Just relax, Jake. Let's go have some drinks and get relaxed. Okay?"

"Okay."

"After the day I just had," she added, "I'm looking forward to getting hammered."

"Okay," I said. "Would it still be too soon to speak of marriage?"

She giggled.

"I'm afraid so, but maybe we could shack up for a while. Would that be okay with you?"

I laughed. It relaxed me.

"Yeah," I replied with my own calm smile. "I could work with that. So, where are we going?"

Okay. I admit it. I looked a little out of place in my two-hundred-fifty-dollar ensemble, which included my off-the-rack sport coat, shirt, pants, tie, and loafers. Oh, hell. Okay. I looked way out of place. I had bought them earlier that afternoon, and in my defense, it was the most I had ever paid for clothes. Maddie didn't seem to mind, though. Hell, she didn't even seem to notice that I had changed.

The bar was someplace that would have, under ordinary conditions, never allowed me in without being on official police business. The line to get in was stretched down the block. They were all beautiful people. Not one gumshoe among them. I tend to notice small details like that.

It was they, however, who eyed me enviously as Maddie walked me into the place like she owned it. The bouncer greeted her with almost goddess-like reverence.

"Good evening, Miss Dumont. You look amazing."

"Thank you, Charlie. He's with me."

"Of course. Welcome to Club Shea, Detective."

Damn, I thought. Was it *that* obvious?

Walking next to her, I guessed it was.

"Yeah. How ya doin'?" I replied, trying to be as polite as I knew how to be. At least as polite as a cop can be under the circumstances.

We had just entered an exclusive club on Broadway, in the heart of the theater district. I was beginning to get that old *I-don't-fit-in-here-at-all* feeling.

I was tragically out of place and underdressed. But, as I was with Maddie, I was extended every courtesy that an "A-lister" would have gotten. I was as uncomfortable as I could be, but I refused to let on. Of course, everyone we met saw right through me, but they didn't flinch.

In short order, we were being led to one of the best tables in the house. On the way, we were greeted by both celebrities and industry executives alike as if we were royalty.

Luckily, I possessed enough couth to hold her chair for her as she sat down.

She expressly thanked me and probably made more of it than she should have, for my sake. She made me feel like a million bucks.

Just as I sat down, the server arrived. I was already nervous as hell, so I ordered two triple Maker's Marks after Maddie ordered a rye Manhattan. *Damn*, I thought. *She owned me already, but if she was truly a rye gal, then I was toast.* News flash! She was, and I was.

The server left us. My eyes took in the room as if I'd never seen a bar before.

"They would never let me into this place unless I was on the job," I finally blurted out.

"You *are* on the job," she reminded me.

"Yeah. I guess I am, at that, but I didn't have to flash my shield."

"Two triples, Jake? Are you *that* uncomfortable here? If you are, we can leave. I want you to relax. You need to relax a bit."

"I am relaxed," I lied. "I'm feeling good. I'm underdressed as hell, of course, but I'm barely a grade above a beat cop. I hope you're not uncomfortable with me. And everyone is staring at us. I'm probably an embarrassment to you. I'm sorry."

"You're fine, Jake. I want you to be yourself. I like you just the way you are. If they have an issue with us, that's their problem."

"But you're someone special. I'm just a gumshoe."

"Stop it! You're my date and I'm grateful. I'm enjoying this."

"I get it. You're enjoying slamming a nobody into the somebodies' faces."

She giggled.

Our drinks arrived. I wanted to chug mine, but I waited just a bit. I tried sipping it, but alas, I ended up drinking it down and went for the other before the waiter got two feet from us.

"Hey, buddy," I called out, slamming the second drink.

He stopped and turned to me.

"Hit me again. The same, will ya? I'm trying to get relaxed."

He was cool about it. He didn't make any off-color comments or give me any strange looks. He just nodded, then took away both empties.

I glanced at Maddie.

"Sorry."

She smiled.

"No need. I want you to just be yourself."

"I'm afraid I'd need about six more before you'd see the likes of that guy."

"Then order more. I'd like to meet him again. He was very interesting."

"You say that now, but…"

I stopped and stared into those blue eyes. I felt so irretrievably lost in them.

She made me feel almost normal. She made me feel accepted. I can't tell you when I last felt so accepted by a woman.

"Jake, have you made any progress on your case?'"

Thank god, I thought. *A conversation in which I could hold my own.*

"It's just getting started, but we're moving along. We've identified the knife involved, but I'm sure you don't want to hear about that."

"But I do. Can you tell me about it?"

"The coroner suggested a Liston blade. In fact, a seven-inch blade. It's a mid-range surgeon's amputation knife, so named after a Scottish surgeon named Robert Liston in the 1800s. They were produced in five-, six-, seven-, and eight-inch blades. It's been suggested that they are commonly found today in Teufel kits."

"In what?"

"Teufel surgical kits. They were kits containing specialized surgical amputation instruments manufactured from 1857 up to 1900, by Jacob J. Teufel. The kit was popular over in London circa 1880s. It's thought that the Ripper might have used it or a similar blade on…uh…you know."

"On his victims?"

"Yeah. Exactly."

"Interesting. So it's an antique, then?"

The server returned with my drinks. I slammed one before he even set the second one on the table. I looked at him. He understood and nodded. He gathered up the empty and departed, sure to return soon with its replacement. *I gotta get a better handle on this drinking*, I thought. But then my eye caught the second drink. I felt better knowing it was close by. I resisted sucking it dry, but only barely, knowing that I could not hold out for long.

"Yeah. That's what I'm told. An antique."

"I see. So it shouldn't be hard to track it down, I imagine."

"Actually, nearly impossible. Liston blades were made throughout the 1800s by the thousands. Teufel kits were manufactured until 1900. That's about the time when Teufel went out of business. There's no way to track down a single blade without some extraordinary luck. You'd first have to locate the owner. And, of course, the owner is most likely the killer. Alone, it would be like finding a specific needle in a stack of needles. Besides…"

I slugged a drink.

"Besides?" she asked.

"Teufel kits generally carried only the knives made by Teufel. A Liston knife was not typically one of them. But some kits were known to have a Liston knife in them. Most likely because the surgeon was more familiar with it and preferred it over the Teufel knife. So, I really don't have anything concrete to go on right now — just my own witless speculations."

"Sorry to hear that. Anything else?"

"The throat was cut from left to right."

"I'm sorry. How is that significant?"

"Well. First off, it suggests that the killer is right-handed. Secondly, all the canonical Ripper victims had their throats cut in the same manner — from left to right."

"Does that narrow it down?"

"Yeah. I'm searching for a right-handed killer who owns a Liston amputation blade. How hard can that be?"

I chuckled.

She smiled.

"Sorry," she said. "That was sort of thick-headed."

"Not really. You sure you want to talk about this?"

"Sure. Why not?"

"Just doesn't feel right."

"I'm fine. But I guess your job is pretty difficult at times, huh?"

"It can be, but I'm sure you don't want to hear about my problems."

"To be honest, Jake, I'm fascinated by what you do. I admire you so much. I mean, you're tasked with solving murders. Very noble work. Your job helps give answers to people who suffer great loss."

"Only if I solve the case. Otherwise, they're left with only questions."

"I bet you're good at your job."

"Twenty years I've been at it and I'm still learning. Just when I think I've seen it all, something like this case crops up and smacks me across the kisser. I'll probably never see everything people can do to one another. Maybe that's best."

"Well, it seems an honorable job. Thank you for what you do. And thank you for being here tonight with me. I feel safe. Are you armed?"

"24-7," I replied.

"Underarm or ankle?" she asked.

"Both, actually. You can't take any chances in this business."

"I hear that."

She lifted her drink. "Here's to you, Jake. My protector."

I think she only did that so I wouldn't feel bad sucking my drink down. I was falling for her hard. I slugged my drink just as my dutiful server returned with two more glasses of courage.

I resisted slugging them and smiled at him.

"You're a savior, you know?"

His only response was another polite nod. He gathered up the empties and left. I didn't ask for more. I had a feeling he would be keeping an eye on me from then on and would deliver others just when I needed them most.

"I'm an alcoholic, you know. And I don't go to meetings."

"Be yourself, Jake. I'm not asking anything from you. I guess if I had to do what you do and see what you see every day, I might be where you are myself."

"Is it still too early to talk about marriage?"

She smiled. "I'm enjoying being here with you right now. Is that answer enough?"

"It's a better answer than I deserve."

My eyes fell to one of the glasses, but I hesitated.

"Jake," Miss Perfect said, "be yourself, please. Don't try to be anything else for me. Okay?"

I nodded and slammed my drink.

"Would you like to leave? Would it be better for you if we went someplace else? You look very uncomfortable."

I was damn sure falling in love with this doll.

"I know a place to get the best steak in town," I said. "It ain't like this, but the food is out of this world. At least to bums like me. Unless you're a veggie gal."

"I'm a meat eater," she replied, smiling. "And we're outa here."

She dropped five hundred-dollar bills on the table like they were quarters.

"Oh, shit!" I murmured, knowing that this place was even more out of my league than I'd realized.

I helped her up from her chair and walked toward the door. I pulled some bills from my slacks pocket. I flipped past the fifty and the twenty to the ten. Then to a fiver. I thought a moment and then flipped back to the fifty. I thought again and flipped back to the ten.

I wrapped it around my detective's card and slipped it into the breast pocket of our server.

"If you ever need anything, buddy, just call me."

"Thanks, Detective. I'll do that."

Somehow I was not surprised that he, too, knew I was a cop. Maybe anyone looking at me could tell. Maybe gumshoes are easy to spot everywhere. Maybe all of us cops have that look about us — that *I'm a mess of a human being, but I don't know anything better to do with my disordered life* look.

CHAPTER 6

From the outside, the hole-in-the-wall restaurant looked like a dive that should have been on someone's to-be-demolished list, but she admitted that she had never tasted a better steak in her life.

I reminded her that while we cops maybe lack the class of high society, nobody knows where the best restaurants and bars are in any city more than we do. She agreed.

I had myself pretty bent by the time our evening was over. She was half in the bag as well. We had a lot of laughs and a great time talking. She had an amazing personality for someone so young and intelligent — and, dare I say it, successful.

Fred, the owner, sat with us the last hour of our night together and bought us more rounds and laughed along with us.

I knew good people throughout the city. In twenty years, I'd found all I needed to find. They all treated me well in return.

I had sense enough to call a black-and-white to help get us home.

At her condo, she invited me up for coffee. I got scared and foolishly turned her down. But in a way, I was a hero. She was a great kid, but she had no business hanging with a guy like me. And for all my shit, I didn't deserve to be with a woman like her. It was better to leave.

I kissed her on the forehead and staggered back to the black-and-white escorted by a uniform. As another patrol car pulled up in front of the building to keep watch for the evening, the uniform drove me back home.

"That's some dish, Detective. If it were me, I would have stayed."

"That's why I'm a detective and you're not."

"Maybe so, but I wouldn't have passed up an opportunity like that."

"Just shut up and get me home before I start crying."

He chuckled.

He didn't know how serious I was.

I thought about what he said later that evening, lying in bed alone, as usual. Maybe he was right. Maybe I was just stupid all the way around. In fact, the more I thought about it, the more I regretted not having stayed for that *cup of coffee*. In the end, though, just before sleep overtook me, I came to the disheartening conclusion that it had been the right thing to do — for me and for my way of life, or more the truth of it, my way of *existence*.

A cannon exploded next to my head. I bounded up off the bed to find the cell phone ringing. I slammed the stupid green icon toward the stupid red one and put the phone to my ear.

"What!" I bellowed.

"Congratulations, Mister Brewer!" replied a happy male foreign voice. "You've just won tickets to a free Caribbean cruise."

I looked at the clock: 3:04 a.m.

"You're an ass bubble," I retorted, then clicked off the phone.

The phone was off, but the cannon kept exploding in my head. It happens sometimes, I don't know why. I shook my head. The cannon fire quieted.

I walked out into my living room and noticed the moonshine reflecting off my 4-by-8 dry ink magnetic whiteboard through the curtain-less window — beckoning me.

I grabbed the eraser and cleaned the board.

Then I flopped down onto the sofa and stared at it. My mind went as blank as the board.

And there I sat, vacantly staring at the clean board with no thoughts winging their way through my empty head.

Then, without warning, a thought went screaming through my brain.

Why the hell did I have a whiteboard in my living room anyway?

I justified its existence by telling myself that it was there to write down thoughts that might arise during my investigations. That I thought better here in the quiet of my own home and could not as easily be interrupted. That my thoughts were purer here, unpolluted by the chaos that typifies the ambience of a bustling precinct.

You'd be surprise at how hard us alkies work at convincing ourselves that lies are truths.

Sure, for a time it works, but then you're smacked in the chops by the unalterable truth. I hated the truth. I hated the fact that I couldn't avoid the truth for very long. And the truth regarding this matter was that I simply couldn't leave my work at the precinct. I was addicted to the action, to the misery, to the unyielding invasion of horrid thoughts of murder. I already had an addictive personality. I was a drunk. Apparently, being an alcoholic wasn't enough. I was a horror junkie as well. A horror/misery/crime junkie.

I guess I lied when I said earlier that I drank to forget all I witnessed during my shifts. I'm an alkie. That's why I drink.

Still, even in my sloshed moments, useful thoughts do arrive. In a flash, I got one that led to many others.

"Why?" I muttered.

I struggled up off the sofa and, grabbing the dry ink pen, began writing on the board.

Thirty minutes later, I sat back down and studied my whiteboard, now covered with words and symbols.

WHY JACK THE RIPPER? read the top line.

Under that I had tried to answer that by asking other scribbled questions.

What is the significance of copying Jack the Ripper murders?

It was particularly violent.

It was particularly angry.
It was particularly infamous.
It was particularly personal.
It was particularly sick.
It was particularly historical.
It was particularly challenging.
It was particularly freeing.

Is the killer looking for fame, recognition, respect?

Does the act of murder and dissection make the killer feel more significant, important, noteworthy, special, intriguing, frightening?

Before the murder, did the killer feel slighted in some way, dismissed, unimportant, insignificant, disrespected, unnoticed, unappreciated, uncontrolled, controlled too much, or deported from a cause?

Was the murder a rebellious response to authority, order, discipline, a lack of justice?

Why not kill quick and clean?

Was the killer unconsciously wanting to get caught, begging to be caught?

The killing was not undertaken as the result of some impassioned spontaneity, a frantic hostility, an out-of-control explosion of rage. Sure, on the outward skin of it, it appeared to be the result of a wild rage of passion. To me, though, the mess appeared almost staged, purposefully messy. And I believed that the butchery had been undertaken carefully, thoughtfully, with purpose, with meaning. It was deliberate, coordinated, planned, and precise.

True, the killing was not gently achieved. That was clear enough. But there was a sick order and design to it.

Another question asked: *Did killing the victim make the killer feel cleansed, spiritually and/or emotionally? Did he now feel repatriated to some great cause? Did he now feel reassembled or reconnected, the very antithesis of dissecting the victim?*

Was he finished?

Are there to be more killings, more dissections?

What was demonstrated by the killer — anger, satisfaction, personal revenge, justification of some deeper wound or consideration?

To be sure, more questions would come to mind in due time, other related thoughts. For now, though, these were offerings of a good start. Those words scribbled across the board and the questions asked on the pre-printed forms gave me enough to consider for a while.

My cell phone rang again.

I looked at the clock on the wall: 4:20 a.m. I glanced at the window. It was still dark outside.

I clicked the phone on. The number in the window indicated that it was from one of the detectives at the precinct.

"Brewer here, hungover and dying a horrible death."

"Perfect," said the voice on the other end. "Then this will be right up your alley."

I was correct. It was another quick-witted detective from my station, Charlie Longstreet.

"Speak to me, Charlie, but not too loud, please. I'm still battling a cannon in my head."

"Don't feel like joking right now, Jake. We got us another one. Just like the other night. Only this one's worse than that. It's bad."

Bad was a gross understatement.

I stepped off the sidewalk of Broadway and 50th into the alley where Doc Harrigan was busy doing his thing. I didn't disturb him. He noticed me but didn't shoot nasty remarks my way. In fact, he said nothing at all to me. I just looked the body over by myself.

The killer had done a thorough slice and dice on another hooker in another darkened alley. As before, her face was carved off and the teeth bashed out and removed from the scene. But I noticed that he'd obviously had more time to spend with the victim on this night, for he had opened her up from crotch to chin. The defatted skin had been laid back and off to the side, exposing everything inside. The collected lump of fat was haphazardly mounded next to the body at the waist. I actually got the sensation that it had just been tossed aside, and that's where it had landed.

But that wasn't the worst of it.

The worst of it was the organs had all been ripped out and dropped next to the body in no specific order. It appeared like a slice-and-toss job all the way.

All the parts were there, but a chunk was missing from one of the kidneys, the left one. Seeing that made me gag. I could only assume, at that moment, that it had been bitten through and swallowed raw. Bile shot up my throat, but I fought it back down before it launched out of my mouth between my clenched teeth.

I hated *cooked* kidney. I couldn't imagine someone taking a bite out of a *raw* kidney and swallowing it. A raw *human* kidney. This case was making less sense every moment. Or it was starting to become painfully sensible. I wasn't yet certain. But it answered one of the many questions on my whiteboard. There were going to be more killings, more dissections. How many more, I didn't know. But there were going to be more of them. Of that, I was positive.

Once again, I quieted my mind and tried to see how the murder might have been committed. I imagined how the murderer might have turned her away from him gently in anticipation of the sex act, or spun her around violently and snapped her neck. Either way, she couldn't have lasted but a second.

Yeah, she might have been turning tricks that evening, but in the end, the trick was most definitely on her.

As what was still left of the corpse was lifted onto the gurney, one of the paramedics discovered another folded note, this time under the body. He handed it to me. I carefully unfolded it. It was again written in blood by a sharp object. I again read it aloud. *"A sorry surgeon am I with skills still to hone, and a*

5th Avenue Whore remains to be sliced to the bone. JTR."

"A rhyming Jack the Ripper?" said one of the uniforms. "That's a new twist."

"Everyone's got to update sooner or later," said another uniform, with a chuckle which launched other chuckles in the alley.

"*SHUT THE HELL UP!*" I shouted. "A girl's been murdered. Would it be as funny if she was *your* daughter?"

The area went deathly silent. My point had stoutly been made.

I understood the reason for the laughter. Sometimes you either laugh or you crumble into tears. Sometimes you don't have a choice. Still, there was a proper time and a place for the twisted behavior of overworked, stressed-out police officers and paramedics. This, however, was neither of them.

"Who was first on the scene?" I asked abruptly.

The patrolman who first cracked wise stepped up. "I was, Detective. A routine look and see. This alley is always dark. I've learned to check it out now and then. Most of the time I find young kids drinking illegally or smoking dope or screwing. Nothing big, though, until tonight."

"You asked around for any witnesses?"

"Sure did. Nothing. No one heard or saw anything. Not that there were many around to be asked. It's usually pretty deserted in this part of town at night."

"What time did you find the body?"

"At 2:10 this morning."

Doc Harrigan wandered over to me.

"Any details for me, Doc?"

"Jake, meet Jane Doe Number 2. Jane Doe Number 2, meet Jake."

"Cute, Doc."

"If I'm not being cute, I'm crying. This is a god-awful mess. I know what you're about to ask. Time of death was about one o'clock. I'm guessing it took only minutes to disembowel the victim."

"That's it? A few minutes?"

"A few minutes is more than enough time for a butcher. And from the looks of it, it was a butcher of average skill. Minutes, Jake. Every organ has been nicked several times. The intestines, both large and small, have several perforations. The damage was done in haste and with lack of care. As I said, a butcher did this. But I will say that the work was very *determined*."

"Determined?"

"No. Not exactly. Very…willful. Very intentional…deliberate. Yes, that's the word I was looking for. Deliberate."

"Would you also say spiteful and serious, Doc?"

"Two excellent words for it. Yes. Very seriously spiteful."

Another confirmed note could be checked off on the whiteboard. This killing, like the one before it, was undertaken in a deliberate manner. The killer was serious. And he had the time to do what he wanted. He thus had the opportunity.

"Ain't there a lot of blood for postmortem work?"

"He was slicing and dicing, Jake. I don't think he cared."

"What I'm saying is that he must have been covered in blood when he was finished."

"Plastic coveralls and other protective gear would have sufficed."

"Where do you think they are?"

"Dumped. Burned. Sunk. Could be anywhere, Jake. It wouldn't be hard to bag it and get rid of it."

"Any chance it might be around here somewhere?"

"The dumpsters in this alley are empty. I suppose he could have discarded it into another dumpster in the area."

"Do you know how many dumpsters are within blocks of here?"

"Nope. I'm a doctor, Jim. Not a refuse engineer."

"Funny, Doc. I'm sure Gene Roddenberry is chuckling right now."

I mentally checked off another line from the board. The killer had the *means* to do what he wanted. I was on some kind of track with the killer. At least I was beginning to think like him. The only missing part of the triad of crime investigation was the motive. I didn't believe for a moment the killer was motivated by the mere fact that the two women were pros. But the face carvings gave me great consternation. It could have only been done for one or two reasons, to deny her the peace of being recognized by a loved one or acquaintance, or to deface her in order to make her identity difficult or impossible.

"Besides someone with medical training, could a skilled hunter, someone who was skilled at butchering his kill, have done this?"

"I believe so. But New York City isn't what I'd call game country, Jake. Not many hunters run up and down Fifth Avenue butchering hookers, I would imagine. And there was very little skill required."

"I agree, Doc. I was just wondering if the skill to do this would be necessarily confined to one with medical training."

"I'll say it again in case you missed it before. A butcher could do this, Jake. In my opinion, a butcher *did* do this. But I got another single stab wound to the heart, just like the first victim. I'm betting it will confirm the same weapon. I think we're being given something of a gift here."

"He's giving us a clear clue?"

"I'd say yes, as well as a challenge."

"Got it, Doc. 'Here's the weapon, boys. Come and find me.'"

"That's about it."

I caught a whiff of something familiar. I followed my nose like a bloodhound to the torn-open stomach of the victim. I sniffed at it.

"Doc, did you catch this smell?"

"I did. Smells like whiskey to me."

"Me too, Doc. I'm wondering."

"I'm ahead of you on that. She was drinking just before she was killed or rendered unconscious. That's my guess anyway."

"Got slipped a Mickey?"

"That's a real possibility. Most likely an ultra short-acting benzodiazepine."

"Come on, Doc."

"Valium, Jake. Drop a couple capsules into a glass of whiskey, and with the added effect of the booze, probably knocked her out cold very quickly. Probably was unconscious at the time of her death."

"Is that some kind of blessing?" I asked.

"Depends on your definition of blessing, I guess. But if you're thinking of tracking down the prescription for Valium, good luck with that."

"I wouldn't waste my time, Doc. I bet over half of this city is on Valium. Maybe more."

"It's common. Hell, I pop one now and then to get to sleep. I'm gonna pop one when I get home this morning. With this vision dancing in my head, I'd never get to sleep without it."

"After all this time, Doc, I thought it wouldn't bother you. I thought this would have just become a normal event for you."

"I'm human, Jake. I know at times it doesn't seem so. But I can't believe anyone in possession of a rational mind could get to thinking this would ever be normal. Without my drugs I'd never get any sleep at all."

"I understand. I stay away from that shit, though. Too addicting."

"Right. Yeah, booze is not addictive at all. Different drug, Jake. Same results."

"Okay, Doc. You got me there."

"Gotta run, Jake boy. You've got your hands full with this one. That's for certain."

"Can't wait for the toxicology report to confirm the Valium."

"I'll get it to you when I can. The lab's pretty backed up, I hear. Good night, Jake."

"What? No parting repartee?"

"Piss off, Jake."

"Good night, Doc."

CHAPTER 7

I sat hunched over my desk, lost in empty, non-cohesive thoughts. *Lost!* Another understatement. I was adrift in a sea of emptiness within the blackness of a universal void — my own mind's abyss.

It was my usual place. But I wasn't normally this lost by this point in an investigation. I had ideas, leads, or paths to follow.

Not this time.

To make matters worse, the department had recently changed out my old computer monitor that took up the better part of my desk. Now a slimmer monitor they called a *flat screen* sat staring at me, mocking me with its forever blinking cursor on an otherwise blank screen. What the hell was the use, I wondered. It might be slimmer and take up less room on my desk, but it was still as useless to me as the old hulk before it. I could no more figure out what to do with it as I could with the other. I hoped they were happy. First they forced me to use this new smart phone which proved to be just as dumb as the last phone, and now they replaced my old screen with this new screen. Damn worthless technology, I thought. It's done nothing so far to help me solve this crime. What a damned waste.

I had no use for any of the new technology, except for the camera on my new phone. That, I could have some fun with sooner or later, I thought. As for the new computer screen, I just stared back at it through hateful eyes for several minutes and then spit a breath at it.

"That's it, blink away at me, you piece of shit. Mock me, but I'll see you crumble away to dust before I put any effort into trying to figure you out."

Yeah, I know. It was a stupid thing to say to that inanimate object, but hey, it's how Jake Brewer rolls.

All the expected reports lay on my desk. I spied the one with my Post-it note that I had handed to Officer James Calhoun, to confirm Maddie's birth record.

It was just as she had told me. Margaret Skimmer, born in Lemmingberg, Ohio, on the date she had told me. I wasn't really surprised.

I picked up file after file and thumbed through them. As I also suspected, there were no fingerprints left at the scene from the killer. No DNA from the killer was evident. No typical evidence like hair or skin from the killer. In fact, the killer had left nothing that could be used as identifiable or prosecutorial evidence. Nothing.

I picked up Doc Harrigan's autopsy report on Jane Doe Number 1. My eyes scrolled past the usual stuff. Officially, Doc confirmed that a Liston blade made the incision to the heart.

I now fully expected that the second victim suffered similar effects of the same blade.

From my previous studies of the Whitechapel murders, it has long been held that the murder weapon used by Jack the Ripper could have been a seven-inch Liston blade, but mountains of evidence have piled up over the years since to discount that blade as the murder weapon. Still, Doc's official confirmation captivated me, if only for a moment.

Besides the murder weapon, though, there was nothing in the report that brought any light to my darkened mind.

I was in a fix, and not seeing any immediate way out of the fix I was in, I sat at my desk staring dumbly at the assortment of useless personal items sitting on top of it.

My eyes scanned across the surface until they came to the second nameplate at the front of my desk. It faced away from me so I couldn't read what was engraved on it, but I already knew what it said. *Detective Nowhere*. It was a ten-year anniversary present from the other dicks in my department and it exactly exemplified my place in life, but more to the matter at hand, it described the current investigation — I was nowhere close to solving this puzzling case. Hell, if the truth be told, I was nowhere close to *beginning* to investigate it the way it needed to be investigated.

Despite the teasing theories put forth by other detectives, the culprit was not the reincarnated spirit of Jack the Ripper. Nor was it the ghost of Jack the Ripper transported to the USA. It was obviously the work of some sick copycat. But of all the crimes that could be copied, why the Ripper's?

No doubt the murders were going to capture the attention of the press as soon as they got wind of them. They loved this stuff. They couldn't get enough of it.

No matter that lives were being savagely taken, they were in the *sensational* business, not the *news* business.

It was a far cry from where they used to be in the days of responsible journalism, driven to much higher standards then and compelled more to inform the public of what was important to know for their safety and well-being, and the reporting of something bizarre for the sake of selling more papers. The news reporters of old would never have resorted to such tasteless chicanery.

Sounds good doesn't it? Of course that's all bullshit. The press has always had a feeding frenzy with this kind of news only for the sake of selling more newspapers. Be it 1888 or 2088, it was all about selling newspapers, baby. That or just being relevant for the day. Tomorrow another organization might scoop them all. But just wait. The next day it might be another who held Top Dog position. Here's a real news flash for you: until the end of time, it will always be so.

The note left by the killer referred indelicately to the Fifth Avenue whore — Miss Blue Eyes, of course. But who were the real whores? The press, surely — whores to entertaining a low-information public and creating a buzz for an even lower-informed group than alerting the public to a real threat to their safety.

Of course, that kind of reporting was making it tough on slobs like me. In the old days I could have appealed to the media to help me to put eyes on this current maniac killer and they would have done so. Of course, they would have demanded an exclusive as trade for their assistance. But I would have welcomed that. It would have been a small price to pay toward the capture of the killer. Today, I couldn't count on that support. If they thought they could get an exclusive from the killer, they would throw me under the bus in between heartbeats.

If the exact details of these two murders were to get out into the public domain, I'd be barbecued. No, the press was not an ally. And it definitely was not a friend to be solicited. It was only a propaganda and indoctrination machine for the evil elite to satisfy an agenda not given for guys like me to know. And it was as much an obstacle to bringing this case to a good close as was the killer himself. I was in this mess alone. And none of the evidence I had so far was making it any easier for me to solve. But like I said, I had no evidence at all to move on.

So Detective Nowhere sat staring dumbly at his desktop not knowing what to do next, but sure wishing he had a triple Maker's Mark neat in his hand and two in the belly already.

I glanced at my watch. 9:15 a.m. I hated finding bodies in the wee morning hours. It made for a horribly long day. You can't just go back home and to bed. Not with visions of torn-out intestines and livers and kidneys dancing around in your head, and without something as strong as Valium, like Doc Harrigan had. What's more, you can't be totally efficient either, being so tired.

My hand twitched. My alternative to Valium was calling me, my hand instinctually looking for a glass. During nighttime it almost always had a glass in it.

It was early in the day, though, and I was already craving a drink. Detective Nowhere came to one conclusion: he was a raging alcoholic for sure. But that realization didn't change the fact that he wanted a drink.

A young officer walked past my desk.

"Coffee, rookie. Black, strong, now."

"Yes sir, Detective."

I interlocked my fingers on the top of my head and put my feet up on the desk. I closed my eyes and tried to visualize the murder scene I had visited earlier. Something about it haunted me.

In my mind I walked through the alley until I got to where the body had been found. While it's true that hookers often used the alleys of the city to do their business, this particular alley wasn't like the rest. It wasn't all that dark. It wasn't all that remote. In fact, I knew of several others that would be safer for a murderer to do his thing and not get caught. Hell, they'd be better for the hookers turning tricks as well.

I revisited one of my whiteboard notes. *Was the killer unconsciously wanting to get caught?* You're an idiot, Jake, I thought. Most murderers, in some sick way, unconscious or not, want to get caught. You know that. Not this one, though. At least not at the moment. This murderer wanted something else. But what was it?

My coffee arrived. I grabbed it and drank a sip. What I wouldn't have given for a shot of booze in it.

I continued my visual walk through the alley. As alleys go, it was a pretty typical one for the city. I turned my mind's eye upward and there I saw the difference. The difference that made it an excellent killing ground. No windows. Well, no windows to residences, that is. It was the back of businesses that fronted Fifth Avenue and to rear of the alley.

At late night, the offices were empty. It was the perfect place to perform postmortem surgery. Hell, nobody but cops on their routine patrols would come here besides the occasional hooker and her john.

Then I considered the first murder scene and damn if it wasn't very nearly the same setting.

I recalled the study of the Whitechapel murders. It was very nearly identical. The murders happened in remote areas where there was little or no activity for long periods especially during those early morning hours.

Damn, I thought. *Could the original Jack the Ripper actually be alive after all these years?*

"Stop it, Jake!"

I opened my eyes and noticed everyone staring at me.

"Did I say that with my outside voice?" I asked.

Everyone nodded.

"Oops! I was visualizing. Sorry about that."

All eyes turned away. It was normal for Detective Nowhere to shout out loud while in one of his vision quests.

I was alone once more.

Jack the Ripper is dead, Jake. Don't start going down that road. It's bad enough to think you might start seeing pink elephants pretty soon. Don't go completely off the track, ol' buddy.

One thing was certain. This copycat had done some studying of the Whitechapel murders. He knew what he was doing. *Jesus*, I wondered. *Do you really think he'll copy the Mary Kelly murder, too?*

The Mary Kelly murder, the most grisly of the canonical murders, reflected what I feared the most. The Ripper had a lot of time to play with. Play? That's not the word I should use here, but you catch my drift. He had the time and privacy to do literally anything he wanted. And what he did to that poor girl has only rarely been duplicated or outdone since. The Ripper truly earned his name that night. He completely ripped apart her body. I remembered the shock I felt at seeing the crime scene photographs for the first time. There was little doubt in my mind that the Ripper did the crime with deliberate and purposeful intent. It was resolute vengeance being exacted on that poor young woman. It was madness — the full spectrum of complete insanity exploding from the tortured soul of the Ripper — the culmination of his perfected skills in action.

These crimes, here in my city, were not of the same caliber of madness. I couldn't yet prove that, but I could sense it. These were being perpetrated for some reason beyond that of simple murder or retribution against prostitutes.

Prostitutes have always been easy prey. The deaths of hookers always seemed more of a *convenience* to me rather than the desire to stamp out hookers for any particular reason.

The murders were carried out by a certain madness, for sure, but this madness had an ulterior motive — one much deeper, much darker. I was certain of that.

Officer John Carleton walked past my desk.

"Hey, Jake. I just escorted your Pretty Blue Eyes to her office. Bill Dodson's on it now."

"Thanks, John. Anything odd last night?"

"She looked pretty much in the bag when you got her home. Is that what you mean?"

"We had a few. She's a rookie."

Carson snickered.

"Compared to you, Jake, we're all rookies when it comes to handling hard liquor."

"I mean anything else odd?"

"Not really."

"The night was quiet?" I asked.

"Yeah. She went in and never came out until this morning, looking damn good."

"Management still won't let us camp outside her door in the hallway?"

"I asked again last night, Jake. The answer is no. The owners association doesn't want cops in the building without warrants. I think they're afraid we'll see some nefarious activity."

John snickered.

"Until they need us," I said. "Then we're welcomed with open arms."

"Yeah. Anyway, I dropped the tail at her office without incident."

"Thanks, John."

Carleton nodded and walked away, then stopped.

"There *is* something odd, Jake. She was plastered last night, but this morning she looked like she hadn't had a drop of booze. She recovers damn fast, I'll give her that."

"Must be her youth," I said. "When I was young like her, I had a high rate of metabolism. I could drink like a fish all night and be normal after only a few hours of sleep."

"You, Jake? Normal? Young? You've got to be shitting me."

"Get the hell outa here."

Carleton smirked as he left.

I felt relieved that Maddie was okay.

Another young officer then walked up and dropped a stack of sealed envelopes onto my desk

"Here's the photos from CSI and the coroner's report on Jane Doe Number 2, Jake."

"Thank you," I replied.

I broke the seal and spread them out on my desk.

Marlon Brando's last lines in the movie *Apocalypse Now* came to me: "The horror. The horror."

For over twenty years I've looked at similar photographs and wondered how one human being could do such things to another human being. Then I realized that human beings didn't do it. Animals did. Insanity did. Hate did. Revenge did. Other kinds of beings did. Those who commit these kinds of crimes had very little in common with human beings.

Still, even after so many years, the photos in front of me shocked me. I can only imagine how the first policeman felt as he entered the room where Mary Kelly's body lay dissected. *Poor bastard.* He probably took to drinking, like me.

It was clear to me that cool, calculating madness was present during all the crimes here and at Whitechapel. But I could not help wonder what the true motive was beneath it all. Something evil or hurtful lay behind the outward slaughter of these young hookers — something deep, foreboding, dark, and terrible.

With the original Jack the Ripper, I believed, there was a terror running under the skin of the man who could do that sort of thing to a woman. There was something injurious about it too. Not only for the victims, but for the assailant as well. He was hurting. He was hurting bad. So was my Jack. Something cancerous was eating at his cold, black heart. My job was to figure it out and stop him as soon as I could — *if* I could.

I spent the rest of the day staring at those pictures and reading and re-reading the autopsy report until my eyes finally blurred.

I even studied the victims. There were few similarities between them. So the killer wasn't targeting a particular hair color, size, weight, etc. The victims appeared completely random, except for the fact that they were both hookers. Of course, without a face, they could have been sisters and I wouldn't be able to tell.

I was missing some obvious clue. I was certain of it. But that clue was hiding from me in plain sight and, in the state of mind I was in at that moment, suffering for a drink as I was, it would remain hidden from me. I needed a drink and that was all I soon found myself concentrating on.

I glanced at my watch: 6:30 p.m. *Where the hell did this day go?* I asked myself. Contrary to what I stated before, regarding finding bodies early in the morning, this day had passed in a flash.

Sliding through the door of Bobby's bar, I noticed the familiar faces of the usual crowd. I exchanged playful barbs with a few as I headed toward the bar.

When I reached it, Bobby had my two drinks already poured and waiting for me.

"I have very strong feelings for you, Bobby," I said as I swept up one of the drinks and aimed it for my mouth.

I got a smirk and a chuckle from him as I chugged it and then slammed the empty glass back down onto the bar.

"Wow! Papa needed that one."

I got a few chuckles from the regulars out of that remark.

I only managed another smirk out of Bobby, though. He was used to me and my ways and he immediately refilled my glass.

I picked up the two drinks and sauntered back to my special table, continuing my exchange of friendly gibes with patrons on the way.

We weren't what anyone would call fast friends. We were bar rats. And there is a certain and simple understanding, a tolerance, a respect — an acceptance, if you will, that bar rats have for one another. We were all alcoholics. Alcoholics understand that no one in a bar is without sin. So there was no need for the ceremonial casting of stones. We were drunks. We knew it. We all accepted it.

Just as I set the drinks down on the table, I heard that angelic voice behind me.

"Would I be intruding on your special place?"

I turned and staggered. Not from the booze, but from the heavenly sight before me.

"Damn. You keep looking better each time I see you."

Maddie giggled. My manhood stirred, but that was about all it could manage. That was enough, though.

She sat down. I slid in behind the table and against the wall, as usual.

"Your special seat?" asked Maddie.

"The Hickok Rule."

"The Hickok Rule?"

"Wild Bill Hickok. An Old West gunfighter. Sat with his back to the door. Got a bullet in the back of the head for it. Thus, the Hickok Rule. Never leave your back exposed."

"Good rule, I guess, if you're a gunfighter."

"Or part of the mafia," I said. "Or a *cop*."

She grinned.

Bobby, god love him, was there in an instant with her Manhattans.

"I swear, Bobby."

"Yeah, yeah, Jake," he countered, smiling.

"You two have some kind of thing going?" Maddie asked.

"It's just our gay way," I replied, knowing what question was coming next.

"You're gay?"

"Nah. I'm so straight you could shoot me from a bow."

She burst out laughing.

I swallowed my drink, waiting for her to recover.

"Okay. You got me," she said.

"So, you a lesbo?"

"No. But I've experimented. I was younger then."

I almost choked on my drink. I hadn't expected that answer from her. But I recovered nicely.

"Whatever floats your boat, doll."

"I'm over it. So, what is it with you and the barman?"

"It's just my teasing way of acknowledging his attentiveness to my special needs. We've bantered back and forth like this for years."

"Well, he's got a great ass," she said, bumping her eyebrows.

I gulped, but again recovered quickly.

"So tell me, Blue Eyes, what brings your light to my dark side of the city?"

"I've been thinking about you all day. I had a feeling this is where I'd find you."

"Yeah. It ain't hard to find me here. This is sort of my home away from home."

"Where is your home, Jake?"

"Around the corner. Right smack dead in the middle of the Kitchen."

"Why here?"

"These are my peeps. I belong here. I bust half of the people in here often. We understand each other. We understand our roles. No judgment here."

"I'd think you'd be concerned with some kind of retribution from those you arrest."

"Not from these folks. I don't usually arrest them anyway. I just have the uniforms pick them up and let them sleep off a drunk now and then in the clink. Their cells aren't usually locked. In the morning they get up and leave on their own. Once in a while someone will stop by my desk to thank me for a square meal and a good night's sleep."

"Interesting life you live, Detective... Detective... What *is* your last name, Jake?"

"Brewer."

"Oh, my," she said, snickering.

"Stop," I said. "Don't start. I've already heard every beer joke ever thought of. I don't even like beer. I'm a hard-liquor kinda drunk."

"Why do you do that?" she asked.

"Do what?"

"Demean yourself."

"I'm not demeaning myself. I'm a drunk. I admit it. What's wrong with that?"

"It comes off sounding as if you disrespect yourself."

"Hey," I said, "I love myself, but I'm a drunk. I don't hide that fact. I don't try to be someone I'm not. I'm a drunk. And if someone doesn't like it, they can kiss my rosy red blooming begonia."

"You *are* an interesting man, Jake Brewer. I don't know why I'm so fascinated with you. But you've got me hook, line, and sinker."

"Let's drink to that," I declared.

We did, for a few hours.

Then we went back to my place, where she screwed my brains out.

CHAPTER 8

When I awoke the next morning, I was alone.

There was no note on the nightstand or anything that she had left behind for me to believe that she was really there the night before.

I wondered. Was it all in my head — my booze-soaked head?

It was certainly possible, I concluded. Most mornings after an especially good…no, that's not the word; an especially *soaking* drunk, I awoke with a devastating hangover and no memory of the happenings of the night before.

That morning, however, it was like I hadn't drunk at all. I was bright-eyed and bushy-tailed.

Still, knowing me, it was entirely possible that I had dreamed the whole screwed-my-brains-out thing.

I crawled out of bed and walked into my living room. And there I saw it.

On the whiteboard, Miss Blue Eyes had left me a note in amongst all my notes.

Jake. I'm starting to fall for you. Love, Maddie.

I grinned. Last night did happen. I felt like Tony the Tiger. Grrrrrrreat!

Early mornings in the department were no different than late at night. Cops hauled in perps just the same.

I ignored all of it. I had gotten laid. The whole world, with all its nastiness, couldn't make me feel anything except joy. You'd think after ten years of celibacy I'd have given up such doings. Well, I had done just that. But now, after being back in the saddle again, so to speak — although I had never ridden a horse in my life — I was thinking about it all the time.

This murder stuff had suddenly taken a backseat to this lovemaking side of life. I wanted more. Dare I say it, I wanted it more than a drink. Well, okay, that was a lie. I also wished I had a drink to celebrate my return to the world of the exotic lifestyle.

I hate it when I'm feeling great and the world just insists that *great* is too good for a sap like me.

Standing at my desk was a young officer. He didn't have a happy look about him.

"Don't tell me you've got bad news, Officer. I'm not in the mood for bad news right now.

"Here's some more photos for you, and the lieutenant wants to see you in his office. *Now!*"

"What for?"

"Like he's gonna tell *me*?"

"Right. Sorry. Thanks."

I grabbed a cup of coffee on my way to the lieutenant's office. It was from the bottom of the pot, filled with grounds, but I didn't care. I sipped of it what I could.

Lieutenant Grayson was hunched over his desk signing paperwork when I rapped on the door frame.

"Get in here, Jake," he said gruffly, without even looking up to make sure it was me.

I set the coffee cup down on his desk and walked to the shelf behind him. I picked up a baseball from its plastic holder and studied it. It was signed by Derek Jeter. I tossed it up and caught it.

Hank dropped his pen and turned and took the ball out of my hand and replaced it onto its holder.

"Sit down, Jake."

I flopped into the chair in front of his desk.

"What's up, Hank?"

"I got a report from one of the uniforms that Miss Hottie spent some time at your apartment with you last night. Is that true?"

"That lying little prick."

"So it's not true?"

"A gentleman doesn't discuss that sort of thing."

"Yeah, but I'm asking you."

"That hurts."

"Can the bullshit."

"Okay. It might be true."

"Is it or not?"

"Well, we messed up the sheets a bit, but when I woke up this morning she was gone."

"Eleven-thirty," said the lieutenant.

"Eleven-thirty? What about eleven-thirty?"

"That's the time she left your apartment and got picked up by the black-and-white unit that was parked outside your building."

"Damn. Eleven-thirty? I thought I was better than that."

"I've had dates *without* sex that lasted longer than twenty-five minutes."

"Twenty-five minutes? That's all it was? Well, there goes my reputation."

"News flash, Jake. You never had a reputation with the ladies. You're a drunk."

"Well, that's true enough, I guess. So, is that why you called me in here, to insult me?"

"No. I called you in here because I want to know what the hell you're doing with her in the first place. She's a material witness in a murder investigation — *your* investigation. She's not your bedroom toy, nor are you hers. I brought you in here to tell you this: If it doesn't stop, and I mean right goddamn now, then I'll pull you off the case. You're losing it, Jake. You're losing perspective. We've got two carved-up bodies and no leads. Get your little head back into your pants and your big head back into the investigation. Got it?"

"Yeah. I got it. Sorry."

"I ain't got time for sorry. Sorry ain't gettin' the job done. Are we communicating, Jake?"

"Yeah. Yeah, I get it."

"Great! Get the hell outa here."

I turned to leave his office when he continued.

"And Jake. The liquor is really getting out of hand. Even for you. The black-and-white unit tells me you just barely made it home last night. You might want to seek some help about that. Do it, Jake. Get some help or you'll force me to retire your ass. At the very least, don't drive when you're in the bag that deep.

Use a bit of sense, if you still have any. Am I getting through to you?"

"Yeah. That too."

"You're the best investigator I got, Jake. No one else even comes close. But I'll do without you before I let you screw up my department. Now, get back to work and get a handle on this investigation before the press gets full wind of it. I'm having a harder and harder time keeping the lid on this."

"I'm back in the game, coach."

"Good. Piss off now."

Grayson was right. I screwed up big time. I believed I could keep Maddie at arm's length from now on. But the liquor was going to be another matter altogether.

Alcoholics can't just turn it off. That's why we're alkies in the first damn place. Grayson had covered my ass countless times before. He was a good guy, better than I deserved. I resolved to get a handle on the booze before I forced his hand.

I got back to my desk. It looked nearly the same as when I sat there last. The photographs, however, still spread out across my desk, were face down. Someone, thankfully, had turned them for me. I had forgotten to do that myself. No doubt I was thinking more about Maker's Mark at that particular moment than the sensibility of anyone walking past my desk. The booze was getting out of hand. I had to admit that.

The new package of photos lay in the center of the desk, still sealed. I gathered them all up into one pile and then moved them into the squad investigation room. It was a large room with window blinds and several tables and wall-mounted, magnetic whiteboards where a team could spread out the evidence for a better perspective.

I decided that this would be my new office for a while.

I spread out every photo in the order of the murders. It was a grisly task. I then sat for the next few hours staring again at them, hoping to spot the smallest clue that might help me identify the perp.

About three hours into my death stare, I heard a knock on the door. It was young Officer Carleton.

"Jake, you got a phone call. Line six."

"Thanks."

I picked up the line.

"Detective Brewer," I said, trying to sound professional.

"Hi, Jake. It's Maddie. How are you?"

I wanted to remain professional, but that lasted for about one second after I heard her voice. I was toast again.

"Hi, there. I'm doing great. Thanks for last night. I really needed that. How are you doing?"

"I'm having a hard time walking."

She snickered. I felt a tingle southward.

"Yeah. Right. I heard about my performance already. I was rudely reminded that you left about eleven-thirty."

The tingling ceased.

"It's the quality of time, Jake, not the quantity."

"You're being kind, but I did warn you. I'm a drunk. Drunks have issues when it comes to that sort of thing."

"I'm not complaining. I just wanted to call to thank you for a great evening. I haven't had that much fun in a long time. I'm usually under tight control and the model of corporate decorum. It felt wonderful to just let loose. I look forward to another night of wild abandon."

"Yeah, about that. It's not going to happen. I got chewed out this morning about our night. You're a material witness to an important investigation and I almost compromised that. Well, to be honest I did compromise it, but we drunks don't always admit it, nor make good decisions when we should."

"I'm sorry, Jake. I suppose I'm to blame for that. I shouldn't have tracked you down the way I did. Can you forgive me?"

"There's nothing to forgive. It was *my* fault, not yours. I'm supposed to be a professional. It got out of hand last night. I've got to reel it in before something bad happens."

"Then I can't see you again?"

"Not for a while. Not during this investigation. At least not unless it's in an official capacity."

"I don't think that's fair, Jake. I like you."

"And I more than like you, but…well…"

"What?"

"I shouldn't tell you."

"Now you have to. You can't tell me that and expect me not to want to know. What is it?"

"Well, we've got a second now. The body was discovered early yesterday morning. And it's a bad one, Maddie — grisly, terribly grisly."

"Oh my god, Jake!"

"Yeah. Listen, you've got to keep this under your hat. If full word of these murders gets out into the public, we'll have panic on our hands."

"I know. I know. I was asked to keep what little I know quiet by your Lieutenant Grayson. I understand completely. But how many more, Jake?"

"What do you mean?"

"I mean, how many more do you think there are going to be before it ends? Jack the Ripper killed five officially, but he is suspected of having killed many more than just five, if you include the ones he's suspected of killing in the U.S. Do you think this guy will try to top the Ripper?"

"Oh Christ, I glossed over that earlier. I had been concentrating on the severity of the murders. I've never given any hard thought to the quantity issue. Damn!"

"Jake, sorry to cut you short, but my meeting is about to start."

We said our goodbyes and then I fell back into my chair, stupefied that I had never given real thought to the number of victims this guy might be trying to achieve. *This could get really bloody*, I sadly concluded.

Officer Carleton walked up and dropped another package onto the desk.

"What ya got now?"

"Something to really mess with your head."

"What's that?"

"Better you see it for yourself."

He walked away before I could grill him. I reached for the package, but Grayson walked in and began lifting the photos from the desk.

"What have ya got, Jake?"

"I've got them in order."

"Fine," he said replacing them. "Are you getting anywhere?"

"Not really, but I'm seeing a pattern, of sorts."

"What kind of pattern?"

"This guy is…how can I put it…methodical and meticulous. No! That's not it. This guy is messily methodical."

"What the hell does that mean?"

"He tears the bodies apart, but he leaves nothing behind that can identify him. Have you ever heard of that?"

"Now that you mention it, no. And you're right."

He looked over the pictures again as I continued.

"Blood everywhere, Hank. Body parts scattered. Crazy vicious butchery and he left no prints, DNA, hair samples. Nothing. Impressive."

"Well, hell let's throw an admiration party for the guy, Jake."

"I'm not saying that, Hank. But what happened to all that evidence? Killers always leave something behind. Where the hell did it go?... Oh, shit!"

"Oh, shit, what?" asked Grayson.

"Hang on, Lieutenant."

I picked up the logs and found the officer's name and phone number. I hit the speaker button and got a dial tone. I dialed.

"Officer Johnson," the voice responded.

"Randy, this is Jake. Listen up. You found the second body yesterday morning. Did you by any chance check the dumpsters in the alley?"

"Yes, Jake. I did. Nothing there."

"Did you by chance check the surrounding alley's dumpsters?"

"I didn't do that."

"Do it. Do it now."

I'm dealing with a DUI right now, Jake."

"Drop it. Tell them it's their lucky day. Inspect all the dumpsters in...say...a two-block radius."

"Okay. What am I looking for?"

"Something bloody, like plastic or whatever."

"Okay. Will do."

"If you find something, don't touch it. Call me immediately."

"Okay."

I disconnected the call.

"You're thinking he wore something to hide his DNA and then dumped it?" asked Grayson.

"Doc suggested that earlier. But I'm betting on it now."

"Someone would have seen him carrying it around."

"Maybe."

"Are you thinking he already had the supplies in the alley?"

"Something like that."

"He'd have to plan the job very carefully to pull it off exactly where he did."

"I'm thinking he's got a car and he picks up the hookers, drugs them, and drives to the alleys. He does them and tosses the garbage in a dumpster on his way home."

"Makes sense. Sort of. But he could drop the garbage anywhere, then. Why have the uniform only check within two blocks?"

"I'm betting he wouldn't want it in his car too long. Just in case. I'll say it again. This guy is messily meticulous. I'm guessing his car is clean as a whistle, too."

"It's a hell of a shot in the dark, but I've seen you do some crazy shit before that paid off. Let me know if anything is found."

"Will do."

He walked out and I was alone again.

I went back to staring at the pictures, looking for anything that could capture blood and might have been left behind.

I studied each photo with a magnifying glass.

After another hour I dropped the magnifier to the table. There wasn't a hint of anything left behind. This bastard was the best I had ever seen keeping the murder scene clean. Clean, that is, for his own traces.

I glanced up at the clock on the wall. Six o'clock on the dot. *Hey*, I thought. *I haven't thought of a drink all day.* At least not since I got my ass chewed. That had to be some kind of a record. Maybe the chewing-out had had its desired effect.

I guess I shouldn't have thought about it, because then that was all I could think of — a Maker's Mark neat.

I arose from my chair and was about to leave when I noticed the sealed package on my desk. I reached for it, but my cell phone went off.

It was Officer Johnson.

"Jake here. Did you find something?"

"No, Jake. And I made a three-block sweep."

"Thanks, Randy."

Disconnecting, I realized that I had gained nothing for the effort and that it had brought me right back to where I had been only a short while ago. Detective Nowhere was nowhere. Time for a drink.

CHAPTER 9

I was sitting in my usual seat in Bobby's bar when she walked in.

She made a beeline for me.

"I know I'm intruding, Jake. I don't want to cause you any problem, but I had to see you."

She sat down. Bobby had a Manhattan to the table within moments plus a couple more shots for me and then he was gone.

I looked at my watch: 8:57 p.m.

"Long day?" I asked.

She sucked down about half of her drink before saying another word.

I smiled. "One of those days, I take it."

She rolled her eyes. "You could say that."

"Is there a black-and-white outside?"

"Actually, he brought me here. I told him I really needed to see you. He offered to give me a lift."

"Might as well. He'd have to follow you anyway. So what's on your mind?"

"Nothing. I just needed to see a friendly face. Anything new with the investigation?"

"Well, it's moving in a positive direction. That's all I can really say at the moment."

"I see. You've been warned to keep it quiet, I presume."

"Just protocol, Maddie."

"I understand." She finished her drink and Bobby had another right there, taking away the empty with a nod and a smile.

"I'm in big trouble, you know," I said.

"Yes. I'm sorry. I didn't realize you'd get in such a fix with your boss."

"It's not that. I'm falling for you, Maddie. That's my trouble."

"Really? How sweet."

"No. It's not. I'm an idiot. I know there's no future in it, for you or for me. I'm an old drunk. You're a rising young star in a city where rising stars need to be careful with whom they associate."

"But Jake, I—"

"Let me finish. I'm a cop. I don't dress well. I've apparently got serious emotional and mental problems. At least, the department shrink seems to think so. It doesn't matter, though. I'm not in your league. I don't want to fool myself. And you, you need to know that. I'm not what you need. Nor am I even what you should want. Not even for a frivolous whim's sake. I'm no good in relations. If you only knew what I see every day. I deal with the lowest forms of life in this city. I'm scarred — beyond what I even know myself. I know I need to get a hold on this drinking, but it's the only way I know to rid myself of the terrors that fill my mind when I'm sober. If being sober isn't terror enough."

She reached out her right hand to lay it on mine, as she lifted her drink to her lips with her left. I pulled away.

"Don't. Don't waste your time with me. Go back home and get on with your life."

I stood up, dropped some cash on the table, and grabbed her arm, pulling her to her feet.

"But Jake," she protested.

I ignored her. She continued protesting, but I didn't listen. I pulled her through the bar, out the door, and put her inside the patrol car.

"Take her home and don't let her leave her place tonight. You got it?"

"I got it, Jake," replied the uniform.

I was instantly struck by the obvious as I slammed the door and the black-and-white pulled away from the curb. What was it that struck me? I had no place else to go, except to an empty, dark, lonely apartment.

I walked back into the bar.

It was one of those nights when the patrons cleared out early. By midnight, I was alone. I drank too much, as usual.

It was 2:15 when I locked the door and staggered home, leaving my car parked along the curb. It was safe. Most everyone knew it was mine. I collapsed onto my bed still fully clothed.

Perhaps the effect of Grayson's warning had faded, or perhaps it was that I was a hopeless slosher, beyond redemption. Or perhaps I just didn't give a damn anymore. Whatever the reason, I lay on my bed, beginning to sober up while failing to fall asleep. I hated that most. Sobering up was like waking up into a land filled with only disappointment and dread.

After two full and useless hours of just lying there staring at the walls and ceiling, I finally yielded to the call of my investigation room. I glanced at the clock on my nightstand: 4:35 a.m.

"Damn it!" I said, getting up.

To make matters worse, I was now sober as a judge. Someone explain that to me. How do you drink yourself nearly blind and then two or three hours later you're sober? *Hell*, I thought, *I'm not even any good at being a drunk.*

Still, a better decision was being reached. I called the department and they sent a black-and-white to pick me up and take me to the office.

I walked into the room with a fresh cup of coffee and began my day by staring once more at the photos. One by one, I again studied them intensely. That feeling of missing something haunted me.

An hour later and five more cups of coffee and two trips to the john to get rid of it, I resigned myself to the fact that whatever might be hiding from me in those photographs was not going to reveal itself to me just yet.

I wandered around the department chatting with the late-shift detectives. For once the city was rather quiet, at least for our precinct. We engaged in the usual detective banter until I'd wasted two hours of their time. I headed back into my den of doom.

It was then that I noticed the still sealed package on my desk — the one Officer Carleton predicted would *mess with my head.*

I opened the package and withdrew the contents.

It was a more complete background report on Madison Dumont, aka Margaret Skimmer.

Over the years it had become SOP (standard operating procedure) for our department to order reports on people who reported strange or wild crimes. Such reports had often been found to be critical to the investigation because more often than not those reporting a bizarre crime were somehow connected to it. Not that they were often the one directly responsible for the crime or even necessarily aware of their involvement in the crime. But they were connected in some way.

In the past, such reports had proved to be highly instrumental in ultimately identifying suspects and facilitating their apprehension.

I slumped into my chair and read for the next hour and a half.

What was printed on the papers before me boggled my alcohol-infused brain, but not so much that I couldn't believe what I was reading, and I read every word with alert fascination.

One solitary piece of paper lay under all the rest. It made me jump to my feet in startled surprise. It was a letter of reference for one Madison Dumont from Shitberg, Kentucky. That wasn't the name of the town, of course. But I didn't care. I had, more importantly just discovered a link to Maddie outside New York. And it wasn't Ohio.

"Holy crap!" I barked. "I need some help with the computer, please."

A younger officer, Patricia Nelson, one of our in-house researchers, came to my desk.

"What do you need, Jake?"

"I need you to sit down and do something for me."

We went on the Internet and, within seconds, using the information in the report, she found what I was looking for.

"Thanks, Patty. Leave the screen on, please."

"Sure, Jake," she answered as she stood up and walked away.

I looked at my wristwatch: 10:07 a.m. My hand shot for the telephone. I dialed the Jackson County Sheriff's office in McKee, Kentucky.

"Good morning," I said when someone answered. "This is New York Police Detective Jake Brewer. Would Sheriff Hagan Duggar be in his office now and available? He would? Great. Might I have a word with him, please? Yeah, sure, I can hold."

I didn't have to wait long.

He answered.

"Yeah, good morning to you too, Sheriff. Yes, indeed. I'm calling from the Big Apple. Yes, you can help me. Might we have a short discussion about Zyree Luttrell?"

Short? Yeah, right. Our discussion lasted almost a full hour. Sheriff Duggar convinced me that a telephone conversation wouldn't be enough to answer the thousand questions that were now forming in my mind, and he invited me down to Kentucky to continue our discussion.

We finished our phone call and I spent the next hour pacing my office before I saw Lieutenant Grayson wander in sleepily past the open door.

"Lieutenant!"

Grayson walked into the room with an odd expression on his face.

"We're not on until swing shift, Jake."

"Yeah, I know. So what are you doing here?"

"I have a meeting with Captain. What's your excuse?"

"We need to have a sit-down discussion, Hank."

"Before my coffee?"

"Yeah."

"About what?"

"Me heading to Kentucky."

After thirty minutes of convincing him that there was something important in Kentucky other than hicks and sticks and stills, I was authorized for a plane ticket to Kentucky.

The next morning at seven, I sat at the gate in LaGuardia waiting to board a plane for the roughly two-hour flight to Cincinnati. I was pleased with myself at how skillfully I had laid out my strategy in Kentucky for Grayson. And although I was shocked when he sat quietly listening and didn't try to tear apart my reasoning for going there, I took it as a confirmation that he also considered it important to the investigation to get me to Kentucky to see what I could uncover.

Then, like a slap in the face, I recognized Grayson's strategy. It wasn't my demonstrated skill that got the ticket authorized. It wasn't my oratory proficiency that convinced him to let me travel. He wanted me gone. He saw my blossoming relationship with Maddie as a problem for him and the department. He wanted us separated to let things calm down. That bastard had played with me like a toy.

I chuckled to myself. That's why he was my boss and not the other way around. He was a manager. I was a grunt. He was sharp as a tack. I was a drunk.

Well, Jake, I thought, either way, you're on your way to Kentucky. They may have their hicks and sticks, but it was their stills that I was really looking forward to. Gotta play it cool, though. If Grayson thinks I'm in the bag too much, he might pull me back home early. I came to the conclusion that I would have to be on my best behavior in Kentucky, for a good while, at least. I didn't want the sheriff to make a call to Grayson and ask him to please get his drunk detective out of his county.

What is that they say about the best-laid plans?

I was pretty much in the bag by the time we landed, courtesy of Susie, the friendly, cute, and oh so accommodating flight attendant, who had the cutest ass I'd ever seen, next to Maddie's, of course. And how she loved showing it off on her many trips up and down the aisle during the flight.

Two and half hours after arriving at the Cincinnati airport, I pulled into a parking stall in front of the Jackson County Sheriff's Department in McKee, Kentucky.

I looked into the rearview mirror and was frightened to see my bloodshot eyes staring back at me. Good thing for me I had developed the ability to drive with blurry vision on my way down from Cincinnati.

Walking, barely — to be honest, staggering — I slipped into the door and strode up to the front desk. I flashed my badge.

"I'm Detective Jacob Brewer. I believe Sheriff Duggar is expecting me."

"Okay, Detective. Let me get him for ya," replied the male deputy manning the desk.

He walked back into an office and spoke to the sheriff. I, meanwhile, tried to determine whether I smelled of booze. I couldn't tell, of course. Drunks are usually the last to smell the booze oozing out of their own pores.

My mind flashed on Susie's fine, tight little ass sashaying up and down the aisle of that damned plane.

I saw the sheriff look up and then spring out of his chair. He came to his door and waved me to him.

"Sheriff Duggar," I said upon arriving at his door. "I'm Detective Brewer."

"Oh, heck, Detective," he said, motioning toward a chair in front of his desk, "everyone just calls me Hagan. That'd be my given name."

"Everyone just calls me Jake, Hagan," I replied, seating myself.

I sort of tumbled into the chair. Hagan noticed, but ignored it for the moment.

"I must say, you New York City boys do things quick-like. Heck, it was like we was just talkin' together a bit ago."

"It was yesterday, but I convinced my lieutenant that it was pretty important that I be here."

Hagan sniffed at the air as he reseated himself.

"Would that be Maker's Mark?"

I was shocked and bit embarrassed. Well, as embarrassed as a drunk can be at being found out.

"Sorry, Hagan. The flight attendant was a real cutie and ever so accommodating. I apologize for my condition."

"Oh, heck. That don't bother me. I'm a bit of an imbiber myself. Don't have the money for that expensive Maker's Mark elixir. I'm more of a local moonshine imbiber."

He chuckled. I felt instantly relieved.

"Maybe you could introduce me to the shine later, if you don't mind? I guess bourbon tends to smell a bit coming out of the pores."

Hagan laughed.

"Shine don't smell, and I expect we'll get to it before too long. Well, Detective, this is wonderful, just wonderful. I've never met a real-life New York City detective before. This is darn excitin'."

He grinned at me.

This was *my* first time meeting with a one-horse-town sheriff, but I didn't let on.

"I appreciate your taking the time to meet with me."

"It's a pleasure. It's a real pleasure, and I gotta tell ya, Jake, you piqued my interest with your case. That Jack the Ripper fella was a special sorta nasty."

"Yes, he was."

"But you askin' about this girl, Madison Dumont; that's a really enticin' mystery to me. I can't say I've ever heard that name before, though. On the phone you said you think she might be from around these parts?"

I opened my briefcase and pulled out a picture of Maddie and laid it in front of Hagan. He stared at it for only a second or two, then shook his head.

"Holy Nellie's on a camel and Bucky's in a ditch! She's a mighty fine-lookin' woman, Jake. Yes, sir, mighty fine, but she don't spark a memory. She one a those fancy models like you see in magazines?"

"No, she's the managing editor for one of those magazines."

"You don't say. Well, sir, if she was from around here, I think I'd remember a good-lookin' gal like that. Heck, I don't think we grow them kinda lookers down around these parts."

He handed the photo back to me. I sat stunned, wondering who Holy Nellie might be and why she was on a camel. And just who was this Bucky guy in a ditch and why wasn't he on his own camel? I was going to laugh at the wonderful absurdity of his backwoods colloquialism, but I didn't know if doing so would offend him. Thus, having no understanding of Kentucky cultural sensitivity, I allowed discretion to guide me and I remained mute on the subject of Nellie and Bucky.

"Yes, sir," he continued. "And a fancy name like that only gotta be a name you'd find in the Big Apple."

More surprising words from the sheriff. It was my reaction as well when Maddie and I discussed it. Here or in Tinytown, Ohio, a fancy surname like Dumont might not be common among these folks.

"Very astute, Hagan," I offered. "As we discussed, she claims to be from Lemmingberg, Ohio, and her real name is Margaret Skimmer. But let me ask you this: There's no record of a Dumont family in these parts, is there?"

"None I know of, Jake. And I growed up here. Like I said, sounds too fancy for around here."

"She said she changed her name because it worked better for her in New York. But that's not what intrigued me as I went through her file. What I caught was that she was using the name Madison Dumont before she went up to New York."

"You sayin' she was Madison Dumont down this way?"

"It appears so," I replied. "But for sure you don't recognize her?"

"Sorry, Jake. She don't bring to mind anyone from around here."

"Maybe we could show the photo around?" I asked. "Maybe someone else might recognize her."

"Sure. You never can tell."

He scratched his chin and then looked at me with sudden worry growing on his face.

"Could I see that photo again?"

I handed it back to him. He studied it intensely for almost a full minute.

"No, sir. She don't look at all familiar to me. I thought for a moment I might have seen her before. But…no, I can't say that I have."

He handed the photo back to me again.

"Jake," he continued, "I'm havin' a hard time imaginin' that pretty woman could kill anyone at all, let alone like the Ripper."

"She's not the suspect, Hagan. She's the witness."

"Witness? Oh, I guess I didn't catch that part."

"Listen, whenever someone reports a violent crime like the one I'm investigating, we run a side investigation on the witness. We've found that many times the witness is somehow involved or connected in some odd way to the crime or to the perp. When my officers ran her name through the system, they didn't find anything on her. At least not under that name. It was like she materialized into being about ten years ago in New York. Except for that information, my people couldn't find a clue about her. One of our officers then discovered this reference letter in a folder on his desk. He doesn't remember pulling up this letter from anywhere. It was just lying in the folder. But what made it special is that it contains a possible reference to Annville here in Kentucky through a work reference."

"Well, Annville is only about ten miles due south from here on Highway 290. You're thinkin' she's really from down that way?"

"I can't say for sure. Like I said, all we found was a letter of reference for a Madison Dumont dated around the time she showed up in New York from a Mister Zyree Luttrell of Annville, Kentucky — in conjunction with a job application to a magazine publisher Maddie was applying to as an intern."

"That would be Zyree Luttrell Senior, I imagine. He used to run the general store down in Annville. Nice man. Could I see the letter, Jake?"

I pulled it from my briefcase and handed it to him.

He sat studying it as intently as he had the photograph. Then he glanced up at me.

"Yes sir. I recognize Zyree's signature. Seen it many a time before."

"So, no doubt the letter is genuine?" I asked.

"No doubt, Jake."

"Could you introduce me to him? I'd like to chat with him."

"You'd like to chat with *him*?"

"Yes. Is it possible?"

"I reckon so, if you speak angel."

"What's that?"

"He's dead. Died about three years ago. Heart attack. Keeled right over onto a potato chip rack and hit the ground dead. Made a heck of a mess of them homemade chips in the process, too. It was real sad. About Zyree, that is. Everybody liked Zyree. The chips wasn't bad either."

"I see," I said, with a hint of disappointment no doubt in my voice. "Well, what else caught my attention during our phone call was when you mentioned your professor friend...uh, I've got his name here somewhere in my notes."

"No need to look. That would be Professor Arnold Hastings you're talkin' about."

"Yeah. Hastings. Is *he* dead too?"

"Not that I know of. I expect you'll want to chat with him?"

"If you could arrange it."

"Sure can."

"Can you tell me a little about him?"

"Sure. He taught criminology at the university up in Lexington for many years. He was originally from here, so after he retired, about fifteen years ago, he moved back here. He's made a life study out of the Ripper murders. He's what you call a *Ripperologist*. He started a whole Ripper group down here a couple years later. It was pretty active until four or five years ago. They used to meet once a month and discuss the murders and any new evidence and theories that came along. But now they only get together every six months or so. And I believe they use the Internet to do that now."

"That's one of the reasons I'm here, Hagan. Who would have thought there would be a Ripperologist in these parts?"

"We're a small backwoods community, Jake, but we ain't totally ignorant of what happens out in the world, so to speak."

"I can see that."

"I studied under the good professor myself when I was a young 'un at the university. Heck, I'm the one got him to move back here."

"Really?" I asked.

"Yeah. Talkin' to him about Jack the Ripper is oftentimes as interestin' as our own homegrown mysteries."

"What mysteries are those?"

"Oh, we got us several juicy mysteries down in these parts. Strange ones. Bewilderin' ones. But the one I'm talkin' about is the mystery of what happened to Reverend Joshua Cousins. He was our local preacher up until ten years ago or so. One day he was here. The next day he was gone. Disappeared into thin air, some will tell ya. We ain't never found 'im either or what might be left of 'im."

"Really? You say he disappeared about ten years ago?"

"Yep. Let me think on that a sec… Yeah, it was just about ten years ago now. Yeah. It was too much to tell you over the phone, but now that you're here maybe you might help me look at the case. We can jump in the squad car and I can deliver ya to all the scenes. Nothin' much has changed around here since then. Would that be okay with you?"

"Sounds fascinating. If you don't mind, though, I'd like to concentrate on *my* investigation for the time being. I'm on the department's dime, you understand?"

"Sure do. You bet."

Sheriff Duggar glanced at his watch.

"It's close to lunchtime around here, Jake. Everything just sorta shuts down at this time. There's a great restaurant here in town called Elma's. It's small, but ol' Gerald's got the best chicken steak in these parts. Would you care to join me?"

"Absolutely, Sheriff."

CHAPTER 10

Sheriff Duggar wasn't lying. The chicken steak was the best I'd ever had.

After lunch we jumped into his squad car and headed south to Annville.

His *little mystery* was intriguing and enticed me to inquire more about it as we drove.

"You say the reverend went missing and was never seen again?" I asked.

"That's right. He just up and disappeared, just like that."

"I must say that *is* interesting. If you have time later, could we chat about that more?"

"Heck, Jake, we got nothin' but time down here. Ain't nothin' really happened since the Rev went missin'."

"How long ago was that, again?"

"Just about ten years ago, I reckon. It was a real mess, too. Reverend Cousins had himself in a bit of trouble up near the end. It was just speculation, mind you. Nothin's ever been proved outright, but there was plenty of allegations and lots of gossip goin' around."

"About what?"

"About the Rev havin', shall we say, *inglorious* relations with some of the young girls amongst his congregation, and then, of course, there was that rumor of his involvement with a young child who turned up dead and pregnant. That kinda thing."

"He was a pedophile?"

"No proof of that. Just speculation and gossip. But if you ask me, I'd say suspicion run high enough to believe it to be mostly true. But it was the way she died that caused everyone sleepless nights for some time."

"How's that?"

"Well, she was found…dare I say it…she was found like Jack the Ripper had got to her. She was all tore up. Parts of her insides missin'. The only way we found out she was with child was from the bloodwork done by Ol' Doc Burns durin' the autopsy. But that weren't the worst of it. Her face was carved off. Like the killer didn't want her to be identified. Isn't that just awful?"

"It is, Hagan. Just awful."

My heart leapt in my chest when Hagan mentioned her face being carved off. It was terribly close to home. I kept that detail to myself, though. I was still in the information-gathering phase of my investigation. I wasn't yet ready to exchange sensitive information that could be crucial to solving my case.

"Can I speak to Doctor Burns about the body's condition?"

"He's dead, Jake. Died about fifteen years ago."

Jesus!" I said. "Is *everyone* dead?"

"I'm still kickin'."

"It was a rhetorical question. You know, we deal with lots of crimes like this. But I didn't expect to hear about them down in these parts."

"We don't get a lot of crimes down here too much anymore. At least not like we used to, when the revenuers was tryin' to break up the stills, but when we do, they's doozies."

"And because of his probable connection to the Jack the Ripper case, you think someone suspected the preacher of the crime and might have exacted some kind of revenge on him?"

"He denied any involvement, of course. And I can't say for sure, but I have always held my suspicions regardin' his participation in the crime. I've maintained that he knew more about it than he said. But then he went missin' and we ain't turned up the body. I can say this, though: it had everyone around here real spooked and wary for quite some time."

"When did the little girl die?"

"Well, let me think about that.... That would be about nineteen years ago now. Shucks, sure don't seem like all that time has passed. But yeah, nineteen years ago."

"Did you get the girl's name?"

"No. We was never able to match her to any database of missin' children. Who she was remains a mystery to us all to this day. I suspect it will remain so forever."

"Was your Doc Burns able to establish an age for the little girl?"

"It was more of an educated guess. He thought she might be between eleven and thirteen."

"How sure was he of those ages?"

"She had barely blossomed, if you get my drift, so he reckoned her to be between those ages. Old enough to get with child."

"Got it. So, the reverend had been under suspicion all those years prior to his own disappearance?"

"Not right away. But as time passed, word spread. He continued to deny any involvement over the passin' years, but people get to talkin' and get to pointin' fingers. It was a real problem for us all for a time. He was very intimidatin'. Shoutin' Hellfire for wrongful accusations made. Threatenin' the souls of those who kept such accusations goin'. People were scared of him. And then, like most things here that lose traction, it faded away and everything went back to normal. If you can call it that."

"Did he have a family? The preacher?"

"Oh, yeah. The missus still lives in the same house."

"Her name?"

"That would be Mercy Cousins."

"Any children?" I asked.

"Two daughters. Kerri Ann and Mary Beth."

"They still live around here?"

"No, sir. They left to parts unknown some time ago."

"Do you know about when they left?"

"Just after their pa went missin'."

"So, ten years ago?"

"That's right."

"Did they leave together?"

"Oh, yeah. Them two was thicker'n thieves. They was always one next to the other no matter where they was."

"Were you able to interrogate them about the disappearance of their father before they left town?"

"Oh, yeah. We might be a bit backwards down here compared to you big-city boys, but we're not altogether incompetent."

"Sorry, Hagan. I didn't mean to insinuate that."

"Just funnin' ya, Jake. I had a chat with both girls myself. I came to the conclusion that they knew nothin' about it. If they was lyin', they did a good job of it. Anyway, I could find no reason to stop 'em from leavin'. Besides, for many years before and after, there was strong rumors floatin' about that their daddy did some things to them when they both was real young. I thought it better to let them go and get on with their lives — maybe get that sort of thing behind them if it was true."

"Their mother never confirmed or denied it?"

"Mercy wouldn't do that. You ain't met her, so you don't know. Mercy was a victim of the reverend as well. I always believed he threatened her in order to keep her quiet about it. I don't know for certain about that, but I believe it."

"I see. So the girls left the area soon after their father went missing and he went missing about ten years ago. Have I got that right?"

"You got it right, Jake. They both took off at the same time. And I ain't seen hide nor hair of 'em since."

"And that is also about the time Maddie Dumont showed up in New York. And I'm guessing no one has really missed the good reverend all that much."

"He was a hard man — very judgmental. He was especially hard on his own kin. I don't reckon many have missed him much. I can say I haven't missed him at all. Since he's been gone, my life has calmed quite a bit."

"Do you think their mama has a forwarding address for the girls?"

"I don't believe she does. But you can ask her yourself if you want to. Would you like to go out and meet her?"

"Yeah. You bet."

"Well, just so you know, she's a bit touched in the head, if you know what I mean."

"I think so. Results of the reverend's abuse?"

"I think so, mostly. She's always struck me as the fragile type anyway. But the reverend certainly didn't help her none."

"Okay. Consider me warned."

We passed a bar. I couldn't help but stare at it. I was doing pretty good with my self-imposed sobriety, except for the plane trip. Oh, hell! I'm lying about it. I wanted a drink so bad I could almost taste it right there in the patrol car. The sheriff noticed me staring.

"You havin' a need for the spirits right now, Jake?"

"I should be on the wagon right now. I'm having a bit more than a need for it, if you catch my drift."

"Shoot, down in these parts that ain't nothin' to be ashamed of. On the way back up to McKee, I'll take you out to ol' Jed's still. You familiar with moonshine?"

"Heard of it. Never had it before."

"Ol' Jed's shine is the best ever. You'll love it. Yes sir, puts the hair back on the dog, as we say down here."

He laughed. It was a great laugh — a real belly laugh. I enjoyed hearing it. But it didn't do much to quell my desire for the taste of booze sliding down my throat. I did my best to sound professional.

"You don't arrest moonshiners down here, then?"

"Heck no. Where do you think we get our drinkin' liquor from? That store-bought rotgut don't compare to our shine at all. No, sir. And darn it all, it would be hard to get on down here without our moonshine. They're good ol' boys. They don't bother nobody. They keep to themselves pretty much."

"The Feds allow it?"

"Heck with what the Feds allow. Everyone loves the stuff. We'd have us a real riot on our hands if we busted the shiners. I even cart down supplies to ol' Jed now and then, when I know ahead of time that I'll be passin' by."

I chuckled. But to be honest, I was hoping he'd offer to go by the still right then. He didn't offer, though, and I was self-conscious about asking, so I let it go. My hand began to tremble some. I slid it under my leg, but the eagle-eyed sheriff noted it.

"Yes, sir, I think you got more than just a simple need for liquor, Jake. I think you got a powerful need for it."

"I won't lie, Hagan. I've been dealing with some issues regarding it lately."

"Well, heck. This just ain't right," said the sheriff.

Hagan stopped the car in the middle of the highway, got out and opened the trunk, and then slammed it shut. He returned with a pint jar with a screw top. He handed it to me and started driving down the road again.

"Now listen, Jake. Investigatin' crimes is hard enough on old boys like us. Take a few swigs of this delight and it might mellow you some — change your perspective, you might say. Steady that hand of yours. But I warn you, this is some killer mash. If you're not careful, it'll jump up and bite ya a good one — get ya to go walkin' on your lips for a spell."

I laughed.

I opened it and took a swallow of the smoothest liquor I'd ever had in my sorry life. It was just what I needed. After a time, things started to stabilize again.

"Hagan, ol' buddy, this is exactly what I needed. I've never had better. Could we keep this to ourselves, though? If my lieutenant knew I was drinking right now, I'd be in for it. He warned me about stills down here."

Hagan snickered.

"We do things a might different down here, Jake. Don't you worry yourself about it."

"All right, then. I know where I'll apply for a job if I get tired of New York."

"Well, speakin' for myself, it would be an honor havin' the likes of you here."

"I appreciate that."

"I reckon you could say that we're a mite more tolerant of the failings of life here," said the Kentucky sheriff. "Things matter here, Jake. Good things matter most. The rest don't matter at all."

I had heard some recital of this subtle backwoods wisdom before, but I had never heard it spoken so eloquently.

"It seems you've got a touch of philosophy in your soul, Hagan."

He chuckled.

"Shoot. Must be the effects of the shine. Expands the mind, you know. At least that's what we keep tellin' ourselves. Sometimes a body needs a small lie or two to keep perspective on the larger issues of life."

He chuckled again and then got serious.

"Folks in these parts, Jake, are simple folks with simple minds. They tell you what they're thinkin' plain and true. They don't pussyfoot around the truth. If you're gonna deal with them like I do, it's best you understand that about them."

"I shall endeavor to do just that."

"Well then, I reckon you'll get along just fine, then."

CHAPTER 11

We parked in front of Luttrell's General Store in downtown Annville and stayed seated in the car for a while. Hagan said it gave the folks who noticed us some time to reconcile with it. I noticed the name on the sign.

"I take it there be kinfolk ownin' the store now?" I asked, dipping into my scant repertoire of country hick accents and colloquialisms. I was probably off the mark a bit, but Hagan went on without remarking on it.

"Yeah, Zyree's son, Zyree Junior. Just, everyone calls him Junior."

I smirked.

"Junior? I heard everyone in Kentucky is named Junior."

"Watch the tone, Jake. I warn you. That's the boy's name."

"Sorry. It just took me by surprise."

"Be on your best behavior now. This town is sorta like moonshine. It'll bite you hard if you ain't mindful of how things are here."

"I don't know what I'd do without you, Hagan."

"To be honest, you'd most likely end up a lump in the forest dirt if you'd come down here on your own. They're not real trustin' of strangers in these parts."

"And *I* was thinking you'd find New York pretty intimidating if you ever got out that way. I gotta tell ya, though. This makes New York look like a play park."

Hagan chuckled.

"Are there many lumps in the forest, Hagan?"

"There are quite a few. I ain't dug into 'em and I hope I don't ever have to."

"And you say life is more tolerant here?"

"Well, some life more, some life less."

I took another pull on the jar. I felt better instantly.

"Ready to go?" asked Hagan.

"To be honest, no. I think I'd rather stay here and take my chances with the moonshine."

Hagan chuckled again.

"I like you, Jake. Let's go."

I screwed the lid back on the jar and regretfully laid it on the floor. I crawled out of the patrol car and was surprised that I could even stand.

As we walked into the general store I spied a young girl working the shelves. She was a knockout. My insides stirred. Hell, everything stirred.

"Hi there, Ida Mae," said the sheriff.

"Hi there, Hagan," the girl replied with a dazzling smile.

"Is your daddy here, honey?"

"Yes sir. He's in the back. Who's that with ya?"

"This here is Jake Brewer. He's a real-life New York City police detective."

"Wow! Really? He's cute. Does he have handcuffs?"

She giggled. My brain turned to gelatin.

"Now, now, Ida Mae," said Hagan. "Don't go botherin' strangers like that. He's a city boy, not used to a country girl's teasin'."

"Who's teasin'?"

She giggled again. My heart pounded so loud, I thought the whole world might hear it.

Jesus, how her eyes sparkled — like polished diamonds. Her long blonde hair stretched halfway down her back. Her body was petite, slim, and firm. Her breasts perky and inviting. I was immediately captivated.

Hagan noticed my brazen interest.

He leaned over close to me and whispered, "She's fifteen years old, Jake."

A sudden vision of a steel-barred jail cell door slamming shut in front of my face made me swallow hard, almost choking on nothing but air. If I could have vanished and gone somewhere, anywhere, and hid, I would have. I could only imagine the look on my face. Hagan didn't have to. He saw it clearly.

He snickered.

"I'm sorry," I whispered. "She looks much older, Hagan. In a really good way."

"Yeah, we grow 'em different down here, Jake."

"I'm *really* glad you're here, Hagan."

He smiled.

"Nice to meet you, young lady," I said, wanting to cry.

"Likewise, I'm sure, good-lookin'," she replied, with a sly, come-hither-and-let-me-destroy-you smile.

I felt tears forming in my eyes.

We walked back toward a set of swinging doors. I felt a little lightheaded and stumbled. Hagan shot out his hand and grabbed my arm just above the elbow and steadied me.

"I think the shine hit me," I said, a half-truth.

"Yeah. The intoxicatin' effects of moonshine and a Kentucky girl's smile will do that to a man," said Hagan with his own smile.

"Women. They're evil, Hagan. The whole lot of 'em. And I can't figure them out to save my soul."

"Yeah. They do have a spell over us less evolved menfolk."

"How do they do it?"

"Some kind of dark magic, I expect."

"They can go from cute to evil in less than a heartbeat and then back again, without missing a beat."

"Some more than others, Jake."

"It's a curse, I tell ya, but damn, I love 'em."

"And that, I think, is their dark magic."

He snickered again.

"Oh, I'm glad this is entertaining to you."

"Relax. That's just Ida Mae bein' Ida Mae."

I was embarrassed. And not having any wish to destroy what little professionalism I still possessed, I abandoned any further retorts.

We walked through the swinging doors and stopped.

"Junior?" he called out loudly. "This is Hagan Duggar. You here?"

From far in the back, in a darker section, a man stepped out from behind some shelving, silhouetted in front of the bright light of an uncovered window.

"Hey, Hagan. How ya doin'?"

"Just fine, just fine. You got a minute to talk to a friend of mine?"

"Why sure, Hagan. Why don't you go into my office. I'll be with you in a jiff."

We moved to Luttrell's office and waited. We didn't wait but a minute or so before he walked in wearing a friendly smile. He stuck out his hand and we shook.

"Hi there, I'm Junior."

"Hi there. I'm Jake Brewer."

"Well, that's nice. Mighty nice."

He and Hagan shook hands.

"Take a seat, Mister Brewer. What can I do for ya?"

"Junior," said Hagan, "Jake's a police detective from New York City."

"Is he now? My, my, a real-life New York City detective in *my* store. My, my. People gonna be talkin' about this, I expect. My, my."

"I expect so," said Hagan. "Listen, Junior. He's got some big trouble back in the city and he's come all the way out here because he thinks there might be a connection."

"You don't say, Hagan. My, my. Wouldn't that be somethin'?"

"Yes, sir, it would," said Hagan.

"What do you want to know, Detective?"

"Jake, sir. Just call me Jake. Everyone does. What I want to know is this. I have a file that has a letter of reference in it that supposedly was signed by your father about ten years ago. It was for a young woman who I suspect is from around these parts, and I'm wondering if you might know who she is."

I pulled the letter from my briefcase and handed it to him.

He studied it intently and looked up at me.

"No sir, can't say it looks familiar. But then my daddy was handing out letters like this all the time, it seemed."

"So it was common for your father to sign letters of reference?" I asked, taking the letter back.

"My pa was real good at giving out references to the young folk. He said it lent legitimacy to those folks looking for a job elsewhere. Heck, I do it myself frequently."

"But you don't know who that might have been back then?"

"Like I said, lots of kids have worked here."

"Could I show you a picture, Junior?"

"Sure."

I pulled Maddie's head shot out of my briefcase and laid it before him. I got the same response from him that I did from the sheriff.

"Wow! She's quite a looker. She one of them super models?"

"Not exactly. Do you recognize her?"

"No, and I'd never forget a woman like that."

Then his face changed. His head twisted back and forth on his neck as he tried to view the picture from different angles.

"You know," he said, "she sorta looks like that girl... Nah! It can't be."

"Can't be who?" I said.

"Well, there's a hint here of a girl who worked here for a short time. I don't recall her name, but she was pretty — real pretty. Not this kinda pretty, but some of the features are similar. Nah, I'm wrong about that. I don't recognize her. Sorry."

"Please think, Junior," I said encouragingly. "This could be really important."

He stared at the picture for almost a full minute. Then he lifted his eyes to meet mine. He shook his head.

"Sorry, Jake," he said. "I don't recollect seeing her before."

"Not at all?"

He shook his head again. "No, sir."

"Well, thanks for thinking about it, Junior."

"Yes, sir," he said.

I lifted the photograph from Junior's hands. A disappointed expression swept over his face.

"Junior, let me ask you this. Would you by chance have a list of employees who worked here back then?"

"Normally I'd say yes, but we had a fire about five years ago. Burnt up a lot of records. You remember the fire, don't you, Hagan?"

"By golly, Junior, you're right. Burnt this very room, didn't it? I remember that."

"Sure 'nuff. Didn't take us long to rebuild, though. Everyone in town chipped in and helped. But the records are gone I'm afraid."

"Have you worked here long yourself?" I asked.

"Oh, yeah. Ever since I was a young 'un. Pa's rules. If I wanted spendin' money, I had to earn it."

"I'd say your pa was a man of wisdom, Junior."

"He had his ways about him," he replied.

"Junior, might you recall anyone else who stood out back then? Anyone special?"

"Well, let me think on that a minute or two. But I'll tell ya, ten years is a long time in these parts."

"Just do your best, Junior," I said.

He did. And it took him about a minute and a half before he looked into my eyes again.

"I remember there was Allie. She worked here over a couple of summers about then."

"She got a last name?"

"Yeah. Allie Shaw."

"Where is she now?" I asked, jotting down what he said in my notebook.

"I expect she might still be up in Lexington."

"In Lexington?"

"Yes, sir."

"Why did she go there?"

"That's where the University is."

"Ah. Which one?"

"That'd be the University of Kentucky. Wanted to become a doctor, she said."

"I see. She left to go to college and still might be there?"

"Yes, sir. I reckon doctors don't get done with their schoolin' real quick."

"But ten years seems like a long time even for becoming a doctor," I said.

"Oh! Well, maybe she's gone by now, then. I don't really know."

"Okay. Can you recall anyone else?"

"Well, sir, there was Becky. Becky Northland. She worked here around that time also. For about a month before she moved away."

"Do you know where she moved to?"

"I only heard rumors 'bout that," said Junior. "Heard tell she was secret with child."

"I see. Any idea who the father might be?"

"We're not sure about that either. She left kinda quick-like."

"Hagan," I said, "anything on her you recall?"

"Yes, sir. I recall her. And I got my suspicions. She was under the counsel of Reverend Cousins for a time. Just before he upped and disappeared, I recollect."

"The preacher. Right. Might he have known who the father was?"

"We're not sure about anything, Jake," said Hagan. "And she wouldn't talk about it. There wasn't much I could do but let her go. She had just turned eighteen. Don't have no idea where she might have ended up."

"Wow! Sounds like a little Peyton Place here," I said.

"I ain't never heard of that place, so I can't speak to that."

"It's okay, Hagan. It was just a fictionalized town on television many years ago."

"Ah. I see. I don't keep up with that much."

"Any other employees, Junior?" I asked.

"Yes, many more, but I can't rightly remember them others right now. Just about everyone in town worked here at one time or another. Too many to recall individually. Especially that far back."

"I understand," I said.

"How about Kerri Ann and Mary Beth?" asked Hagan.

Junior's eyes opened wide in recall. "Yes, sir. They both worked here for a while when they was real young. Sad about them, huh, Hagan?"

"Yes sir, Junior. Very sad."

"Sad?" I asked. "What was sad about them?"

"Reverend Cousins. Their daddy," said Hagan.

"Of course," I said.

"They was his girls," said Junior. "Kerri Ann and Mary Beth Cousins. They was the reverend's daughters."

"Right," I said. "Hagan told me that."

I scribbled more into my notepad before I again looked into Junior's eyes. "Any truth, you think, to the rumors that he might have been fooling around with some of the young girls in the area?"

Junior's eyes darted around the room as if he was either searching his mind for the right answer or creating a lie. I had seen that look many times before when questioning people.

"Yeah, Junior," I said. "I already heard about the pedophile rumors."

I studied his reaction. I could tell there was more to it than just the reverend having an unnatural fondness for children.

I looked at Hagan.

Hagan was on to him as well.

"Now, Junior," the sheriff started, "ain't nothin' to protect."

"Is there something else, Hagan?" I asked. "More rumors about the reverend?"

Junior's eyes steadied in his head.

"That's all they are, rumors and gossip. Hagan, you know that nothin' ever came to light about them stories."

"I know, I know. You and the preacher got on well. I know that. He didn't come down here to talk about that, though. He's tryin' to connect his case with that pretty young woman in the picture you just saw. That's all he's tryin' to do."

"Junior," I said, "I understand your reluctance to share intimate details about people and events in your town with strangers. To be honest with you, I'm a lot like you. I don't easily share with those I don't know well. I'm especially protective with information that might harm those I know well. And I know that the only reason you're even talking with me right now is because I'm with Hagan. I'm not offended. In fact, I'm impressed with your integrity."

Junior seemed to buy into my little ruse instantly. I saw him relax in his chair. I was also convinced that their secret, Hagan's *little mystery*, might well have a lot of truth to it.

But I was more interested in my case.

"Do you have any idea about what might have happened to Reverend Cousins, Junior?" I asked.

"No sir, Jake. It's a real mystery," he replied.

I continued. "I heard that the Cousins girls might have had some tough times here when they were young. It's a terrible shame that there are kids who have to live through such tragedy. I feel for them. I really do. But I'm here to discover information that might help me solve a real bad string of murders back home. That's all I'm really interested in at the moment."

"Jack the Ripper–type murders," said Hagan.

Junior's eyes lit up.

"You don't say."

"I do. Yes sir, I do," replied the sheriff.

Hagan then tapped me on the shoulder.

"Junior's one of those Ripperologists I told you about. Meets with the professor like I said."

I'd found my in with Junior. And I planned to take full advantage of it.

CHAPTER 12

"I know pretty much all there is to know about the Whitechapel murders," offered Junior. "Them was fascinatin' murders back then. Are you aware that up until then, there ain't never been murders like that on record anywhere in the civilized world? And they only been duplicated rarely since."

"Wow! You're amazing, Junior," I said, trying to butter him up without coming across as totally patronizing. "And you're dead right about that. Very astute observation."

"Well, thank you, Jake. Kind words. My, my. Yes sir, kind words. Of course I ain't professional like you, but I'm workin' on some theories of my own."

"Well, I'd like to hear them. Maybe after I wrap up my investigation we can sit down and chat about your theories. Meanwhile, I've got someone up in New York City trying their dead level best to duplicate the Ripper's dark deeds."

"Wow! You don't say. My, my. That's somethin', all right. My, my."

"In fact, I think this fella is trying to one-up the Ripper. He's created a real mess for me. I'd appreciate any help you can give me. I'd certainly credit your consultation when the time comes."

"Ain't this somethin', Hagan? A real New York detective wants me to *consult* with him on his investigation. Wait until I tell the professor and the other fellas. My, my. Yes, sir. My, my."

He was mine now. I owned him. Now, if I could only get him to recall who worked here and left the area around that specific time frame.

"What can I consult with you on, Jake?"

"It could be critical to my investigation if you could recall a girl who worked here back then, calling herself Maddie Dumont, who got a reference from your daddy and left soon after."

Junior scratched the stubble of his beard for several seconds before responding.

"I'm sorry, Jake. Like I already said, lots of kids come through the store workin' on their school vacations and for the summer. Heck, most of the young 'uns in town and surroundin' have worked here or are about to start workin' here. As you might have guessed already, we're not big on industry around these parts. There's just my store, the gas station, and the feed store, and that little bitty local bank down the street. Except for farms round about, there ain't many places to work in town. The young 'uns get bored real fast and move around a lot."

"I understand, Junior. Just think on it a bit more if you could."

"Yes, sir. I will. I promise you. I'll give it some more thought. You gonna stay in the area for a while?"

"A couple days more. That's all my boss will let me stay here. I got a lot of work to do between now and then."

"All right, then. I'll give the matter lots of thought and call Hagan when I'm done thinkin' on it."

"Junior, when is your next Ripper meeting?" I asked.

"It's not for a couple more months. We use video conferencin' now. But I reckon I could call everyone and get a real-life-together emergency meetin' quick-like. What you got in mind?"

"Let me think on it a bit, but perhaps meeting with you all with your finely honed minds might be able to open a door in my investigation."

"Wow! Heck, that would be somethin'. My, my. I think the boys might be all excited about that. I'll make some calls today and get back to Hagan on it. My, my. Wouldn't that be somethin'?"

"That would be fine," I said. Trying to use their own lingo and style, I continued, "That would be just fine. I'm obliged to you, Junior."

The smile on his face would probably be with him for quite a spell, I reckoned. (Sorry, I couldn't let that one slip by.)

I could fit in here well, I imagined. I could just see it. Then I laughed. It was an inward laughter, but I did find some sick humor in all of this. Maybe I was laughing at these yokels, but in my mind, they deserved it. If they allowed one of their preachers to molest children here and tried to cover it up, I'd wish that I could find a way to arrest them all and burn this backwoods town to the ground.

First things first, though. I had to find a firm connection to the reference letter and Maddie's employment application. If there was one. And I just knew there had to be.

After being here as long as I had, I'd convinced myself that there was more to Maddie Dumont than I knew.

I was suddenly nervous about it. A part of me was scared to think what I might discover about Miss Blue Eyes down here. But hell, I was always nervous or scared about something. That was one of the reasons I drank so much.

Of course, it was just one of the many lies I told myself to justify my errant behavior. To be truthful, and I hate being truthful with myself, I was simply an alcoholic. And that's the honest reason why I drank so much. Glad I got that off my shoulder.

Hagan slid into his seat of the squad car and chuckled.

"You're amazin'," he said.

"Oh, yeah? Why is that?"

"You must be a musician, because you played Junior like a fiddle. 'Sit down and chat' about his theories. Dear me, I almost popped a chuckle at that one."

He chuckled again.

"You adapt pretty quick, I'll give you that."

I sniggered.

"Was it that obvious?"

"Not to Junior, it weren't. You've got that boy ready to jump off a cliff if it gets him fame from *consultin'* with you. Yes, sir, by golly, you're a quick study, Jake. Darn quick."

"You and I okay with what I did?"

Hagan chuckled once again.

"I'm goin' to school on that one. You read him like a book. I'm darned impressed."

I noticed the jar of moonshine on the floor. I reached for it, twisted off the cap, and took a giant swig.

"You gonna share that?" asked Hagan with a grin.

I laughed hard, wiped off the rim with my shirt sleeve, and handed the jar to him. He reared back his head and drained it. I was wounded by his action. It was like I'd just lost my best friend.

I think he noticed my disappointment. He winked at me.

"Don't fret, Jake. I got a few more pints in the trunk."

I think my relief clearly showed on my face, but the involuntary sigh gave me away for sure.

"Good to hear that," I added to the sigh.

"Let's get down the road a piece and I'll stop and pull two from the trunk. It's not good for the sheriff to be seen pullin' liquor from his trunk in broad daylight."

"I get it. You do things differently down here, right?"

"You're gettin' good at this understandin' stuff."

I laughed. It felt good.

We sat on the shore of a small pond at the end of Pond Lane on the north side of Annville. About half of our pints were already consumed. Both of us were pretty much shitfaced, but still functioning. Nowhere near a hundred percent, for sure, but at least beyond my expectations, being new to the ways of the shine and all.

We had been sitting there for over an hour laughing mostly at stupid cop stories. Sometimes it just feels right to relax. We hadn't forgotten about meeting Mercy Cousins. It was just that priorities seemed to have shifted some over the last hour. And you must realize how important it was for me to correctly sort out my priorities.

Hagan was definitely a good ol' boy who understood the people of the area. His twenty-seven years on the force, twenty-three of them as sheriff, came with a price, though, like it does for most cops. He claimed that his job broke up his marriage. Of course, he added, the young soldier who happened to be passing through McKee at the time and caught the eye of his too-long-left-alone wife might have had something to do with the demise of his wedded life as well.

Hagan was not the kind of man who held grudges long. He moved on with his life after his wife moved on with hers.

He stated that getting a divorce was probably the second-best thing that had ever happened to him. The first was, of course, becoming a cop. With his life unfettered now by a woman who wanted to know his whereabouts all day long as well as other neurotic demands of the evil female mind, he reclaimed the joy of his fishing, hunting, and sports-watching life.

Overall, I'd have to say that Hagan Duggar was a pretty happy guy. And unlike me, a very stable personality drunk or sober.

"Well," he said, standing up and dusting off his behind, "I reckon we best head on over to Mercy's and get her interviewed."

"Do we have to?" I protested.

"No, sir. We don't gotta do nothin', but if you need to get your investigation completed, then we ought to get to it."

"I hate it when people use sound logic against me."

Hagan laughed.

"She should be home about now. She works sewin' up quilts for some local store up in McKee."

"Hey, Hagan, you think we'll have time to stop by Jed's still later on?"

"Oh, sure enough. We gotta go right past it on the way back up to McKee. I ain't forgot about it. Heck, I need to get resupplied myself."

He laughed again and I just couldn't help enjoying his laugh. It made me wish that I could avoid going back to New York altogether.

CHAPTER 13

We stopped in front of Mercy Cousins' home. She was out on the porch, sitting in a whitewashed rocking chair and sipping something that looked like iced tea. She took notice of the sheriff's car stopping in front of her home, but she didn't budge. She just sat there quietly rocking and sipping tea like she didn't have a care in the world — almost daring us to interrupt her peaceful moment.

"Now remember, Jake. She's a bit touched. She'll likely as not carry on a normal conversation and then, without warning, she might just go quiet and get to cowerin'. Sometimes she might even go to talkin' to someone you and I won't see."

"Does she get violent?"

"Oh, no. Nothin' like that. The psychiatrist that examined her after her husband vanished likened it to PTSD. The reverend used to beat up on her pretty good. That much we know is true. He did have a temper, especially after suckin' down too much of the shine. There was many a night he'd come home liquored up to the gills and start tossin' the house, screamin' that the devil had infested his home and turned all his womenfolk into demon whores."

"Jesus Christ," I blurted. "It's a wonder that woman can function at all after that kind of treatment."

"She's gettin' better. She used to not look at anyone straight in the eyes. The Rev used to pop her a good one for lookin' at him when he was yellin' at her.

Said she was defyin' him with her sassy look. Said he felt like the Devil hisself was starin' back at him — challengin' him. So he smacked her around until she stopped her starin'. Sometimes she still goes to cowerin' when a man talks to her, especially a stranger. So expect that."

"Okay. I'm warned again. I sometimes get the feeling I've entered the Devil's den down here."

"Sometimes I get to feelin' I'm in the thick of it myself. You ready?"

"As I'm going to be," I answered.

We exited the car and started for the porch. She didn't move a muscle. I started to think that fear of my approach had paralyzed her. But as we neared, she became animated.

"Who's that with ya, Hagan?" she asked. Her rocking started to accelerate.

I couldn't help but notice that she was a very pleasant-looking woman. She appeared to be in her late forties, nicely shaped, petite frame, with short blonde hair and a not unattractive face. She wore no makeup, but her skin was soft and supple-looking. It was hard for me to imagine her getting beat up by her pervo husband. It's always the dainty ones that take the beatings from those men whose manliness I have always called into question.

"This here is Jake Brewer, Mercy," said Hagan. "He's a New York City police detective. He's just here to ask you a few questions. Will that be okay with you?"

"What kinda questions?"

Her rocking sped up even more. It was obvious that she was quickly becoming uncomfortable and wary. I smiled as friendly a smile as I could.

"Mrs. Cousins, I'm investigating a crime in New York City. That's all. I could sure use your assistance."

"I don't know nothin' about New York City," she said, her eyes falling toward the porch. "Why you wanna ask me questions have to do with New York City?"

"It's just some questions about your two girls, Mercy," said Hagan.

Her eyes immediately lifted up to Hagan. "They in some kinda trouble?"

"No, no. Not at all," I said, trying to be as reassuring as I could. "Are they in New York?"

Her eyes shifted over toward me. "Don't know. Don't know where they are. They don't call or write."

"That's a real shame," I said. "I'm sorry to hear that. Is it possible that they headed to New York?"

"Couldn't say. They just left. But I can't imagine they'd go there. They don't know nothin' about big city livin'."

"Mrs. Cousins, can you recall when they left home?" I asked.

"They been gone a good long spell. Years. Ten years or so, I reckon."

"Could it be longer than that?" I asked.

"Could be, I reckon. But it ain't so."

"Could it be eleven or perhaps twelve years?"

"I said ten years, didn't I?"

"You did. Forgive me, please. Have you heard from them since they left?"

"Is there something wrong with your hearin', Detective? I said they don't write nor call."

"Right. You said that."

I was testing her; she seemed to be in full command of her faculties. I pressed on.

"You aren't curious about where they might be?"

"No. They're old enough to manage their own life."

"I see. What are their ages, if you don't mind?"

"Mary Beth would be twenty-six and Kerri Ann would be twenty-five."

"I see. Do you miss them?"

"What kinda question is that? Of course I do. Hagan, why he askin' questions like that? Is there somethin' wrong with him?"

"Now, Mercy. Have some patience. He's asking questions that need askin' is all."

"Fool's questions, if you ask me."

"My apologies, Mrs. Cousins. About your husband, now. Have you heard from him lately?"

"No. And after he run off, I don't think of him anymore."

"He ran away?"

"I believe so. Probably with that Tilly Watson. They was lovers, you know — sinful lovers."

"You know that for sure?"

Hagan dropped his hand on my shoulder. He was giving me a hint. I fell silent.

"Now, now, Mercy," he said. "You don't know that for sure. We talked about that, didn't we?"

"We did, Hagan. But he ain't here. And Tilly ain't around no more neither. You put it together yerself."

"That's just a coincidence, Mercy. I've already told you, Tilly's known to be up in Lexington right now, working in a store. And Joshua ain't with her."

"So you say, Hagan Duggar. So all you say, but how do I know you all ain't lyin' to me, and them two is carryin' on up yonder?"

"'Cause there ain't no reason for anyone to lie about a thing like that," said the sheriff. "We all want for your happiness."

"I know, I know," she said, slapping away an invisible hand. "But I think he's lyin'. No. No, you don't. Don't go believin' what anyone says right out like that."

I recognized immediately that Mercy Cousins was having a conversation with someone invisible to me, just as Hagan had warned me that she might. I had seen this behavior dozens of times as well. It was a product of stress — a defense mechanism.

I glanced at Hagan. He bumped his eyebrows. He knew it too.

"Mrs. Cousins," I said loudly, "I need you to relax now. No one is trying to hurt you."

The strength of my booming voice quieted her instantly. She fell into a stupor and remained in that state for several seconds. Then it was like a light had been turned on again. She returned to us, only she wouldn't look me in the eye and I could see that she was feeling intimidated.

I stepped forward and crouched down below her. Often, someone cowering feels inferior and is afraid to look up, fearing the intimidating position. By crouching below her, I was hoping to make her feel that she was in a superior position, both physically and psychologically. It worked. She blinked. She looked directly at me.

"Mrs. Cousins," I said softly, "would you by chance have a picture of both your daughters you could show me?"

"I ain't got none. Joshua wouldn't allow a camera around us. He said cameras was of the Devil and they captured souls."

Jesus, I thought, the reverend was really messed up. How could a town allow this deranged man access to anyone as a preacher? Preachers in most communities are extremely influential and often possess very dominant personalities. They commanded respect and obedience from their congregation. It's often a simple thing for them to control the behavior as well as the complete lives of their flock. A preacher who is deranged could be as wicked as he or she wanted to be and justify his or her behavior by stating that it was *God's will.*

I had run into this type of behavior control before. It would be very difficult to break the believers away from the master. Mrs. Cousins had obviously been a victim of great abuse by her husband. And I had no doubt that his daughters had been at least as abused.

I pulled out Maddie's photograph and showed it to her. I caught the slightest hint of recognition in her eyes, but she didn't respond.

"You recognize this woman, don't you?" I asked softly.

She didn't reply.

"Mrs. Cousins, it would be really helpful if you could answer me. Do you recognize the woman?"

"Help him, Mercy. If you can," said Hagan.

"Tilly Watson. It's Tilly Watson. She got that evil look about her. Like a siren callin' men to their doom."

Holy shit, I thought. Her brain has left the building. So much for that hint of recognition.

"No, Mrs. Cousins," I said. "This isn't Tilly Watson. Her name is Margaret Skimmer. But of late she is living under the name of Madison Dumont. Maddie for short. Do you recognize her?"

"It's Tilly Watson, I tell ya. She's a seducer, this one. Got Joshua's soul. It's best you stay away from her."

I looked up at Hagan. He shook his head.

"Okay, Mrs. Cousins," I said. "Thank you."

Then an idea struck me.

"Mrs. Cousins, would you mind if I wandered around inside your house for a bit?"

"What for?"

"I'd just like to get a feel for what your life might have been like when the reverend was around. Would that be okay with you?"

"You can wander around if you like, but you couldn't possibly understand what life was like when that devil was here and about. I'm glad he's gone. I don't never want to see him ever again if I can help it. Him and Tilly Watson can go to blazes and stay there."

"I can certainly understand that. Thank you. I'll go inside now." I glanced up at the sheriff. "Hagan, would you please go with me?"

"Be delighted. Okay, Mercy, we're goin' inside now. You just rest yourself here a spell."

"They ain't nothin' in there to see, but go on in if you want to."

Hagan and I stepped through the doorway and I was struck with a sudden feeling of evil. As I've already stated, I've never been psychic, but this feeling was overwhelming. I was assaulted by varying visions of pure wickedness. I believed Hagan felt it too, because his face turned almost white with some kind of unseen fright.

"Do you feel it, Jake?"

"I do, Hagan. I could almost cut it with a knife, it's so thick."

"I ain't never felt comfortable in here." He shivered. "Dear lord, I think the hand of evil just dropped onto my shoulder."

"If you say so," I replied.

The home was simple and plain, the furniture clean but worn. The walls were painted off-white. The floors were mostly of stained wood, but scuffed and scratched. It was an older home, cut up into small rooms, each with a door.

The kitchen was outdated, but clean. Mercy Cousins may have been off her rocker, but she was a good housekeeper. Everything was in its proper place. The appliances were old, but were clean and apparently functioning.

"Hagan? How many times have you been inside this home before today?"

"Several times, Jake. Like I said, I ain't never been comfortable here, but it never felt so heavy as it does now."

I discovered the girls' bedrooms. They were as plain as the rest of the house. And true to form, there wasn't one photograph in either of them. I opened the closet doors. The closets were empty.

Walking down the hallway, I found the door leading up to the attic. I glanced back at Hagan and pointed to it. He shrugged his shoulders. I opened the door and started up the stairs, first flipping on the light at the foot of the staircase.

"What are we lookin' for again, Jake? I've plum forgot."

"Any idea who these girls are in relation to my investigation. They're the only ones, apparently, who left the area around the same time Maddie Dumont showed up in New York. I'm not saying the girls are related, but I'd like to find a clue to where they might have gone from here if not to New York."

"You changin' your mind about this Maddie Dumont, then? Is she becomin' a suspect?"

"No. But her application for employment had the letter of reference from Zyree Luttrell attached to it, remember? It's made out in her new name."

"Yeah. But we ain't never had any Dumonts down this way that I know of. At least not permanent like — none at least that I'm aware of. And if the letter was made out to Maddie Dumont, like you say, then nobody remembers her. So now I don't see how Maddie Dumont is a part of your investigation except for bein' a witness like you said before."

"I get that. That's what makes it all the stranger. What does Maddie Dumont have to do with Annville, Kentucky? There's an obvious connection, Hagan, but I'm stumped as to what that is."

"Heck, Jake. This is the part of an investigation that makes me want to walk away and go fishin'."

"As I see it, that's what an investigation is all about. A fishing trip."

"Now you put it that way, I guess it is. But it's not the kind of fishin' trip I like."

"I wish you knew someone who had seen Maddie with the Cousins girls. That sure would be helpful."

"I'm most of the time up in McKee, Jake. I can't say that they never knowed one another. But I don't know who would know such a thing except for Junior."

"I'm wondering, then. I'm wondering if they did know each other and the Cousins girls followed Maddie to New York. They might all be in touch on a regular basis there now."

"Yeah, I suppose it's possible. Now don't take this the wrong way, Jake, but the Cousins girls weren't all that much to look at. At least back then they wasn't. I don't see what a real looker like Maddie Dumont would have in common with the Cousins girls."

"I've seen changes in women's looks that would shock you. A little makeup, new clothing, new hairstyle, and you might not even recognize them if they came and stood right in front of you."

"You're right, Jake. You're right."

"Maybe that's Maddie's only connection with Annville. Maybe she drifted through the area. Needed some money, worked for a time at Luttrell's, then moved to New York and went through a complete makeover. Transformed from a backwoods girl to a New York fashion magazine editor."

"I suspect you're right about that. And maybe the Cousins girls hooked up with her and they all moved to New York and become somethin' they couldn't possibly hope to be here."

"I have to say, Hagan, that's what has been rattling around in my brain of late, and it makes about as much sense as anything else."

"Things don't always have to be complicated, Jake."

"No, they sure don't. And that could explain why no one seems to recognize the photograph."

"Even Mercy might not recognize her girls now if they went through the change," added Hagan.

"No offense, but I don't think Mercy is positive which planet she's on."

"You're right," he said. "I have to say it. You're right. Let's look through this attic and see if we can find anything else."

The attic was nearly full of old clothing and other stored items. The clothing looked like they had once belonged to Joshua.

"She must be expecting him back," I said.

"Kinda looks that way. Either that, or prepared for him if he does show up."

I spied an old metal shipping chest. It wasn't locked. I opened the top and peered in.

About a thousand moths flew up into my face, startling me. I yelped and fell onto my back, then joined Hagan in laughing.

"Jesus Christ!" I said. "It was like a horror movie."

The moths scattered and hid themselves away until not one could be seen. I crawled back up onto my knees and reached into the chest. It was full of clothing that the moths had been dining on. Everything was full of tiny holes. They were of little interest, but then I spied an odd-looking piece of paper and tugged at it. It was an old travel ticket — the passenger side of an airline voucher. I studied it with increasing shock.

"Hagan. Look here! It's an old used voucher for an airline seat to New York."

Hagan squinted at it. "Sure enough, Jake. Well, I'll be."

"It's made out to Joshua Cousins and it's dated just over ten years ago."

Hagan studied it and added, "Just a few months before he disappeared. I never knew Joshua to travel to New York. I'm surprised at this."

"Do you think Mrs. Cousins would mind if I kept this?"

"Heck. We can ask her."

If it were true that Joshua Cousins had once traveled to New York, then it was a possibility that he could have gone back there. Perhaps the good reverend wasn't missing after all. Maybe it was just that he hadn't yet been discovered in New York. And then it struck me. New York would be a haven for a pedophile. I ran my theory by Hagan and he agreed that it might be possible.

"Could you find him in New York?" he asked.

"I could try, but if he changed his name, I might not have a chance. And New York is a place where a lot of people change their names and disappear into the crowd."

I jammed my hand down deeper into the chest and struck something hard. I moved some clothing aside and my heart sank into my stomach. It was a book about the Jack the Ripper murders. When I pulled it out of the chest and showed it to Hagan, he shrugged his shoulders like it was no big deal.

"You don't get it?" I asked.

"Yeah, I get it. What's the big deal?"

"The reverend had a Jack the Ripper book."

"Yeah, he was in the professor's group."

"You didn't think it was important to tell me this?" I asked in shock.

"He's missin' goin' on ten-plus years, Jake. I didn't think it any longer relevant."

"Hagan, let me point out that I'm holding a plane ticket to New York, a book about the Ripper murders, and we've got a missing preacher who not only thought his daughters were whores, but also is suspected of being a pedophile, and I've got a murderer in New York trying to be Jack the Ripper. Are you following?"

"I see that now, Jake. I get it. You think Joshua went to New York and is killin' young women."

"I'm not saying my suspect is Joshua Cousins, but it sure deserves a thorough investigation. I mean, you've never come up with a body, right? It could be possible that he moved to New York all those years ago and for whatever reason now he's gone from sex with minors to murdering hookers."

"I always saw him as a certified nut job before he went missin'. But I had no evidence he ever did anything wrong. My hands was tied."

"Where did his daughters move to, Hagan? That's my big question. Oh, no! What if they followed him to New York? What if they followed him so they could kill him? Could that be possible?"

"I don't see how, Jake. It's been ten years. Wouldn't they have found him by now?"

"I suppose so. I'm just throwing out guesses."

"Besides, Jake, them two girls was naïve to the wicked ways of the world and sweet as honey. I can't see them hurtin' anybody. I most certainly can't see them followin' their daddy to New York to be with him. Not if…you know."

"I do, but what if the gossip was true? What if Joshua molested his daughters? I wouldn't think they remained naïve to the wicked ways of the world long. What if their minds snapped and they went after him to do him harm?"

"That's a lot of ifs, Jake."

"There's always a lot of ifs at the beginning of an investigation."

"I still think you would have come across his death before this."

"New York is a big city, Hagan. It might be possible that they found him and killed him and then moved on with their lives in the city."

I felt around in the chest some more, and my fingers hit something else that was small and hard. I gathered it up and brought it out. It was a button, but not any ordinary button. It was a button with a swastika engraved on it. I showed it to Hagan.

"Oh, my," he said. "Oh, my. There might be some truth to all them rumors after all."

"What rumors?"

"Among all the rumors spread about Joshua, one of them was that he was a member of the American Nazi Party. But I got a file on all of them. Joshua's name was never found linked to them and I never found one shred of evidence to the contrary."

"Until now, that is," I said.

"You're right about that, Jake. Until now."

I emptied the chest and found nothing more incriminating than the button. I knew the button was circumstantial at best, but perhaps this trip to Kentucky might have proved to be well worth it.

CHAPTER 14

Sitting in my hotel room at nine o'clock that evening, I stared at the twelve gallon jugs of moonshine on my dresser. Jed, the moonshiner, was a kick in the pants and now I had enough shine to keep me mellow for weeks. Who am I kidding? I'd have it finished in days, if it wasn't for work.

Of course, to an alcoholic, finding booze like the shine was like a thief, or a banker, finding millions of dollars in cash with no owner in sight. They know it's wrong to keep it and spend it, but you just know they're gonna do it anyway. And they probably won't tell anyone about it — ever!

But just how was I going to get twelve gallons of moonshine back to New York? I got a brilliant idea.

I went to the front desk and asked the night clerk to find out how many hours it would take to drive back to New York.

She connected her desk computer to the hotel's Wi-Fi in seconds. I was impressed by how she knew how to do that. Within a few more seconds she looked up at me and smiled.

"Twelve hours, sir," she said.

"You found that out that fast?" I asked, stunned.

"You should be able to connect your cell phone to our Wi-Fi yourself."

"You don't know me. I barely learned how to take a photo with this thing."

She laughed.

I thanked her and flipped her a ten spot, then went back to my room.

I could do twelve hours standing on my head. I could get all my babies home, the gallons safe and sound, and no one would be the wiser. Especially Grayson.

I could effectively slosh my way to bliss and never see the inside of Bobby's bar for quite some time. Everyone would think I was on the wagon. And I'd be on the wagon, all right. I'd be on the wagon to *Hammeredville* for days. I'd put in for some vacation time and stay thoroughly blitzed in my dreamland bliss.

My phone rang and my delusion vanished. It was Grayson.

"How are you, Lieutenant?"

"You're sloshed, aren't you?"

"I'm on my own time, Hank."

"I bet you've discovered a still out there and you're stocked with moonshine about now. How far off the mark am I?"

Damn, I thought, *he's good.*

"Nah. Nothing like that, Lieutenant," I replied, taking a pull from the jug.

"Why don't I believe you?"

"I've made some progress out here," I said, wishing to change the subject quickly before I confessed.

"Oh, yeah? Tell me about it."

I told him about all I had discovered down here and then recited my theory regarding Maddie Dumont and the good reverend's possible involvement. To my surprise, he seemed to agree.

I then asked him if I could stay a day or two longer and follow up on some other leads. Again, to my great surprise, he agreed.

"It sounds like a cesspool down there," he said.

"A cesspool here, a cesspool there. What the hell is the difference anymore?"

"I guess you're right about that."

Then it struck me!

"Hey! Why are you so damned agreeable? What gives?"

"Okay, Jake. I'd like you to stay away for a few days more. Some things are happening up here and I'd like you out of it. That's what gives."

"Okay, but can you tell me why?"

"Two words. Maddie Dumont."

"What about her?"

"She's called me about ten times so far. Three times tonight alone, wondering when you're coming back."

"Oh, shit! Does she know I'm here in Kentucky?"

"Yeah, you bet. I even gave her your address.... What do you think I am, Jake? A complete idiot?"

"Of course not, but I hope she doesn't catch wind of where I am. She's got some kind of connection down here, I'm positive of that. But exactly what it is, I haven't got a clue yet."

"She's interested in you, Jake. And that's really troubling. I've kept a lid on it, but I don't know how long I can keep it on. What the hell did you do or say to this chick, Jake?"

"I have no clue about that either."

"That's bullshit."

"Well, I might have told her that I had feelings for her."

"Great, Jake! Thanks for that."

"Where does she think I am?"

"I told her you've been temporarily transferred to another case as an undercover officer, and that you're incommunicado for a while. She didn't take it real well. I told her I don't know when you'll be back in the office."

"Sounds good to me."

"Yeah, but she calls me every few hours for an update. I'm beginning to sense some panic in her voice."

"Why's that?" I asked.

"You tell me."

"I can't. Lieutenant, can you help me? Check the records and see if the not-so-good reverend might be up in New York and confirm his association with the Nazis, if you can. I think it's a long shot, but if he is up there still using his real name, we might also have a suspect for the Ripper copies."

"The Nazis? Are you serious?"

"As a heart attack. I've discovered some circumstantial evidence that he's somehow connected to those loony tunes."

"And if I can't find him?"

"Then we're no worse off than we are right now."

"I'll call if I find anything. Meanwhile, keep the moonshine to a minimum. Are we clear?"

"I hate it when you do that."

"I know. Question: Is it as good as they say it is?"

"Better. Goodbye."

I clicked the phone off.

There was no use pretending to hide it from Grayson. He read me like a book. But I was elated to not have to return to New York right away. I really did want to explore the hidden places down here a bit longer without having to rush my investigation.

I was troubled more about Maddie, though, or whatever her name really was. I wondered what was going on with her, but without contacting her directly, which would have been a huge mistake, I was just going to have to trust Grayson to keep me covered. I really had no idea why she needed me to be back in New York. She was hot. She was exciting. And I certainly was interested in her. Apparently, she was more interested in me than I gave her credit for. But she had become a person of interest in the Ripper copy crimes. Grayson was right. It was better for me, her, the investigation, and the department that I stay out of town for a few more days.

I suddenly didn't feel like drinking alone. I dialed Hagan's number. He picked up.

"Hi, Jake. What gives?"

"I could use a drinking buddy."

"Get over here, then."
"Where's your house?"
"I'll text the address to your phone."
"I'm on my way."

I told Hagan what Grayson had told me. He chuckled about it, but it made sense now to him. Then we got to chatting about the state of affairs in his neck of the woods.

"I like havin' you around, Jake. You give me a new perspective on what's goin' on down here. It's real easy to let things fall away into normalness. Things become real regular, real fast. Know what I mean?"

"I do, Hagan. And I agree. Sometimes things need to be shaken up."

"You really think Joshua took off to New York?"

"I think it's possible."

"You think he's the one killin' them girls up there?"

"It's just a hunch, but I've got nothing to lose by checking it out."

We sat in his living room pulling on our respective jugs of shine. I was growing in bliss every moment. The shine really mellowed me out. Or maybe it was that I wasn't in New York, surrounded by all the garbage that was my usual life. It really didn't matter.

Either way, I was blissful and I didn't want that to change.

I told him about Maddie Dumont and her calling into the department like she did. He snickered.

"Does sound like a Kentucky girl. Once they get their claws into a man, they don't let go too easy."

"Do you really think she might be from these parts?"

"Heck, Jake, I don't know what I'm talkin' about. I get to settlin' in, drinkin' my shine, and anything becomes possible."

Hagan laughed. I laughed as well. It felt good to just sit, laugh, and drink.

We both fell quiet for several minutes. I think we both had discovered that perfect moment. When nothing needs to be said. No action needs to be taken. When bliss settles gently down upon you and it all seems perfect and right. But perfect and right doesn't last long with me. Finally I stirred.

"I wonder what happened to the girls," I said.

"I was thinkin' on that earlier myself," Hagan replied.

He took a few pulls on his jug and then leaned back into his chair and shook his head.

"It's hard to say, Jake. They weren't what you'd call attractive and neither of 'em had blonde hair. They was dark-haired — dark brown and sort of homely-like — plain, simple, and not what you'd call real slim neither. They wasn't fat or nothin'. They just wasn't real slim neither. I mean, they was pleasant enough to look at, but they weren't all that attractive to most down here. Simple, like I said. Plain."

"Well, that ain't Maddie. She's hot as hell. And almost a death knell to a lonely old alkie like me."

"The kind, I expect, that don't need to be seen through liquored-up eyes?"

I chuckled. "No liquor required. You saw her picture. She's stunning."

"Ain't she, though," he said. "I saw me a girl like that once. Scary, ain't it?"

"Yeah. Hey, Hagan. Can you tell me more about the Nazis down here?"

He chuckled.

"That was a switcheroo." He laughed. "They ain't what they used to be, Jake. All old-timers now mostly. They're pretty much harmless. They meet formally once or twice a year, but they get together more often at the local waterin' hole. They use it as an excuse to get together and drink."

"So, they're not forming lynching parties and hanging black people?"

Hagan laughed that great belly laugh again.

"No, Jake. I think you're mixin' them up with them KKK boys. Nah, nothin' like that. Besides, there ain't many black folk down this way to start with, and them that are stay pretty much to themselves. But they're nice folks. Mostly farmers. Good people. We don't have those kinds of problems down here. And I wouldn't stand for that sort of thing if it did exist. No, everyone gets along pretty good. We just don't trust strangers. That's our weakness. But all this mistrust come from outa the revenuer days back during Prohibition. Them federal boys come down here lyin' and gettin' on with folks just so's they could find the stills. Now we see all strangers as revenuers until they prove different."

"I understand. And I can't hold it against anyone for thinking like that. So the Nazis aren't something to be concerned with?"

"Nah. Like I said, mostly old men about to die out. Like an old dog. Just growlers now. Heck, they barely got one workin' tooth in their head among 'em."

I laughed.

"I suppose, though, that the reverend could have found them too weak for his tastes and moved on to New York," I said.

"I s'pose he could have," said Hagan. "But why start killin' hookers now? Why not start years before this? Besides, killin' hookers don't sound like the Nazi way of things to me. Them ol' boys was more into marchin' around in their uniforms and talkin' socialist crapola. Them here ain't never been the violent type that I can recall."

"The timing's got me troubled as well, Hagan. The timing of it doesn't make any sense."

"Personally, Jake, I think you're barkin' up the wrong tree. I think he's dead and buried out in the Dan'l Boone somewhere."

"The Dan'l Boone?" I asked.

"That's what we call the Daniel Boone National Forest down here. The Dan'l Boone."

"Okay, got it. Please continue."

"What I was gettin' at is folks down here have been known to do that, ya know? Kill somebody and bury the body. Even if there ain't evidence. They just get it in their mind that a body has done them wrong and they take care of it in their own way. Then they won't breathe a word of it to no one ever. We've got several missin' persons and unsolved murders down here goin' back a long time — long before my time. There's lots of revenuers who went missin' years ago. The ATF don't send agents down here anymore. I guess they got tired of havin' to hire replacements."

I chuckled, then got serious again.

"So you don't think there's any good reason to go out and dig into some of those lumps in the forest dirt?"

"No reason I'd care to undertake. And for the sake of everyone, what's buried out there should stay buried. Besides, whoever might be out there ain't been missed. You follow me?"

"I hear you. For the time being, I guess we'll just have to wait and see what my lieutenant digs up. Oh...can we meet with the professor tomorrow?"

"Darn it all. I forgot to tell ya. Sorry about that. I already called him and set it up for late tomorrow morning. He's all kinds of excited to talk to a New York City detective about his theories."

"Great. Can't wait."

Hagan chuckled again.

CHAPTER 15

As I have already stated, for us committed alkies mornings come too damn early. But then we aren't really at our best in the afternoons or evenings either. But on mornings-after, especially to a brain still much too booze-logged for its own good, it was a monumental chore to find a reason to get out of bed.

Still, I managed to roll out of the sack at 7:00 a.m., and met Hagan for breakfast at Elma's Country Restaurant just down the street from the Old Town Motel.

A country eggs and bacon breakfast got something into my belly besides moonshine. In no time at all, I was feeling spry and ready to roll.

We sat and chatted about various unrelated things until it was time to go meet Hastings.

We arrived at the professor's home, in a newer subdivision about two or three miles east of the city center, exactly on time at ten o'clock.

He was already seated out on his porch when we pulled up in front of his house. He immediately leapt up off his chair and waved.

"Good morning, Professor," said Hagan, exiting the car.

"Morning to you, Hagan. Is that the New York City detective with you?"

"Sure is."

"Well, come on, then. Hurry up. I must tell you, Hagan. I hardly slept all night with the excitement of meeting the detective here."

"Hold on. We'll be there in a bit."

Introductions were pleasant and brief. Professor Hastings wanted to dive right into his theories about who Jack the Ripper just had to be — based upon *his* research, of course.

I was forced to listen politely, but I was wishing I was back at my motel sucking on some shine by the time he was done.

He was thoroughly convinced that most everyone had it wrong and that the killer was, in fact, James Kelly, who was first identified by an author named Terence Sharkey. What made it more interesting for the professor was the fact that a New York City detective by the name of Edward T. Norris, who performed his own investigation for a TV program, seemed to have confirmed the professor's findings, although Norris and the professor had never met. But a colleague of his, Jack Shafer, had consulted with the professor about Ed's theory over several months some time ago.

I didn't tell the professor, but I knew Jack very well. I worked with him as well, and as a fact, was under his command. He was what we called a *fast mover*, and while I was moving in the direction of the bottle, Jack was moving quickly up the chain of command.

Jack and I, on many occasions, had spoken long hours on the merit of his theory that James Kelly was

Jack the Ripper. He made his argument sound compelling, but I saw too many holes in it to jump off the cliff with him. Still, Jack and Ed could be one hundred percent correct, for all I knew about it.

I could just imagine what the professor would have done if I'd told him about Jack and me. For once, though, I knew when to keep my big mouth shut.

From the professor I had heard nothing but broad speculation. It has always amazed me that whenever there is information tending to discount a subject or a theory, it has always either been disregarded completely or minimized so as not to spoil the expected results.

As common with most academic types, he absolutely believed he was right about everything and couldn't understand why the world didn't beat a path to his door to shower him with all manner of awards and other accolades. He even saw a big movie contract in it for him.

The truth is this, as far as I'm concerned: the original Ripper's identity will most likely never be discovered with certainty. And I couldn't care less. My Ripper, however, *would* be unmasked. Period.

After an hour of patiently listening to him...well, okay, that's a damn lie. I actually had clicked him off right away and was daydreaming about that jug of sweet shine waiting for me back in my motel room. At any rate, I finally had my chance to discuss what I had come for.

"Professor, in the matter of Reverend Joshua Cousins, can you tell me how deeply involved in this group he was?"

"Certainly. He was very much involved. He was fascinated with the case. In fact, he kept the most detailed file on the case of us all. He even tracked down and purchased his own Teufel kit, believing that Jack the Ripper must have owned one."

That comment perked me up.

"Would that be the surgical amputation kit produced by Jacob J. Teufel?"

"Very good, Detective. Yes. The very same."

"Did the reverend's kit, by chance, contain a Liston knife?"

"An astute question, Detective. Not originally. But he later augmented his kit with a Liston blade. I'm very impressed by your knowledge, Detective. Very impressed, indeed."

"Thanks, Professor. Do you recall the length of the reverend's Liston blade?"

"Yes, of course. He was so very proud of it. Seven inches, Detective. It was a seven-inch blade. You appear to have an extensive knowledge of such knives."

"I've done some studying lately. I've learned that many Teufel kits contained a set of Liston blades."

"Again, most impressive, Detective. But I do believe you're headed down the wrong road."

"How's that?"

"You're referring to the knife reportedly used in the Ripper murders?"

"Yes."

"There's no evidence that the murder weapon was a Liston blade. That reference came from a movie some years ago, Detective — more correctly, from the mind of the screenwriter. But yes, several old Teufel kits have been discovered with Liston blades. But Teufel did not supply such blades in his kit. He had designed his own set of blades for the same purpose. Liston blades were typically the personal property of the surgeons who preferred them over Teufel's knives."

"Yeah. Come to think of it, that's right. I've heard that."

"But the blade used in the Ripper canonical murders was similar. However, from my research, the only blade that fits the description in the autopsy reports exactly was either a knife used in upholstery work of that time or one commonly used by butchers of that era.

"For a time, there was some speculation that it could have been some type of a surgical knife, but that theory has never been given serious consideration. There were no knives commercially made back then that could have better fit the description given. Except, perhaps, for the Liston knife. And that would have been a good knife to use. You are aware, though, that no actual murder weapon was ever discovered?"

"Yes. I'm aware of that. But you say the reverend had a copy of the knife and a large case file?"

"At first his case file wasn't so extensive. But he really got into the case and expanded it over time. As for the Liston blade, as I've already said, when he first purchased the Teufel kit, it contained only the instruments manufactured by Teufel. It was several months later that he found the Liston blade. He claimed to have found it up in New York. And yes, he had quite…"

"Wait! You said he found it up in New York? He traveled to New York?" I asked.

"Don't know if he actually traveled to New York, Detective. I believe he said he found it in a catalog. Had it sent down from New York, I think."

"Oh, I see. What about the case file?"

"As I was about to say, he had an extensive file. But it didn't really help him."

"Why's that?"

"It's no secret that he disagreed with my findings and had his own suspect in mind, but he never produced the unequivocal evidence necessary to back it up properly."

"And who would be his killer?"

"He was of the opinion that Jack the Ripper was a man by the name of Carl Feigenbaum."

"I've heard of him."

"Well, you should know that although the theory is appealing, it is unfounded. It was based upon the lack of evidence, or circumstantial evidence at best. Joshua, of course, ignored what he didn't like, just like all the others."

The thought immediately struck me that all the others might include the professor himself. But I held my tongue.

"Did you challenge him on his findings?" I asked.

"Absolutely. We all did. That's what we do here. Challenge all findings and theories until we are left with what seems most reasonable and logical. That's why we are of the consensus that Jack the Ripper was James Kelly. By the way, Jake, are you aware that Feigenbaum wasn't even his real name?"

"I am. It was something like Zahn, or Zahm, I believe."

"Once again, quite impressive, Detective."

"Thanks. Tell me, how did the Rev react to you all challenging him the way you did?"

"It made him very angry and frustrated."

"That's it?"

"Apparently that was enough, because he left the group."

"He quit your group?"

"Certainly did. And about three months later he disappeared."

"Now, that *is* interesting," I said. "Did he ever seem the type of man who might ever want to duplicate the Whitechapel murders?"

"Detective, this may seem brash and arrogant, but over time I have come to believe Joshua capable of that and much, much more. Mind you, my belief is based largely on my own personal intuition about the man."

"Okay. You said much, much more, though. Like what?"

"May I assume that you've heard the rumors about him and several young children?"

"Yes, I have. Do you have any information regarding that, Professor?"

"May I remind you, Detective, that I spent almost thirty years teaching criminology?"

"I know."

"Well, you can't teach it unless you understand both the material and the criminal mind."

"Agreed. But what are you getting at?"

"He was an odd sort, Detective. Very clever and deceptive, if you ask me. It is my opinion that the only reason he was not arrested and charged for those various crimes was because he knew how to cover them up. Now I'm speculating here, but he *was* quite intelligent. In an evil way, but quite intelligent. Of course, his nonsensical rhymes never furthered my opinion of him."

"Rhymes?" I asked, now very intrigued.

"Yes. He was of the strong opinion that had Jack the Ripper sent rhyming notes to the police instead of his boring letters it would have added distinctly to the allure and mystery of his murders. Joshua wrote several himself as demonstrations. But they made no sense and seemed too adolescent for me to take his efforts seriously."

"Might you have some of his rhymes, Professor?" I asked.

"No, Detective Brewer. I have none of them."

"That's too bad. He does sound like a nutcase."

"As I said, Detective, he was eccentric. But despite his peculiarities, if we were back in Whitechapel in 1888, I'd have him at the top of the suspects list. As for the charges of pedophilia, yes, Detective Brewer, I have no doubt that the rumors were true."

"Interesting. So, after he quit your group you never saw him again?"

"Oh, no. I'd see him frequently around town. Hard not to in a town this size. We were cordial with one another. He utterly captivated the other members, though. And I must admit he was not a boring fella. He kept things lively here in the group. But I'll tell you this. I wouldn't be one to ever go out into the Dan'l Boone with him alone."

"I understand. So he never participated in the group again?"

"No, but against my advice, some of the others from the group went over to his cabin and tried to talk him into coming back, but he refused."

"His cabin? You mean his house?"

"No, Detective. I mean his cabin. His cabin out in the Dan'l Boone."

"He had a cabin in the national forest?" I asked.

The professor nodded.

I glanced at Hagan. "Hagan, did you know about Joshua's cabin?"

"Of course. Everyone knows about the cabin."

"Is it nearby?"

"Oh, yeah," replied Hagan. "Twenty minutes or so to the door."

"Did you ever check it out?"

"Absolutely. The day he was reported missin', I had two deputies run out and look it over."

"Did they find anything?"

"Nothin' suspicious to their eyes."

Chatting with the professor had been helpful. Still, circumstantial evidence reigned supreme that day and seemed par for the course. I could draw out nothing actionable from our discussion. I assumed that no one else ever did either, which is why the reverend was never arrested.

"Well, somewhere out there in the universe," I said, "lies the answers I need. I expect I'll find them if I keep searching."

The professor smiled graciously.

"It seems you are searching for your destiny, Detective. I wish you good fortune in that endeavor."

"Actually, Professor, I subscribe to the notion that no one can search for their own destiny. Rather, it is destiny that discovers the one who searches with honest intent."

"Very interesting, Detective. You are quite the philosopher, it seems."

"Nah. To be honest, Professor, I think I heard those words spoken in a booth next to me as I sat shitfaced in a bar."

Both Professor Hastings and Hagan laughed.

"Well, then, Detective Brewer, I hope your destiny discovers you at its soonest opportunity during your honest search."

"Thank you, Professor."

A quick admission here. I found no good reason to allow the professor to think I was brilliant. Besides, to be discovered for what I truly was would have only taken one more philosophy-laced question. It would have then been very apparent that I was nothing more than an alcoholic shamus who retained a few still-enabled neurons somewhere in his booze-soaked brain.

I don't believe in pretense. Say who and what you are and let the chips fall where they may. And before you think it a noble position to take, don't be fooled. It was just easier for me to tell the truth than to try and recall a lie.

We often fail to recognize the blessings come from truth before the cursings come from lies.

No, that didn't come from my mind either. I think those words came from the same source as the other ones, or from somewhere similar.

And while there are alcoholics who hold possession of beautiful and brilliant minds, there remains a common denominator for us all. We're drunk more often than not. And all that brilliance is no match against the manic and incessant demand for alcohol. And for all that, alcohol remains not the destiny, but rather the undesired fate of all alcoholics.

I thanked the professor for his time and was invited to join the group. They had been chatting recently using Skype. I guess old dogs *can* learn a few new tricks after all. I lied and told him I'd give it some thought even though I had no interest in doing so. But he didn't notice my lie.

Every now and then, I guess, a lie is more appropriate than the truth. I'm such a damned hypocrite.

After bidding Professor Hastings goodbye, we crawled back into Hagan's cruiser and sat for few moments in silence.

Finally, I blurted out.

"We have to go back to Mercy Cousins' house, Hagan."

He looked at me and nodded.

"I believe we're thinkin' on the same line, Jake. The Teufel kit?"

"Yes. The Teufel kit. I didn't see it when we were looking around, but I didn't exactly have that in mind at the time."

"Well, she's workin' right now, but I guess we might visit her again about the same time we did yesterday. Would that be alright with you?"

"Perfect, Hagan. But I've got another favor to ask of you."

CHAPTER 16

"Sure," was Hagan's response to the favor I had asked of him.

The favor was to put my own peepers on the Rev's cabin.

"We can be there in twenty minutes," he added.

Hagan's estimate of time was perfect. Within twenty minutes we were standing on the porch of the old cabin.

Something about it creeped me out instantly. Bizarre, pornographic, violent images of the Rev and young girls played in my mind. Most likely it was my overactive imagination at work, but I still found it creepy and I couldn't stop the thousand or so invisible wolf spiders from trekking up and down my spine.

I lifted the door latch and entered the cabin. There was no lock on the door. The inside was eerie and plain. Nothing in it but an old, olive drab–colored Army surplus cot, a potbelly stove, and a rickety old table and chair. One window, with a dirty pane of glass, faced a small creek that slowly meandered through the acreage. The cabin offered no conveniences of electricity or plumbing.

What was so fascinating about this place was that anyone in their right mind would want to spend any time at all here, I thought.

Moments later I walked around the outside of the cabin and then out into the forest for some distance. Hagan followed along quietly, allowing my full senses to survey the area. I couldn't help but see lumps in the earth rising up like domed mountain summits. I kicked at a few of them, a bit terrified that I might expose a hand, a head, or some other rotted body part. The lumps I kicked at were just natural mounds of earth, though, and I wasn't at all unhappy about that.

We then walked down near the creek. It was there, inching along its banks, that I was overwhelmingly struck with the nauseating sensation of death, of torturous violence and raging anger. I looked around. Dozens more lumps that could have held decayed bodies popped up out of the earth. My stomach quaked, but I forced its contents to stay in place. Barely.

I turned toward Hagan.

"Hagan? Do you feel it?"

"Holy Nellie's in the bottle and Bucky's in a tree, I feel it, Jake! Can we go back to the car now?"

I cut Hagan a look that said I agreed with him. We left the area quickly and slid back into the patrol cruiser and sat breathing heavily in silence for several minutes, both of us anguishing from the assault of invisible insects on our skin.

Now, I must admit it, I still didn't know who Nellie and Bucky were. And while I suppose that Bucky was treed as a result of some poor choice he made, Nellie was dead on with being in the bottle. I found myself sucking on a flask of shine an instant later.

Good thing, a flask. It limited my intake by virtue of its small volume. I had found one in a local store the night before. Of course I filled it often. I had to. It was easy for me to suck it dry quickly. And I nearly did so after returning from our little hike to the creek.

Okay, after successfully and totally weirding myself out, I now sat staring at the cabin through the car window. The wood was old and worn and unpainted. The roof was completely covered with a thick green moss. More spiders skittered across my back. I tried to shake them off and was unsuccessful.

As I sat in the front seat of the patrol car sucking on my flask, my earlier sensation returned. I convinced myself that this area housed some kind of hidden horror. I couldn't put my finger on just what it was, but something hideous had happened out here. It wasn't an ancient thing, either. What I was sensing was recent or at least not long ago.

Was I just picking up on some latent energy left by the reverend? Or *was someone or something calling out to me*? Not certain of what was giving me this feeling, I kept it to myself.

I turned to Hagan, who sat very quietly in his seat staring out at the forest and sipping from his own jar of shine.

"Hagan, how thoroughly have you swept this area?"

"I had two deputies out here for about three hours."

"And you said they found nothing odd?"

"I said they found nothin' suspicious. Everything out here is odd to me. It gives me the heebie-jeebies, ya know what I mean?"

"I've been getting the same vibes. Something wrong was done here — something evil, something violent, something final."

"Yes, sir, I've been gettin' those exact feelings myself," agreed Hagan. "Every time I come out here, I go back jittery. I don't like it out here at all."

"I understand. Have you got cadaver dogs around?"

"No. I'd have to bring them down from Lexington."

"You might want to get them out here."

"Don't know if we got that in the budget, but I'll certainly look into it. You ready to go?"

"Can you give me a minute?"

"Sure."

I got out of the car and went back into the cabin and sat down in the chair and closed my eyes.

As I did back in New York, I cleared my mind and allowed it to travel where it pleased. Within moments, I was seeing all matter of evil being performed in that cabin. There was no doubt that the Rev had brought some of the young girls out here for his various and nefarious reasons. I saw his deeds, or what could have been his deeds. I felt the girls' fear and loathing. My visions scared me, but I didn't rein them in. I let it all go and then, just for a flash, I saw the reverend's face become frightful. One of his hands flew up to protect his face and then I was back in the cabin — alone.

I jumped up off the chair and went back to the patrol car, slipped into the seat, and finished the flask.

Hagan noticed my discomfort.

"You okay, Jake? You look like you've just seen the devil hisself."

"I believe I have. There *was* evil done here, Hagan. I'm positive. And I really think you need to bring out cadaver dogs. Most of those lumps might just be dirt, but there are some that are probably much more."

"I'll try to get it authorized. You gonna be okay?"

"Yeah. I'm just spooked."

"Me, too. It gets dark early here in the forest. I'd like to get the heck outa here before it does. Besides, Mercy should be home any minute. Let's visit with her before we start back up to McKee."

"Let's go!" I agreed heartily.

We pulled up in front of Mercy Cousins' home. Junior was on the porch with a bag of groceries in his arms. He must have arrived just before us.

When he saw us, he became fidgety. It was probably only something a seasoned detective would notice, but I saw it. It was like he had been discovered doing something naughty. And immediately, in my mind, he had.

"Hi ya, Junior," said Hagan as we approached the porch.

"H...Ha...Hagan. How you doin? Detective Brewer. I...I...I was just bringin' Mercy some groceries, is all."

"Yes, Hagan," Mercy added. "Just some groceries I needed."

"Fine. Fine," replied Hagan. "Don't mean to barge in on your visit, Junior."

"Not visitin', Hagan. Just...just bringin' Mercy some groceries." He turned to Mercy. "If you don't mind, Mercy, I'll just put these in your kitchen for ya and be on my way."

I wanted to laugh, but I dared not, for fear of Junior pissing his pants in panic. It was a surprise, of course, but not that much of a surprise. We had interrupted the liaison between sinful lovers. It was clear to me. I didn't see the recognition in Hagan's eyes, though.

Junior swung open the screen door and slipped inside quickly.

"Why you back, Hagan?" asked Mercy.

"Just have another question for you, Mercy."

"I told you what I know before. I don't know nothin' more."

"The medical bag that Joshua owned," Hagan said. "You have it around here, by chance?"

Junior burst out the door and made his way past us. He looked like he was seconds away from a full-on panic attack.

"So long, Mercy. 'Bye, Sheriff. Detective."

"So long, Junior," replied Hagan.

"Wait, Junior," said Mercy. "I'll get the money I owe ya."

"No, don't bother, Mercy. We can square up later. I gotta run."

Junior almost sprinted to his car. Before we knew it, he had it started and in gear. He hit the accelerator and was down the road in seconds. Hagan didn't take any special notice of Junior's desperate dash. Instead, he concentrated on Mercy's reaction to the missing Teufel bag.

"Mercy," Hagan said, "about that bag of Joshua's. You mean to say it ain't about?"

"I ain't seen it, Hagan. He kept the darn thing in his car. But it ain't there now. You can look if you want."

"No, no. That's fine, Mercy. I just wanted to ask."

"Why you lookin' for it, Hagan?"

"Just wonderin' where it might have got off to. Don't trouble yourself with it."

He turned to me.

"Jake, you got anything more for Mercy?"

"I don't. Thanks, Mercy. Sorry to intrude upon your peace."

"Fine," said Mercy.

Hagan crawled behind the steering wheel and stared at Mercy's front door in dead silence for several seconds. It was closed; Mercy Cousins had disappeared into the home immediately upon our departure.

"Something peculiar just happened, Jake. I don't rightly know what it is, but I got a sense of it."

I chuckled.

"What?" he asked.

"You're serious, Hagan?"

"I don't know what I am beyond confused at the moment."

"I think the sense you got is the thing happening between Junior and Mercy."

"What are you talkin' about?"

"Junior and Mercy have a thing going on."

"A thing?"

"Junior's banging Mercy. We interrupted them."

"Junior and Mercy? No. Junior's married. A nice woman, too."

"Maybe too nice."

"Now, Jake…"

"Hey, I may be wrong, but I think I know sinful intent when I see it."

"You sure about that?" asked Hagan.

"Let me put it like this. I don't believe she's paying for those groceries with cash."

"I swear, Jake, I'm gettin' too old for this line of work… Junior and Mercy?"

"Like I said, maybe I'm wrong, but then *you* explain why Junior was stuttering and stammering and dashed off like he did."

"My Lord," said Hagan. "Ain't that somethin'."

"Well, it seems when the Rev's away, Mercy will play."

"The longer I live here, the more I don't see. Jake, I would not have ever picked up on that."

"I'm not as in tune with this place as you are. That's all, Hagan. But if he's trying to keep this secret, what else might he be trying to keep secret?"

My phone rang. It was Grayson.

"Did you find anything, Hank?" I asked abruptly.

"Hello to you, too, Jake. And yes I did."

"Cut the shit. Tell me."

"First, where are you?"

"In the sheriff's patrol car about to head back to town."

"Okay, good. There's nothing on Joshua Cousins that I could find. Nothing, at least, that matches your description of him. That doesn't mean he's not here. We just couldn't find his name anywhere. Nor could we find pictures of him.

"As for the Nazis, they won't release their membership roll without a court order. That wasn't a surprise, of course."

"I'm not surprised you couldn't find anything on the Rev either, Hank. He's a ghost down here as well.

Sure left his mark on folks down this way, but not in a good way."

"Jake," Hank started, "Maddie Dumont called me again."

"Oh, yeah?"

"This time, she was talking about having some new evidence regarding the murders. Says she needs to speak with you about them."

"Oh, shit. Do you believe her?"

"No. I think she's using it as an excuse to get in touch with you."

"What did you tell her?"

"I told her to tell me, but she won't do it. Says it has to be you and only you."

"What should I do, Hank?"

"Nothing, right now. I told her you were still undercover and I had no way to get in contact with you, but I don't think she bought it. And she won't cough up what she says she knows."

"Hank, I'm positive as ever that she's got some kind of connection down here beyond a simple letter of reference. I just can't figure it out at the moment, and I can't find anyone who recognizes her, let alone might be in contact with her still. I'd really hate for her to get wind of where I'm at. I'm worried she might make contact with someone down here and disrupt my progress. This backwoods area has got some really nasty secrets. The sheriff has been great to work with, but I'm afraid he's as much in the dark as I am when it comes to Miss Blue Eyes — or the Rev, for that matter."

"I'll keep putting her off for now, but I don't know how long I can do that."

"Can I come home?"

"Not right now. Keep looking for anything that can move us forward."

"I will. I'll continue to show her picture around. Maybe we'll get lucky."

"Get lucky, Jake. If you can. We can sure use it."

"Thanks, Hank. Is there anything else?"

"One more thing. A chunk of kidney was delivered to the department last night."

"Did it fit the missing part from Jane Doe Number 2?"

"You know the answer to that already. Good call, Jake."

"At least it wasn't eaten. Any note?"

"Of course. The expected. Right out of Ripper lore."

"Jesus. What a mess. Anything else? asked the grizzled detective, worried that there might be."

Grayson snickered.

"Is that one of the side effects of the shine, Jake, referring to yourself in the third person?"

"I'm trying to separate myself from all of this insanity here. I've got my own insanity to deal with, as you know. How about it? Anything else I need to know?"

"Nothing that can't wait for your return."

"Speaking of that. I was hoping to drive back, Lieutenant. That is, if I have your permission."

"I don't blame you. I imagine it would be tough trying to get all those jugs of moonshine onto a plane."

"I *HATE* it when you do that, Hank."

Grayson chuckled and disconnected the call.

"You and your lieutenant work together real good, I see," said Hagan.

"Yeah. He's great to work with. Keeps me on my toes, I'll tell you that."

"You ain't allowed too many secrets neither, sounds like."

"No kidding. Sometimes he makes me feel like I'm wearing a wire."

Hagan chuckled.

"I take it he knows about the shine, then?"

"Knows about it? I pretty much have his permission to drive it back to New York."

Hagan laughed. After a second or two, I joined him.

"Can you tell me more about the phone call?" he asked.

"It's Maddie Dumont. She's been giving the Lieutenant heartburn regarding my whereabouts. I have a horrid idea that she knows where I am and might be panicked that I'll discover something more than what she's told me so far about her and her connection with the area."

Hagan gave me the strangest look.

"What?" I asked.

"I'm just thinkin' out loud here, Jake. But what if she knows somethin' more about Reverend Cousins than we know?"

"I've been thinking the same thoughts, Hagan. And if she does, it sheds a new kind of light on Miss Maddie Dumont."

Hagan stopped the car in the middle of the road.

I thought it odd that he'd stop in the middle of the road. But he was the sheriff, so I guess he could do as he pleased.

"Jake, could I see that photo again, please?"

I pulled it out and handed to him. He stared at it. After a bit, he nodded his head.

"Got something?"

"Yeah, Jake. Somethin'. Somethin' is comin' back to me now," he said. "Bit by bit."

"I'm listening."

"I recall hearin' of an incident down at Luttrell's quite some time back. I heard it said that Reverend Cousins got into a pickle with some young gal that was goin' through the area."

"Okay."

"I don't recall all the details, but I do recall it bein' said that this young girl knocked Joshua on his backside for touchin' her where he ought not touch her."

"Was this young girl Maddie?"

"I don't recall her name, Jake. But starin' at this photo brings back hints of recognition. I don't recall the girl lookin' anything like this, though. I think I'd remember one like her. But I do see hints of things similar."

"Did this happen ten years ago or more?"

"I don't recall that, Jake. It just flashed through my mind quick-like."

He handed the photo back and hit the accelerator.

"I don't even know why I recall that incident," he added.

"Any witnesses?"

"Just Old Man Luttrell. And I don't recall the context wherein I heard about it either. Just that I did. Strange, huh?"

"I've heard stranger. And I wouldn't put it past Maddie to coldcock some guy like that. She's tougher than she looks. Has to be, to run a magazine in New York."

Hagan's eyes opened wide. He hit the brakes and stopped the car again in the middle of the road. Then he sat rubbing his chin. I could almost hear the gears of his brain grinding.

"I remember more about it. One night I got a call from Luttrell Senior hisself tellin' me that Joshua'd come into the store and was tryin' like the devil to put the make on this little gal that had come in. She wouldn't have none of him, though, and at one point she smacked him across the face. Sent him hard to the floor."

"No kidding?"

"Laid him right out, apparently."

"What happened after that?"

"Zyree said the Rev skedaddled right quick. I figured it was over and he got what he deserved, so I didn't bother to send a deputy down to write up an incident report."

"Like I just said, that could be her. She's a strong woman. Anything else about it come to mind?"

He hit the accelerator once again.

"No, sir. That's all."

"Things are starting to make some sense, Hagan."

"Well, Jake. There you go."

"Yeah," I replied. "Now I'm probably jumping off a cliff here, but what if it *was* Maddie? I could then understand why she might be panicked about me being down here to discover her possible part in the Rev's disappearance."

"You're thinkin' she had a more serious run-in with him later and mighta done more damage to him?"

"I don't know what I'm thinking at the moment. But I'm even more positive that there is more to that little darling than I knew before."

"While I'm at it, Jake, I'm gettin' to think that Joshua Cousins is still around here somewhere. Somewhere below ground, but here. I've been havin' trouble with your theory that he moved to New York. You don't know Joshua, but I don't see him in New York. He never came off as the sophisticated type. He was powerful down here — a big fish in a tiny pond sorta thing. But up in New York, he'd be a minnow in a big ocean. I can't see him toleratin' that. He had a heck of an ego."

"But that might just be what makes him such a great suspect. Who'd expect a backwoods preacher to be a Jack the Ripper copycat?"

"Hmmmm. See, I'd never think of that. That's too complicated for me. I guess that's why you're workin' in New York and I'm workin' here."

"I don't know. You know this area well enough. I don't think I could survive here long."

My stomach grumbled.

"How about a chicken steak?" I asked.

"Sounds good to me," Hagan replied with a wide grin.

CHAPTER 17

Fortune sometimes favors the fool to confound the wise.

From the bed in my motel suite, I considered that statement. As I lay on my back staring up at the ceiling, I guessed that, in my case, it might be true.

I came to Kentucky to discover what this area's connection to Maddie Dumont might actually be. I never guessed I'd discover a suspect for the crime in New York here in Jackson County.

Reverend Joshua Cousins fit the bill perfectly. He had the history of violence, the morbidity of being a pervert, the temper, the guile, the intelligence, the knowledge, and the equipment.

Professor Hastings was exactly correct. If this was happening in Whitechapel in 1888, I'd have my number one suspect.

But this wasn't Whitechapel. And this wasn't 1888. Everything I had on the not-so-good reverend was sorry circumstantial. And to make matters worse, he was missing and undetermined to be living in the New York area. He was a suspect now, but he wasn't a rock solid one. That thinking brought me back to the Cousins girls.

No, I didn't suspect them of being connected to the murders, but they began to fascinate me. *Where would two backwoods-born girls, who had been molested by their father and suffered terrible psychological trauma as a result, go once they left the area? What were they doing now? How were they making a living? Why haven't they ever contacted anyone back here after they left? Were they even alive? Did they actually leave the area? Could they be two of the lumps of dirt in the Daniel Boone National Forest, put there possibly by their father just before he left town? Did they, perhaps, know something substantial about their father that he had to keep from getting out?*

More questions than answers filled my mind. Well, that and the bliss created by the moonshine. But the moonshine wasn't going to give me the answers I searched for.

For now, I'd have to put aside the idea that Joshua Cousins left the area for New York to become a serial murderer. Of course, a part of me would love for it to be him. He deserved a reckoning, one way or another. I'd love to put him away just for something I could probably prove in court immediately — beating up his wife. For the rest of it, though, I'd have to put it on the back burner until I could cement it all together. I knew I was onto something big here, but what it was, was still a mystery to me.

Hagan was called back to his office on the way back into town, so he dropped me off at the motel.

For an hour I had just lay there and thought. Well, once again, that was another lie. I lay there, drank some shine from my newly acquired haul of twelve gallons of Kentucky shine from ol' Jed's still, and thought.

My mind kept drifting back to the cabin. Something terrible had happened there recently. Of that much I was certain. Those lumps in the forest floor held a fascination that was now haunting me.

I glanced at my wristwatch: 5:45 p.m. The small neighborhood hardware store was about to close. Good for me, though, that it was just across the street. Because I got it in my head that I was being called back out to the cabin to explore one or two of those mysterious lumps.

I'm sure it was a strange sight for those in McKee to watch a New York City detective walk across the street back toward his motel room carrying a shovel, a pick, a large lantern, and a five-gallon bucket. But as I was pretty much in the bag and seeing double, it mattered little to me what they thought.

I walked to Elma's and ate a chicken-fried steak, swallowing a couple beers in the process, and then walked back to my motel room. The streets were empty. That was good, because I didn't want to talk to anyone at that moment. I was alone in my head, planning my drive out to the cabin later that evening.

Yeah, it was dark and I was still feeling creepy, but I just had to know what was under those lumps down by the creek that had chilled me earlier.

I was still pretty drunk, but that didn't stop me from loading up my tools into my rental car and aiming it toward the Daniel Boone National Forest.

It was about thirty-five minutes later that I stopped in front of Joshua Cousins' cabin. I was certain to be trespassing, but since the Rev had gone missing, I didn't figure anyone would be out to stop me.

I fired up the gas lantern, shouldered the shovel and pick, and grabbing the bucket, I walked straight toward the creek and those mysterious lumps of dirt.

Arriving at the first strange-looking lump, I turned the bucket over and sat my butt down on it.

I quieted my mind and went into one of my trances, searching my mind for which lump to begin digging into.

I kept getting glimpses of nefarious doings in among those trees. But not one of them aimed my thoughts toward one of those lumps.

I opened my eyes and sighed.

"Nothing, Jake. You got nothing. Might just as well start with the lump in front of you."

And that's what I did. But after the first two shovelfuls, I realized that the lump was hard soil. I would need to pick it before shoveling. That alone gave me pause. A recent grave wouldn't need picking unless it had been covered a very long time ago. And a very long time ago was not what I was feeling.

Just then I noticed glowing eyes gathering around me from deep in the forest. It appeared that the lone human, making digging noises, made for some entertainment for the forest-dwelling inhabitants.

I reached down to my side and laid my hand against my Glock nine millimeter. It was there. First round chambered and ready. Knowing that calmed me a bit. I just hoped I wouldn't have to pull it and defend myself against some wild beast looking upon me as a late-night snack.

It was then that I acknowledged my stupidity to come out here at this time of night to start digging. Why didn't I just wait for tomorrow's morning light?

Don't bother trying to work it out. I couldn't find a good reason either. My liquored-up brain said come out at night and so here I was. Scared, drunk, and digging, but not necessarily in that order.

I grabbed the pick and slammed it into the lump several times, loosening up the dirt. Then I grabbed the shovel and removed the dirt, creating a good-sized hole.

After a minute or two, I clearly saw what had created the lump. A huge tree root. Not a rotting body.

"Damn!" I uttered as I realized that I was, of course, digging next to a large stand of huge oak and hemlock trees.

"Damn city boy," I muttered.

I covered up the hole and moved to another lump. I checked it out first. There was no tree of any kind near the lump. I was standing on top of just dirt, as far as I could tell.

I put the shovel to the earth and stepped on the edge. The shovel penetrated easily. That scared me.

Now this just might be a grave, came the next thought to my brain, seeing that the dirt was loosely packed.

Just then I heard a strange shuffling noise from somewhere out in the darkness. I stopped digging and looked up, my eyes straining to see the source of the sound. I could see nothing.

I thought, if I start hearing banjo music, I'm the hell outa here. There was no music. Just the rustling of leaves and the snapping of dried twigs. The intruder wasn't even trying to be stealthy.

Something heavy was moving about under the cover of the darkness — surrounding me. Then I thought of an elk, or a deer. But then I considered that a bear might be skulking around in between the trees. Suddenly, this little must-do adventure changed to a must-not-do adventure. I lost my inquisitiveness quickly.

I'm from the city. In the city you can see what is coming at you most of the time. Out here, though, I had no idea what might be coming at me from the blackness.

What the hell was I thinking coming out here to dig during the night? It's something only very stupid characters do in horror movies. No one in their right mind would actually do this. So what the hell was my reason? I surmised that Kentucky shine had to be at the heart of any blame.

The sound grew louder. I dropped my shovel and grabbed my Glock. I then slid over next to an oak tree while my eyes began another search for the source of the sound.

I could best describe the sound as footsteps moving across the ground — heavy footsteps. As if something very large was moving toward me or parallel to my position. I couldn't determine which it was.

Okay. I was scared. I admit it. And without any booze over the last hour, I was sobering up. I hated that even more, because too often much more crap happens when you're suddenly aware of your surroundings. I preferred being sauced and blissfully unaware. Now, reaching near sobriety, I was having to take responsibility for what was happening to me at the moment.

The footsteps stopped. I raised my Glock and aimed at where I thought I had last heard the footsteps. All was silent now. The lantern was lit but it was not very effective at lighting up the forest beyond ten or fifteen feet. And what was preying on me was well beyond the light of the lantern.

Jesus, I thought, what if it was someone who didn't want me digging into the lumps? Maybe it was *the* someone who'd buried things and people out here in the first place. What if I'm to become one of the lumps for daring to come out here and investigate?

Okay, I vowed in that instant that I would never ever sober up to this degree again. It was better for me to stay sloshed — forever.

Through the silence, my mind still wondered who it was out there in the darkness and what they might be thinking of this now scared-to-death New York detective. Maybe they were messing with me. Maybe they were testing me. Maybe they were having some kind of sick fun at my expense.

I considered yelling out and challenging them. But a second later, I realized that was a very stupid idea. I mean, what if they accepted the challenge? I buried that idea quickly in the back of my sobriety-cursed brain.

So, standing next to the tree, what was my next move?

The answer came in the form of a high-pitched hiss. I heard it only for a split second. Then the steel-shanked arrow struck the tree inches from my face. I turned away in complete shock and fright.

As I did, something came out of the blackness and struck me across the jaw. It felt like a two-by-four. It hit like one, too. I fell to my back on the forest floor. Then a deep, resonating voice spoke in a low volume, almost whispering.

"Big mistake you comin' out here, city boy. I reckon now you gonna need a lesson on that."

I tried to raise my head, focus my eyes, and speak, but I couldn't form the thought of even moving my head, let alone focusing my eyes or forming a verbal response. I then lost sight of the light of the lantern, too.

I felt the gentle slap against my left cheek first. I opened my eyes and was greeted with a bright light.

"What the…" I mumbled.

"You with me now, Jake?"

I immediately recognized the voice of Hagan Duggar.

"What happened?"

"You got buffaloed, as far as I can tell. Can you stand?"

"I think so."

I stood up on not-so-steady legs. Hagan got my bucket and turned it over so I could sit down. My head felt like it was going to split into two halves. My vision remained blurry.

"I got sucker-punched. Felt like a two-by-four hit me. I didn't see who it was."

"You lucky I came upon you when I did. My headlights caught two big fellas. They skedaddled the moment my lights hit 'em."

"Did you get any better description than that?"

"Nope. But you're one lucky S.O.B."

"Yeah. I fear that if you had arrived any later, I might have ended up as another lump out here in the forest. There's something out here, Hagan. I'm sure of it now. Someone sure didn't want me digging out here."

"Now calm yerself, Jake. It was prob'ly just some shiners who clubbed ya. There's lots of stills workin' up in these parts. They don't like people up here they don't know. Now, I don't believe they woulda done you too much harm, but I do believe they was plannin' on puttin' a scare into ya. And it wouldn'ta been a little one neither."

"Well planned, then. Because it worked. But how'd they know I was even up here?"

"Trust me, Jake. Shiners know it when someone comes around that don't belong. Besides that, a stranger carryin' diggin' equipment in town and then speedin' off in the middle of the night tends to attract attention. I got the call right away."

"Sure glad of it."

"Yes, sir. I figured you might be headin' back out here. Now why you out here diggin' into them lumps at this time of night?"

"I know there are bodies out here, Hagan."

"Okay. But why you gotta come out here durin' the night? We coulda come out here in the mornin' if you wanted."

"I get ideas, I act on them. I didn't really think about it being dark until after I was out here. I'll tell you this, though. I won't be doin' it again."

"I expect not. Okay, then. We ought to get you back to town and checked out by the doctor. He won't like it none that I'm gonna get him outa bed, though."

"I don't need a doctor. I got smacked, that's all. I've gotten smacked before. Gonna have a sore jaw, but I guess I'll be thankful for that. Better than becoming a lump in the forest."

"Did you find anythin' for the diggin'?" asked Hagan.

"Just a reason not to be digging out here at night."

Hagan chuckled.

CHAPTER 18

We often find ourselves in places or situations where we need to be for reasons much larger than ourselves. I've always believed that. But being here in this lazy backwoods area of Somewhere U.S.A. is not what I would have considered possible only a few days ago.

I awoke early the next morning and, as I expected, my jaw was bruised and sore.

I walked to Elma's for breakfast by myself. I needed time alone to think.

Since I had been there more than a few times with the sheriff over the last few days, I was now accepted without suspicion.

In fact, I was greeted with smiles and nods as I entered. A cute little waitress approached me, smiling.

"Good morning, Detective."

Then she studied my jaw. She grimaced.

"Should I ask how that happened?"

"Let's say that I walked into a tree and call it good," I replied.

She shook her head and smiled sadly.

"I'd watch out for that tree, if I was you."

"I'll do that. Trust me."

"Will Hagan be joining you this morning?"

"Not this morning, unless he just shows up. I'm by myself."

"That's just fine. Booth, right?"

"Yes. Please."

She guided me to a booth and turned over a coffee cup. I didn't even have to tell her anything. She just poured the coffee into the cup and laid the menu down in front of me and walked away.

Moments later she returned to take my order as if she already knew what it was.

"A country breakfast again, Detective?"

I closed the menu and grinned.

"Am I that predictable?"

"Most folks have favorites. I think yours is the country breakfast."

"You're right about that. Thank you."

She wrote it down on her pad.

"Would you like me to bring you some ice for that bruise? It's a dandy."

"Nah. I'll be fine. It ain't my first time messing with a tree."

She giggled, nodded, and walked away.

Sitting there waiting for my breakfast, I got to thinking about what she had just said.

Everyone does have their favorites — drinks, food, habits, ways of doing things that make them who and what they are — giving them their own unique personality or life signature.

A criminal is no different. They have their *usuals* just like everyone. They have their favorite places to eat, to visit, to hide the bodies of their victims. And it has been my experience that where one finds a body there are often others in the same area, or very close nearby.

Most of us, I think, believe in the saying, "If it ain't broke, don't fix it."

A criminal mind works similar to most others. If something is working, don't change it. Don't change where you hide the bodies if they haven't yet been found. And if no one is finding the bodies, keep burying them there.

Reflecting on what I had experienced out at Joshua's cabin, I returned to the conclusion that someone had been using that surrounding area as a body dumping ground.

It might not have been the area immediately around Joshua's cabin, but I was willing to bet money that it was. They might even have thought it through well enough to believe that if the bodies would ever be discovered, it would cast immediate suspicion on Joshua Cousins first and foremost. And since he had been under suspicion for other crimes committed throughout the region, he would be a natural suspect for any body uncovered. The fact that he was missing would be reason enough not to go looking for anyone else.

And while everyone's eyes were cast onto the reverend, the real killer could sneak away safely — move the operation, as it were, to somewhere else and begin again.

The real question for me, then, was who, if anyone in the local area, might have been burying bodies?

Hagan may have been right about it being some shiners who smacked me last night, but someone else has been out there doing bad things. My senses were screaming at me.

I remember Hagan telling me that they had several missing persons and unsolved murders going back a long time. Someone, I felt, was keeping dark secrets. I concluded this also: the land around the cabin would give up its secrets, if there were any to give up, if only someone were willing to look hard enough.

I was willing to press Hagan to seek the funds necessary to get some cadaver dogs out there. Although this most certainly wouldn't be the time for me to start opening cold-case files, if my senses were accurate and bodies were discovered out near the cabin, they just might help me in my investigation. Heck, I thought, maybe Joshua Cousins wouldn't be missing for much longer.

My breakfast finished and the table cleared, I sat drinking coffee, rubbing my bruised jaw, and scribbling in my notepad while thinking about how to proceed with my own investigation.

I started to review my notes just as Sheriff Duggar stepped up to me.

"'Mornin', Jake. Am I disturbin' you?"

"Hagan. I was just thinking about you. Glad you're here. Sit down and join me."

He sat down and the waitress brought him a cup which she promptly filled with fresh black coffee.

He squinted at my jaw and whistled.

"He battled a tree out in the Dan'l Boone last night, Sheriff," the waitress offered.

"And it got the best of him, too, I think."

"You gonna eat something, Sheriff?" asked the waitress.

"Not today, Jo Ellen. Coffee will be just fine."

The waitress nodded and departed.

"You still thinkin' on things, are ya?" Hagan asked.

"I have been. I certainly don't know for certain, but I believe bodies are buried out near the cabin."

"Can I finish my coffee before you start tellin' me things like that?"

He snickered.

"Sorry, Hagan, but I've been doing some hard thinking."

I told him about my theory of favorites. He thought a bit about it and eventually agreed that it had some merit.

"I'll have to ask the mayor to let me speak at the city council meetin' about the funds I'd need to get them dogs out there. We're not a rich county. Ever' dollar is pretty much already spoke for."

"I completely understand. I face the same restrictions back home. We have a bigger bowl of money than you, but essentially it's all spent as well. But if I'm right about bodies being out there, Hagan, I might have the answers I need to move my investigation forward."

"It won't happen quick, Jake. That I promise you. We're not a fast-movin' crowd down here, except in the case of a fire or accident. Most likely it'll happen, if it does at all, sometime after you've gone back home."

"Would you like me to have a talk with the council?"

"They only meet once a month unless we got an emergency. They're not expected to meet for another three weeks."

"Okay, then I guess we do the best we can until then."

"What you got on your mind today other than diggin' holes in the forest?" he asked.

"I don't know."

"You still want a meetin' with the Ripperologists?"

"I don't think so. I don't have time to massage egos."

"I hear that. I was hopin' you changed your mind. Them fellas get a bit creepy for my likes."

My cell phone rang. It was Grayson.

"Can I come home now?" I asked.

"Getting tired of the easy life, Jake?"

"No, but I've learned a lot since I've been here."

"Like what?"

"Like, a New York City police detective has no business walking around in a Kentucky forest alone late at night."

"What are you jabbering about now?... Never mind. I didn't call for an idle chat. I called to tell you to come home. Captain is about done with us all. He says you gotta get back here and clean up the mess you've made."

"Would that be the Maddie Dumont mess, Hank?"

"That would be it. She's threatening to go to the press if you aren't back in town real soon."

"I thought you told her I was undercover."

"I did. Apparently she didn't buy it."

"Does she know I'm in Kentucky?"

"I didn't tell her, but I'm guessing she knows."

"I was afraid she'd play the press card sooner or later. She's a tough gal. She knows how to play the game. If she knows I'm here, my goose is probably cooked."

"Better your goose than mine. I'm played out. I can't handle her anymore."

"Hank, I'm out of things to do here anyway. But we've gotta find the Rev if he's up there."

"*You've* gotta find him."

"I hear ya."

"Jake, drive your damned moonshine back if you want, but get back here quick. In fact, bring *me* some moonshine. I think I'm going to be needing it."

"I'm on my way."

"OK."

He disconnected the call. I sat dumbfounded.

"You goin' home, Jake?" asked Hagan.

"Yeah. But what I'm going home to isn't clear. I'm either gonna go back on the case or I'm gonna get booted off the force. Either way, it's not gonna be good."

CHAPTER 19

I made a call to Lieutenant Grayson's cell phone the moment I hit the city limits of New York. We agreed to meet at my apartment.

"I know I chewed your ass out about this," said Grayson, sipping on a glass of shine while he plopped down onto the sofa next to me. "But I sure needed it. Damn, this is good stuff."

He noted my jaw.

"Make a new friend in the backwoods, Jake?"

"It's the lesson I learned. Don't go about disturbing moonshiners out in the forest."

"Hope the lesson sank in."

"I'm right fond of the shine, I reckon," I said, speaking in my best Kentucky accent. "So let's us agree that it was worth it."

"Okay. You've been in the backwoods too long, I can see that. Now get your head back here."

"Too bad we don't have a precinct out in Kentucky, Hank," I offered. "I'd put in for an immediate transfer."

"Jake, if you ever become sheriff of Jackson County, I'll be your deputy."

"You'd leave the high-powered glamour of New York for the backwoods of Kentucky? Who are you kidding?"

"Shit. All they'd see here is my ass going away. I mean it, Jake. You become sheriff and I'll work for you. If it wasn't for the bottle beating the hell outa you, I'd be working for you right now anyway."

I laughed.

"Wouldn't that be something?"

"Okay," Hank said, chugging down the last of the shine in his glass, "back to reality. So, what do you think we have here?"

"I'm not sure. But I went to Kentucky to discover what I thought might be important information regarding Maddie Dumont. I had no idea I'd discover the likes of the good ol' reverend."

"He sounds like our typical freak up here."

"From what I've gathered, I think he'd qualify as a freak almost anywhere. The exception being D.C. or L.A. Hell, he'd be just one of the good ol' boys in either of those two places."

Grayson smirked and poured himself another glass.

"Sure would. But he certainly fits the bill as a pedophile rapist around these parts, I'll give you that. But a serial murderer? A Jack the Ripper kind of murderer? The profile doesn't fit that, Jake."

"Hey, I would never have guessed that some backwoods town in Kentucky would be a hot spot of Ripperologists either."

"There is *that* little twist to consider, I guess."

"Hank, I thought, after so many years in this cesspool, I had seen it all. Well, guess what?"

"Yeah, Jake. I get it."

"Could some backwater reverend become the new Jack the Ripper? Is that really possible? It scares me to think it might be. And this city is prime real estate for him."

"How are you going to investigate him, though? There's no evidence he's here in town."

I remembered the airline ticket stub.

I jumped up and went to my suitcase, pulled out the used ticket stub, and handed it to Hank.

"I found this in Mercy Cousins' home. Can you have someone research this for me? I'm looking for purchase information. Like who purchased it? How was it purchased? When, exactly, was it purchased? Things like that."

Grayson nodded.

"I'll see what I can find out. Ten years ago, huh? Wasn't that around the time he went missing?"

"You bet."

"You think he's come back?"

"It's possible."

"Where are you going to start looking for him?"

"A pedo of his pedigree has certain needs — certain tastes. I'll put the word out into the cesspool and we'll have to sit back and wait to see what turd rises to the top."

"Thanks for the image, Jake. That one won't go away anytime soon. But I like seeing your head back in the game. You know, Jake, you've changed some."

"How's that?"

"I expected you to be shitfaced about now."

"I'm slowing down, Hank. I've come to realize that being out of control hasn't been all that helpful. I can't say I'm completely done with my drinking, but I don't expect to end up on my lips anymore."

"That's good, but if I keep seeing murders like I've seen recently, I might pick up where you've left off."

"I've learned this much, Hank. Drink enough shine and all manner of visions disappear for a time."

"Then here's to the bliss of blackness," said Grayson, raising his glass in a toast.

I felt a slight nudge to my left side and raised my head from the pillow.

"What?" I said sleepily, not knowing if the poke was real or dreamed.

"Welcome home," a sultry female voice cooed.

I turned my head and found Maddie lying beside me on her side.

"Hey, you. How did you get in?"

"A girl has her secrets."

"Apparently."

"Well, to be honest, I used to have secrets, but I guess the cat is out of the bag now."

"It's my job, Maddie. There was no trace of Maddie Dumont until ten years ago. I just needed to know more about you."

"Well, now you know."

She pressed something against my ribs again. This time it hurt.

"Ow!" I bellowed.

Looking down, I found the muzzle of my ankle snub-nose thirty-eight pressed hard against my side.

"Careful! Careful!" I pleaded. "It's got a hair trigger."

"Then don't move," she said.

"Maddie, don't be angry. It was just a routine investigation. So you changed your name. There's no crime in doing that. And I certainly agree with your reason."

"I came to you for help and this is what you do to me; treat me like a suspect?"

"No. Maddie. You don't understand. You're not in any trouble. It's just SOP."

Maddie rolled off the bed and backed away from me.

"Put the pillow over your face, Jake."

"Put the...what? No!"

"The pillow. Hold it up to your face, Jake."

"Why?"

"Because I'm going to shoot you in the face, and I don't want to disturb your neighbors. No use in ruining a good night's sleep for them, is there? Now kiss the pillow, Jake."

"Jesus, Maddie! No! Why are you doing this?"

"Jake! Hello! I just explained why. Are you deaf? Or are you just a stupid drunk?"

"Okay, Maddie. I get it. You're pissed. I discovered your little secret and you're pissed. I'm telling you, it's not a big deal. Lots of people come to the Big Apple and change their names."

"Jake, dear. I'm through talking. Bury your face into that goddamned pillow."

"Don't do this, Maddie. You kill a cop and they'll never stop looking for you."

"Funny, your lieutenant didn't say anything about that. Oh, that's right. He was having a hard time talking with his throat cut."

"What? You didn't. You didn't kill him."

"No? Would you like to go see for yourself? Okay. Before I finish you off, go into your living room and take a look. And don't you try and make a move against me. I'm a great shot. I don't miss."

I slid off the bed, very slowly.

"Keep your hands where I can see them, Jake. If one disappears, your face goes next."

Holding my hands up near my face, I walked to the bedroom door and bent my head around the corner.

"Oh, Jesus!" I said, seeing Grayson's body on the floor.

I moved through the doorway and into the living room. Grayson was dead, all right, and lay sprawled on the carpet surrounded by a black pool. Blood looks black in the absence of light, by the way. And it was a huge pool of black.

"Jesus, Maddie! I can't help you around this one."

"You don't need to help me. It was self-defense all the way."

"Self-defense?"

"Sure. Two drunk detectives trying to rape a witness. I had to defend myself, your honor."

"You'll never get away with it."

"I got away with all the murders in Kentucky. I think I can work my way out of this one, too."

"Murders? You killed people in Kentucky?"

"You don't think those lumps of dirt just grew up out of the ground by themselves, do you?"

"Why, Maddie? Why?"

"It seems that when a woman tries to reach out for help, men need to take advantage."

"Did you kill Reverend Cousins?"

"Who's that?"

"Don't bullshit me."

"Oh, the child rapist. No, I didn't kill him. Do you want to know who did?"

"Then he *is* dead?"

"He's one of the lumps in the dirt, sweetie."

"Who did it, Maddie? Who killed him?"

My cell phone rang.

"Let me answer that, Maddie. It might be the precinct."

"So?"

The phone rang again.

"Maddie. It might be important."

"Not to me."

The phone rang again.

"If I don't answer, they might send a black-and-white to check up on me."

"Good. They'll find me in a state of terror and panic, my clothing ripped."

She ripped her blouse open.

"Help me, Officer. I've just been attacked and had to defend myself."

She grabbed the neckline of her pullover sweater and ripped that. "I'll be a wreck. 'Bye, Jake."

She pointed the gun at me. The phone rang again. She squeezed the trigger. I closed my eyes. Instead of a shot, though, I heard the phone ring again.

I opened my eyes. The goddamned phone kept ringing.

"Oh, Jesus," I said.

I rolled over in bed and reached for my cell phone. I clicked it on.

"I'm alive."

"What?"

"I mean…"

"Jake! Jake, wake the hell up!"

"I'm awake. I'm awake."

My senses partially returned. It was Grayson on the line.

"Hank?" I said. "You're alive?"

"Wake the hell up, Jake!"

"Okay. I'm awake. I'm not happy, but I'm awake."

I crawled out of bed and went to the living room. There was no body.

"Get your shit together, Jake."

"I just had the strangest dream, Hank."

"Don't care. We've got another body. And it sure as hell ain't no dream. It's more of a nightmare. I'm texting you the address. Get your ass over here."

Grayson disconnected. I moved back to my bed and flopped down onto it face first.

"I'm alive!" I shouted into my mattress in exulted relief.

Obviously, I had backslid a little. That happens to alcoholics now and then. The road to sobriety isn't without its potholes of temporary failings. Did I say backslid? I lied. To backslide you first have to stop sliding. I'd been drinking the shine steadily since my return. No matter, though, I'd keep lying to myself as long as it kept making sense to me.

I don't recall what time Grayson had left my apartment the night before. The night sat hazily in front of my brain. I do recall laughing a lot. About what I can't be certain, but as out-of-control drunk nights go, I was left with a fun feeling.

I parked my car just outside the yellow police barrier tape.

As I lifted the tape to slide under it, Grayson spotted me. He was talking on his phone. He motioned me over to him.

I waited for him to finish, not yet ready to witness the scene. Not really certain my stomach was yet stable enough for that.

He finished his call. Put his phone back into his pocket and smirked at me.

"'You're alive?' What the hell was *that* all about?"

"A drunk's fog, that's all. I'm okay now."

"I thought you were slowing it down."

"I ran short of speed bumps."

"Yeah. I get it.... Well, prepare yourself. You won't be sober too long after you see this."

"Anything new?" I asked warily.

"See for yourself."

I started for the scene. Grayson didn't follow. I stopped, turn back to him, and pointed with my thumb.

"You going?"

"Nope. Been there, done that. Lost my cookies. I don't need to see it again. It's all yours."

"That's inspiring."

I walked back into the alley and noticed the usual players milling about. CSI was busy doing what CSI does and Doc Harrigan was bent over the body as usual, only he was stuffing a muffin into his mouth as if he was sitting in a restaurant and not staring down into the shredded bowels of a bloody corpse. *MEs*, I thought, shaking my head. They're a strange breed of humanity.

Okay. Mentally, emotionally, physically, and spiritually (if I really had possessed any spirituality), I was completely unprepared for what I saw. After gagging on the larger stomach chunks that rose into my throat, I successfully forced them back into my alcohol-anesthetized stomach. Still, I could only stare in disbelief.

The scene made the Ripper's Mary Kelly murder seem like a Monet painting.

I don't think a cadaver class at a medical school could ever be as grisly.

I gagged again, but I held whatever was in my stomach at that moment, most likely nothing that wasn't alcohol related, down. I knew I was one of the few who did.

The body was that of another young woman. I could only tell that by the breasts that were sitting where her eyes used to be on another carved-off face. I could only assume that the teeth were missing from her mouth. The rest of her was practically indecipherable as being the body of a human being. For your sake, dear reader, I'll leave it at that.

I stepped up to the body and squatted.

"Doc," I said.

"'Morning, Jake. And please note that I refrained from saying *good* morning because, as you can see for yourself, it isn't."

"Yeah."

"How do I write this one up, Jake? Tell me. I'd love to hear your take on it."

"I don't follow, Doc."

"It'll take me a ream of paper to describe this one, Jake. I'll be writing up the autopsy report for days, if not weeks. The injuries are so severe and so many, I don't know where to begin. It's like describing the injuries of a person who was blown up."

"Well, at least it hasn't affected your appetite."

"I gotta eat, Jake. It's not like I could sit quietly at home this morning and fix a nice breakfast. How the hell am I going to write this one up?"

"I don't know, Doc."

"Look at the scene, Jake. Blood everywhere. It's like the killer went on a splashing kick. There are parts of her slung against everything. Jesus, there are parts every-damn-where."

"This was rage, Doc."

"Ya think?"

"This was a message to *me*. He's pissed. He's really, really pissed."

"So you're making this about you?"

"What I'm saying, Doc, is this is now personal. This is something between the killer and me. He's letting me know that I'm not in control of this investigation; he is. And he wants me to know that he knows I've been gone. He's punishing me. I see that without any doubt."

"Funny you should say that, Jake."

"Why?"

Doc Harrigan reached behind him and pulled out a plastic bag. He held it up to my face.

"Because he left you a love letter. And he even rhymed it again."

I took the bag from his hand and held it up to read it. It was to me, all right. But it had nothing to do with love.

To Jake.

Love is bliss, but not like this.
Love is true, but not for you.
Our dear Jake is on the wagon.

He fights to tame the unruly dragon.

But have no fear, our true Jake is near.
But I'm not done. So let's make it more fun.
This whore will prove that I'm far from finished.
But for our dear Jake, his mind is diminished.

Our poor detective, he needs more incentive.
But as for me, I'm feeling very inventive.
Jake sits alone, so morose and dejected.
I hope poor Jake is not feeling rejected.

My work continues with more to come.
I shall work harder before my work will be done.
His Fifth Avenue Whore is feeling protected.
But soon I'll have her fully dissected.

Jake, Jake. This one is for you.
The next one, tee hee, will be for me.
Stay tuned, you traveling lover boy.

JTR

Okay, the truth. This note *really* freaked me out. But inside it were clues. I had to calm myself and think it through.

I pulled my cell phone from my pocket and stared at the evil device, still having no idea what most of all the little colored pictures meant on the face of it. I gave up.

I walked to the CSI guy and tapped him on the shoulder.

"Tim," I said, "is there a way I can photograph this note with this damned thing? I can take a normal photo, but how do I get an up-close shot?"

He chuckled.

"Still in rebellion against technology, Jake?"

"Cut the shit and just show me how to do it."

It took several minutes for him to enlighten me on the workings of modern-day cell phone technology, and I finally figured out all the whiz-kid jargon and snapped the photo.

"Thanks, Tim," I said, handing him the plastic-protected note. He didn't respond except for a quick nod.

Walking around the crime scene, I noted that no one was talking very much. It was somber to the extreme.

I walked back to Doc Harrigan.

"I know you'll do your best to describe this, Doc. But I wouldn't worry too much about it. The message he wanted transmitted has been received."

"I still have to do my job, Jake. I'll have the report to you when I can. This is going to be a goddamned novel by the time I'm finished, though."

"Novels are fiction, Doc."

"Then it'll be an essay instead. Either way, this is gonna be long."

"We're in big trouble, Doc. You know that, don't you?"

"No, Jake. I'm just the ME. You're the one in big trouble. If you don't put this bastard down soon, it'll get a lot uglier for everyone."

"I know, Doc. Trust me on this. I know."

"I know you do, Jake. But this one isn't going away until you put him away. I'm not supposed to say this, of course, but I wouldn't try to capture this guy alive. I'd try like the devil to put him down. There's not going to be any graceful end for you. You're just going to have to do it and take your medicine for your actions, Jake. I don't see a big win for you here. Think of it as putting down a rabid dog. There's no saving a dog with rabies. You're right, this is personal. It's gonna come down to you or him, Jake."

"Thanks, Doc. I'll keep that in mind."

I turned and started walking away.

"Jake!" shouted Doc. "I hope it's you."

I turned and nodded, but kept walking out of the alley.

"Jake!" shouted Doc again. "Here's another rhyme for you. When you're doing battle against the bottle, don't be quick to hit the throttle."

I stopped, turned, and stared at Doc Harrigan, not knowing what to say in response.

He smiled and continued, "Go get some rest, Jake. You look like shit."

I didn't fire back anything witty or brash. Doc was right. I just nodded.

A thought then struck me. Everyone thinks I'm on the wagon. *How did they all come to such a conclusion?*

CHAPTER 20

"Ah, to where doth that maiden's fair sense fall, now that she hath slipped into the madness of womanhood?"

For many of us, during the innocent blossom of our youth, fun comes and goes with the snap of a finger. However, for us who have lived too long, whether by the snapping of digits or not, the fun passes quickly. And that fair sense of things then falls into madness with ever hastening surety and we, the wretched survivors of youth, are often left worse off than when we started.

My beautiful and innocent sense of life had departed from me long ago. If memory serves, that's about the time my ass slid into the bottle a bit deeper than I had ever intended. Whatever the reason, though, my life had ceased being any kind of fun. And now I had only the madness to look forward to each and every shitty day.

I had a killer going on a rampage, slicing up hookers as if it had become a personal vendetta against anything fair and righteous.

Sitting in my office, I stared at the picture of the note on my cell phone. I decided I needed to see it up close.

I walked out of my office, grabbed the first rookie I saw, and stopped him.

"Need to print this out. Can you do it for me?"

"Sure, Jake, but it's really not that difficult. Let me show you how."

"Don't waste your time. I just learned how to take close-up pictures with it earlier today. I thought I'd go crazy figuring that shit out. I think maybe technology has it out for me. Just do it."

He chuckled.

The kid, that's how I thought of him, clicked a few buttons and handed it back to me.

"Should be printing out now."

"Thanks, kid."

As he walked happily away, my eyes followed him in both jealousy and dread. He was living in that beautiful sense of things right now. I was jealous of his youth, his innocence, his hope. At the same time, though, I dreaded the day when he would suddenly come to terms with the realities of this world and discover what a shitty and terrible place it really is. That's the day when the madness of adulthood would swallow him whole.

I walked to the printer and retrieved the hard copy.

Plopping down into my chair, I read the letter from the start.

Okay, I thought. This freak obviously knows I'm back on the case. It was also fair to assume that he knew I had been out of town and maybe even where I was. He could have gotten some of that information from the newspapers that were crucifying me and the whole department for not yet capturing him. But how could he have known where I was?

That was the most disturbing question. It could mean that someone in the department had spilled the beans on my whereabouts. It could also mean that there was a spy among us. Or, at the very least, someone who had an agenda that wasn't in the best interests of the department.

Whatever the reason, I was being purposefully abused, betrayed, and tossed under the bus.

I was used to that kind of treatment. I wasn't bothered about being the butt of uncomplimentary media reports. I had learned long ago to shake the media off my shoulders and concentrate on solving my cases.

I pulled out a blank piece of paper and began jotting down notes from reading the letter.

As I had done before, I began with writing down my reactions to the killer's words. I was looking for an immediate guttural reaction to them.

After an hour, I had scribbled five pages of *reaction* notes.

What I learned from that exercise was that this killer was becoming fixated on me. He was either falling in love with me or he wanted me dead. Considering my history, I suspected it was some part of both.

It is common for deranged criminals to develop fixations on the cops trying to capture them. They have something going on that is extremely personal, and someone is interested and involved in their lives. No matter the actual circumstances, someone is taking the time to care about them. At least that's what the psychobabblists have told me.

We were involved with each other on a very personal and intimate level now. I started to think that the murders were being committed for the similar reason that a cat brings a dead bird to the doorstep of its owner's home — as some kind of offering or even homage.

What concerned me was that he was becoming very acquainted with me and my *delicates*, as I liked to refer to them. My *delicates* were the personal things about me that only a few knew of — my shortcomings, my vulnerabilities, my messed-up ways. Ah, to hell with it. I might as well call it what it is. I was a raging, messed-up, bat-shit-crazy alcoholic. Okay. There it is.

My alcoholism, that delicate condition that I mentioned before once or twice, wasn't exactly a secret, but it wasn't something that was common knowledge either. And it certainly wasn't something the department wanted the public to know about. So the knowledge of it wasn't widely spoken of nor largely distributed. But the killer clearly knew that I was a slosher and was, for a very short time, sort of on the wagon. *How could he have found out about that? How did he know that Grayson had reprimanded me for my condition earlier and ordered me to get it under control before I left for Kentucky?*

I thought about that first.

After a time of hard thinking, I came to the conclusion that the killer might be stalking me or at the very least be following me about town. He might even have seen me in Bobby's bar drunk on my ass, which would be a normal sight there. Hell, he could have even been sitting right next to me drinking. Now that struck me with a sickly chill.

It scared me a little. *He* scared me a little. I felt the fear, then cringed when I realized that I wasn't, at that particular moment, exactly demonstrating a mountain of manliness.

Facing your own vulnerabilities is hard to take. It's not easy or desirable to do. At Bobby's bar, everyone was relaxed and accepting of our condition. We were all from different walks of life. Some were high-powered brokers, some real estate executives. Some were car mechanics. Some were bartenders and waitresses. Some were rich as hell. Some were living from paycheck to paycheck like me.

But in Bobby's we were equals. We were alcoholics, kindred spirits. No one was better than anyone else. We were vulnerable and we knew it and accepted it. Millionaires and paupers, we were equal in the eyes of alcohol.

But a murderer is something different. He may have been a brother alcoholic, but he crossed a line that no one has a right to cross. And for that alone, I was determined to put him down or capture him. If he really was one of us *conditioned* sorts, then I had to put him away simply for making us excessive imbibers look worse than we were. I guess you could call it *drunk pride*.

That thinking gave me some badly needed inner strength that buffered me against any further infusion of fear or consternation. I reset myself mentally and continued to search the letter for clues I could use against him.

He knew me well, I had to give him that. But I was now set on knowing him equally well. So well, in fact, that I'd find the way to stop him.

I then realized that I hadn't heard from Maddie since my homecoming. I wondered if she was aware of my return. Then troubling questions filled my already bruised mind. *What if she shows up again? How am I going to deal with that? Was she now aware that I had been to Kentucky and not undercover?*

I stood up and went into Grayson's office.

"Are we certain that Maddie doesn't know that I was in Kentucky?"

"*I* didn't tell her. Why?"

"Does she still call you?"

"I haven't heard from her in a few days. I'm hoping she got tired of calling."

"I'm wondering if she stopped calling because she knows I'm back."

"How would she know that?"

"I'm not exactly invisible, Lieutenant. I was just at another crime scene with the press all over it."

"Well, Jake, as far as I know, she doesn't know you're back home."

"She hasn't followed up on her threat to go to the press?"

"She hasn't, not that I know of. Let me ask you this, Jake. What are you going to do if she shows up in front of you? Have you thought about that?"

"I have."

"Well?"

"I plan to lie like the lying bastard I am, of course."

"Stay away from your usual haunts. That might slow her down some."

"I was thinking the same thing. I've got my hooch at home. I don't really need to go into Bobby's for a while."

"That's a good start. But don't answer the door at home either."

"Do you still have uniforms with her?"

"During the night only. Captain pulled the day watch because of the expense."

"I get that. Do we know she's at the office now?"

"No. We don't know where she is at the moment."

"Do uniforms pick her up at night?"

"No. They're just posted across the street from her condo entrance."

"Are they ever sure she's in her condo at night?"

"We *are* professionals, Jake. Yeah, we see her going into her condo at night and coming out in the morning. It's been that way ever since we started this detail. Are you pushing at something?"

"No, I'm just lost at the moment. I guess that's all I can expect right now."

"You got anything from the letter yet?"

"I think the bastard is tailing me. He knows a lot about me."

"Yeah, I gathered that myself."

"Well, now that I'm back in town, maybe he'll slow down his rampage a bit. I imagine the media has made your life an ugly mess."

"Not me, but Cap might be thinking about getting a taste of your moonshine pretty quick."

"Getting rough for him, huh?"

"You could say that."

"I'm going to slow that down some. It gives me horrid nightmares."

"You've said that before."

"Yeah, well, I mean it this time."

"You've said *that* before."

"Okay, okay."

"Listen, if Maddie does show up, you'd better deal with it delicately. You hear what I'm saying?"

"Got it."

A very quiet week passed. No murders. No Maddie. No progress in solving the case. Still, I suspected that all was not what it had seemed. I felt a rumbling going on deep below — as in the undercurrent of the city. The press wasn't pushing the story much. I guess they needed more blood to sell more papers. Now that things had quieted and actually gotten boring, no one was really interested.

I spent most of my time building a profile of the killer, and it was all pointing to Reverend Joshua

Cousins. It was as if I was being led directly to him. And that seemed outrageously convenient.

All I had on him was circumstantial, but I was used to that. That was my normal foundation. I mean, generally, if I had anything of an evidentiary nature, I'd have my suspect in custody. What I had at that moment, however, was more like a roadmap to an indeterminate destination. But even without a defined destination, to get to where one needs to get to, one just simply follows the path or road. If one does that with care, eventually one arrives at one's destination or, at the very least, where the road might lead becomes clearer.

The road I found myself on was leading me back to Kentucky. I was convinced that there was some connection to Annville. But what that was specifically still successfully eluded me.

I was tired. I was sitting in my chair with my feet up on the desk, ready to head home, when I got a phone call. I answered and heard, "I hear you're looking for some church asshole."

"Who is this?" I asked.

"Never mind who this is. You looking for the church asshole or not?"

The voice sounded so familiar.

"Depends," I said.

"Depends on what?"

"Which church asshole we're talking about."

"I see. You wanna play games."

"No games. I just wanna know that I'm not wasting my time here."

"Okay. That asshole from Ohio, or Tennessee, or somewhere out there in Hicksville."

I recognized the voice, finally.

"It's Kentucky, Manfred. And yeah, I'm looking for the asshole. You know where I can find him?"

"No, Jake. But I know who he is."

"So what is it gonna cost me to find out?"

"He was into some shit. I know if you're looking into him, you'll probably end up looking for me. I don't wanna be drawn into his shit."

"What makes you think I'd come looking for you, Manfred?"

"Your boss was asking if he was part of our membership. I know you're gonna come searching me out sooner or later to continue the conversation. I wanna stop you before you get too much into our business."

"Okay. Can we meet and chat?"

"That's why I'm calling."

"Where?" I asked.

"Remember where we met last time?"

"Yeah."

"Tonight. Eight o'clock. Alone. If you ain't alone, I'll pass."

"Eight o'clock. Alone. I'll be there."

He disconnected the call.

I walked into Hank's office.

"I gotta make a meet tonight. The Nazis want to talk about the Rev."

"Oh, yeah?"

"Yeah. I just spoke with Manfred. Eight o'clock tonight."

"Will you need backup?"

"No. He won't show if I don't come alone."

"You trust him?"

"Hell, no. But if I want info, I gotta go on his terms."

"I don't know about that."

"Manfred called *me*. He's scared. I'll be fine…I hope."

"Okay. It's your call."

CHAPTER 21

I'd had run-ins with the Aryan Nations before. They'd never ended well, and I guessed this one would turn out much the same. Someone always came out of the meeting with a bloodied face and an aching head. Sometimes it was them, sometimes it was me. But I needed to tie up this dangling end. If the Rev did have some ties with the Nazis, this meeting had the potential to give me a lead or two. Maybe, with enormous luck, it would put me on a path to solving the case without too much of my blood being spilled.

A two-ended alley in Hell's Kitchen was set as the meeting place. I knew it well. It was a damn scary place. I had to remind myself that I was told to come alone or they'd walk. I needed the meet, so against my better judgment, I showed up alone.

The paths of fools are paved with regrets. At least this fool's path normally was.

I arrived exactly on time, stepping into the darkened alley alone. I stood waiting for several minutes and got the impression that I had been stood up. Foolishly, I wandered deeper into the alley. I was completely alone in that black abyss.

After ten minutes more, I turned and began walking out of the alley, frustrated and wondering why the Nazis hadn't made their promised appearance.

I walked about five paces back toward the street when a door opened in the building on my right.

Two bald-headed giants stepped out into the alley and directly into my path.

What passed for my life flashed before my eyes. It wasn't much of a life even at that.

"I was wondering if my visit was wasted, fellas. I was expecting Manfred."

"Do either of us look like Manfred?"

"No. You're much prettier."

Yeah. It was a smart-ass remark, but I figured I was going to be dead within the next minute, so why not show a little disregard for my own life.

The giant on my right stepped forward and took a healthy swing. I ducked under it and moved forward and laid a full-powered punch squarely on the left jaw of the second giant. A searing pain shot up my arm as a trickle of blood slipped over his lip and dribbled down his chin. He only blinked.

"Ah, shit," I blurted. "That was my best shot."

He sneered at me. At that moment I sensed danger behind me and ducked again. A fist whisked over my head and caught the second giant exactly on the jaw where my fist had just struck. This time his eyes glazed over.

I spun around and stepped away from the space between the two behemoths. The first giant watched his buddy fall with a thud to the pavement.

"I'm just here to talk with Manfred, sport."

He turned his face toward me and crouched as if he were about to pounce on me. I appropriately noted the seething expression on Gigantor's face.

"I'm just here to talk," I repeated.

"You made me hit Fritz," he snarled.

"I didn't make you do anything. It was your choice."

Still in a crouch, he took a small step toward me.

I pulled my nine millimeter.

"Don't make me shoot you in the knee. I hear it really hurts."

He straightened up. I could almost hear his thoughts. He was trying to decide if the pain of a bullet in the kneecap would be worth the joy he'd feel from bashing my face through the back of my skull.

"Trust me," I urged. "A bullet in the kneecap is much worse."

I was hoping he'd take my word for it, but my wonder was answered by the step he took toward me, teeth bared.

I aimed at his left kneecap.

"STOP!" said a voice off to my right.

Gigantor stopped.

My eyes glanced in the direction of the voice. To my relief it was Manfred Eichmann, the other participant of the requested meeting. I've never believed that was his real name, but that's what he called himself, so I flowed with it.

"Good timing, Manfred. Saved your boy a trip to the emergency room."

"I doubt it, Jake. You would have only pissed him off."

I didn't argue. He was probably correct.

"I was wondering if you'd decided against the meet."

"I wondered myself," he responded. "Come on in. We'll talk."

"No offense, Manfred, but I actually feel safer out here."

"Jake. Think about it. If I was going to do you harm, I wouldn't have called off Klaus."

Strangely, that made sense at the moment. I smiled.

"Guess so," I replied.

I sat down with my back against the wall while Manfred pulled the cork from a bottle of Maker's Mark and poured the golden liquid into two short glasses.

How considerate of him, I thought. A kind gesture before he had me killed.

He handed it to me. I chugged it nervously. He smiled and then grabbed the bottle and set it before me. Without hesitation, I grabbed it and filled my glass to the rim. I chugged that too, and then filled the glass half full and set the bottle back down on the table.

"Thanks, Manfred. I really needed that."

"I can see that, Jake. Relax. I'm here to talk like you wanted. Now, what is it you want?"

"A guy by the name of Reverend Joshua Cousins. Ever hear of him?"

"That's the asshole."

"Great. We're off to a good start, then. I found some circumstantial evidence in Kentucky that suggested he might be connected with your organization here in New York."

"What kind of evidence?"

"A coat button embossed with a swastika and a used stub of a plane ticket to New York."

Manfred's eyes wandered around the room for a few seconds, then fixed on me again.

"It was a long time ago, but I remember him. It's hard not to. He was a douche bag, Jake."

"The date on the ticket was from just over ten years ago."

"Yeah....that's about right. He came looking to join our membership. He came dressed as a German officer. He had the whole thing, man. The crop, the monocle, the whole thing. He was hilarious.... He was a shithead, a pitiful puke. A real wannabe. But he was hilarious."

"That fits the description of his reported self-delusion. Did he join?"

"Nah. I got tired of him real quick. We threw him out of the building. He bounced twice across the sidewalk before falling off the curb into the street. We laughed our asses off the rest of the night thinking about him."

"That's it? That's all you remember about him?"

Manfred thought for a moment. His eyes flickered as if recalling some memory. Then he smiled.

"There *was* something else," he recalled. "He offered a certain service as consideration to allowing him to join."

I perked up. "Oh, yeah?"

"Yeah. He told us he had a delivery system set up to bring party treats to the city. Offered us a stake in it. You know, offered to share the profits."

"Party treats? You mean drugs?"

"No. Meat."

"Prostitutes?"

"Yeah. Hookers. He said he had a line of very young talent that he could ship in on a regular basis."

"Young talent?"

"Very young talent. Kids."

"He offered you a stake in a child prostitution ring?"

"Yeah. If we'd allow him membership, he'd provide the little quim."

"And you passed?"

"That's about the time we prepared him for launch."

"Impressive, Manfred. I woulda thought you'd take him up on the offer."

"We're not animals, Jake. Our agenda doesn't include going to prison for child prostitution. We have a political agenda. We're socialist fascists, not perverts."

A witty response filled my head. A second later, it didn't seem so witty and I realized it most likely would have caused me some pain. So I passed on it.

"You have standards, huh, Manfred?" I said instead.

"Don't push me, Jake. I'm being obliging here."

"You are. My apologies. So you launched him out the door then?"

"No. Not right then."

"Oh, yeah? Why not?"

"He begged me to hear him out."

"So did ya?"

"Yeah. He was a weird shit, but he fascinated me."

"How's that?"

He hesitated as his eyes wandered around the room again. Finally, they focused on me once more and he graciously added: "He said he was working with some grocer in his hometown that would recommend the girls come to New York for modeling gigs."

"But wouldn't the parents escort them?"

"No. No parents. He said these were runaways."

"So they couldn't be traced easily."

"Yeah. That's what I thought. He said he picked out the best lookers and he and this grocer asshole worked it out that the girls would come to New York to get into fashion modeling. That's the ruse he used to get them here."

"And there were no modeling gigs for them when they got here."

"That's right. They would offer them a place to stay while they were waiting for their modeling career to take off. Eventually, though, they'd drug 'em and shit, and they'd go into the pornos or the hooker houses. Sometimes, he'd sell the blondes to the Saudis here in New York. They love blondes, you know."

"Yeah. I've heard. Anything else?"

"Said they had a pipeline to LA as well. Said some of the little jailbaits wanted to be actresses. He gotta kick outa crushing their dreams. He insisted it was a real money maker for them. Said they were grossing hundreds of thousands of dollars a year from their operation."

"Did you believe him?"

"Not really. He didn't look like any kind of entrepreneur that was pocketing that kind of cash. He didn't look like anyone I'd wanna do business with anyway. He looked more like Colonel Klink. He had a saying…now, what was that?"

Again his eyes went to wandering and then a broad smile filled his face.

"Oh, yeah. 'Save 'em, then sell 'em.' That's what he used to say. He'd counsel them through his shit church, send them to New York, and then sell them, or whatever. He was a real piece of work, that one."

"Save 'em and sell 'em," I repeated, scribbling the words onto my notepad. "Damn pervert…. So, was that about the time he went airborne?"

"About then. Have you caught up with him?"

"No. Not yet. It seems he disappeared about the same time."

Manfred chuckled.

"Seems like someone else didn't care for the little shit as well."

"Can't say. But it was after his return to Kentucky from New York that he disappeared."

"Then it had nothing to do with us. Is that right?"

"Looks that way, Manfred."

"Good. Anything else, Jake?"

"Yeah. One more thing. Thanks for the meet, and can I expect to make it home tonight without bruises? Or am I about to experience flying, pavement and curbs?"

Manfred chuckled again.

"I like you, Jake. Get the hell outa here before I get a sudden urge to see an airborne detective."

"In that case, my ass thanks you, my ribs thank you, my elbows thank you, my face thanks you, et cetera, et cetera."

Manfred laughed uproariously. I left while he laughed.

CHAPTER 22

For the first time in weeks I was seeing light at the end of a very long tunnel and believing that it wasn't just the headlight of an oncoming train that would soon roll over my ass.

I walked along the sidewalk, heading back to my apartment, and couldn't resist the urge to call Hank. He answered.

"You're still alive," he said, "So can I assume it went well?"

"Better than well. Would you like to hear about what is going on in Kentucky?"

"Sure."

After I finished talking, all I heard was silence. I wondered if I had talked him to sleep. I was about to ask him if he was still on the line when he blew a breath.

"Wow! I never would have guessed that," he said. "So you think this grocer he mentioned was Luttrell?"

"The time frame was ten years ago, so I'm guessing it was the old man. But who knows, maybe Junior is continuing the family business. He did tell me that he still provides youngsters with the letters of reference. It is therefore likely that he's a chip off the old block."

"I like it, Jake. But it doesn't bring us any closer to wrapping up our own little mystery, does it?"

"Right now, my key suspect is the reverend. I don't know how to find him, but I'm hoping Sheriff Duggar might be able to put some pressure on Junior to disclose what he knows. Maybe Junior and the reverend are still in contact secretly."

"Would that the detective gods agree with you."

"Listen. I'll call Hagan first thing in the morning. Let's see where he can go with this info. Right now, I think I'll head to Bobby's, if that's okay with you."

"I hope Maddie doesn't catch wind that you're there."

"She knows or she doesn't. Don't worry, Hank. I can handle it if she shows up."

"Okay, Jake. Good job. I'll see you in the morning."

I disconnected the call and continued walking the three more blocks to Bobby's bar in deep thought.

I sat in my usual booth in Bobby's with a single glass of Maker's Mark on the table in front of me, still full.

My mind was a blaze of action. I was tuning in to every scenario that I could invent regarding the reverend and any possible connection with Maddie.

I was just about to invent another scenario when the room went completely silent. My senses picked up on it just in time for my eyes to focus in on the three MS-13 gang members who had obviously just walked in only seconds before. I could have heard a pin drop.

I carefully slipped my nine millimeter from its holster under my left armpit and pulled it down under the table. My thumb found the hammer and pulled it back. I then sat still as I could, waiting for the second when I expected the air to suddenly start filling with hot flying lead.

The room was too dark to pick out any detail. Seconds later, the man in the middle stepped forward. I couldn't make out his face nor see his eyes, but they, no doubt, were scanning the room. I saw his head stop. His eyes had discovered their target. That target was me.

Leaving two members on either side of the door, he moved directly toward me. As he got closer, I recognized the face.

"Hola, Javier," I said, pointing the muzzle up toward his chest from under the table. "A bit out of your normal area of operation, aren't ya?"

"We ain't got no normal area of operation, Jake. It's *all* ours, if we want it."

"I see. And you're wanting my bar tonight, Javier?"

"No, I came looking for *you*."

"Well, amigo, you found me. What do you want?"

"I got something you might want."

"Oh, yeah? What's that?"

"See for yourself. It's outside."

"Outside? You want me to go outside with you?"

"That's it."

"What do you have for me, Javier?"

"I'd rather show you."

"Do I need to call for backup?"

"Nah, homie. It's a gift and this one's on me."

"A gift? For me?"

"That's what I said."

"Ah, you shouldn't have. I didn't get you anything."

"You want it, or not? I ain't got all night to dance with you."

"Okay," I replied, standing up and holstering my weapon.

He only smirked when he saw my piece being holstered.

"I come in peace, bro. For now."

"Cool, homie. Let's go see my gift, then, *bro*."

I walked out the door and was stunned to see Maddie being held in the arms of a huge gang member. She was unconscious.

I turned to Javier.

"Oh, Javier. Peace, you say? You got big trouble, bro."

"Calm down. Calm down. We didn't do nothing, Jake. I swear. She came into one of our bars. She was in the bag already. I knew she was yours. Then she passed out. I brought her here. Like I said, it's a gift."

"That was thoughtful of you, Javier."

"Not being thoughtful, bro. I know you. And I know that if anything happened to her, you'd come looking for me. I thought I'd save you the trouble."

"It rather looks to me like you saved *yourself* some trouble, but hey, I respect the effort. So, on behalf of the NYPD, I owe you a thanks."

I held out my hand to shake.

"No, homie. I ain't gonna shake your hand. I hate cops. Blue lives don't mean shit to me. But you been square with me in the past. I ain't forgot that. The way I see it, this makes us even. I don't owe you shit now."

"Fine," I replied, withdrawing my hand. "Then from me personally, thanks."

"We cool, bro?"

"Yeah, Javier," I said. "We're cool. Until you get out of line again."

"When I do, we'll dance, bro."

"That we will."

No more words were exchanged. The big gang member handed Maddie over to me. She smelled of booze. She was definitely in the bag. I nodded to Javier. He nodded back.

The gang got into their cars and took off.

As they drove away, I blew a breath of relief. To be honest, I'd thought I was gonna die the moment I saw him walk into the bar. But, as it turned out, it was Javier who was spooked and worried. It was true, if they had harmed Maddie I would have been on his neck. It was good to see the bad boys running a little scared for a change.

I carried Maddie through the door, past the gawkers, and laid her down in my booth.

Bobby was there an instant later with a cup of coffee. He nodded and walked away. I knew he'd be back with more coffee later without me having to ask for it.

At first she grumbled, moaned, and resisted when I tried to get her to drink the coffee. It took some time and three spills, but I finally got her to sip from the cup.

It took about fifteen minutes before she was fully awake and aware of her surroundings, albeit still a bit loopy.

"How did I get here, Jake?" she asked groggily.

"If I told you, you'd vomit."

"Tell me."

"So you're into vomiting, then?"

"Don't be cute. Just tell me."

"You were delivered here by MS-13 gang members. It seems you staggered into one of their bars and passed out. They recognized you. They knew what I'd do to them if anything happened to you, so they tracked me down and here you are. It's amazing, really. They're not usually that smart. They wouldn't say it, of course, but I think you scared the hell out of them when you walked into their bar and were recognized."

She cut me a disbelieving look.

I nodded, confirming my words.

She guzzled the coffee and then grabbed my Maker's Mark and swallowed that.

"Yeah," I said. "That'd pretty much be my reaction as well. So tell me. What was it that got you so loaded you visited our friends of the MS-13?"

"I've missed you."

"Yeah, I'm not buying that exactly."

"What is with you, Jake? You're not nearly as sweet as you were before you went undercover. Did something happen?"

I chuckled.

"I think we both know that I wasn't undercover."

I got a sly smile out of her.

"So, how was Kentucky?" she asked.

"You know Kentucky."

"Yes. I do know Kentucky. So glad I'm no longer there."

"Okay, doll. Enough games. Tell me about Kentucky and tell me all of it."

"You mean such as what was I doing there?"

"Let's start with that."

Bobby arrived with a fresh cup of coffee for Miss Crush-My-Nads and a fresh Maker's Mark for me. I left it on the table untouched. She sipped at the coffee, eyeing my Maker's Mark.

"Are you going to join me, Jake?"

"I'm good for the moment. Kentucky, please."

"Fine. It's not a big mystery. I was passing through the area and needed some money. I got a job, got paid, and left with a needed letter. The end."

"Nah. Nice try, but that's not how it went."

"Oh, really? How did it go, then?"

"Let's have a chat now about one Reverend Joshua Cousins."

"Oh. That freak."

"Yeah. That freak. Tell me about the run-in you had with him."

"You know about that, then?"

"Yep."

"Not much to add, I'm afraid. He hit on me, I hit on him. The end.... But! The truth? I think my hit was much better."

She giggled.

"Did you know the Cousins girls, Mary Beth and Kerri Ann?"

"I knew them. They came into the store a few times. They were only kids. I didn't get to know them all that well."

"Did you get along with Zyree well?"

"Well enough to get the letter I needed."

"How about Junior?"

Maddie chuckled.

"He was fun. He was another freak, of course. A real pervo. I wouldn't let him touch me. Well, not a whole lot more than a bit. But he was fun to manipulate now and then."

I listened to her. The only thought that went through my mind was why she was being so candid with me. Of course, I was asking questions that I suspected she was already prepared for. But she was giving me answers. She wasn't volunteering any useful information, and her answers were more teases than answers, but she wasn't denying knowing anyone. And she knew the catchwords like *freak* and *pervo*.

I concluded that she was toying with me. I figured that much out. But I was toying with her as well. I was testing her. And I think she was testing me as well. I had the feeling she was searching for what I had discovered, or should I say uncovered, about her time in Kentucky. My questions thus far were more like foreplay. I hadn't yet gotten down to the real questions. But I was about to. I decided to just open it up and see what jumped out at me.

"That was a fun warmup round. I enjoyed that."

"What are you insinuating, Jake?"

"Nothing. I enjoyed the foreplay. But let's get naked and to the meat of the matter, shall we?"

That seemed to surprise her. I don't think she was ready for me to jump in like that. But then, this gal was a player. For all I knew, it was she who was playing with me. Still, I thought I'd take the chance and press her a bit more.

"I've been answering your questions, Jake. I don't understand."

"You've been toying with me, doll. In fact, you've been toying with me all along."

"What do you mean?"

"What I mean is that Javier and his MS-13 boys would never show up here unless he was paid to. He's not the sharpest pencil in the box, but he's smart enough not to piss me off by coming to my bar unless he had a very good reason to. And the only reason I can think of involves dead presidents. How much, doll?"

"Jake. Stop it. Why are you being like this?"

"Sure, I admit it, you looked drunk when I first saw you, but the show is over, doll. You can handle your booze better than I ever hope to. I've been out with you. So, how much did you pay Javier to bring you here tonight?"

Maddie dropped her head to her chest and remained still and silent for almost half a minute. Then she raised her head and stared at me.

"A thousand dollars, Jake. I paid him a thousand dollars to bring me here."

"Nice try. Javier wouldn't leave his turf and risk what he risked for a lousy grand."

"Okay, okay. Ten thousand."

"Bullshit, doll."

"Fine! Twenty-five thousand, okay? Twenty-five grand to bring me here. Are you happy now?"

"Getting there. So, how do you know Javier?"

"His sister, believe it or not, is one of the models we use in our fashion layouts. Nice girl. Smart girl. Nothing like her brother. But I needed to get to you. She asked her brother to help me. There you have it."

"Okay. So why all the dramatics? Why not just call and ask to get together?"

"I knew you'd say no. Your lieutenant is an asshole, in case you weren't aware. I know he's ordered you not to see me. It was the only way I could think of to get here that made sense and gave you the plausible deniability I thought you might need. I'm sorry, Jake. I wanted to see you. I'm guilty of having feelings for you. So sue me."

She was laying it down pretty thick now. I wanted to burst her bubble, but I had my own agenda. I decided to play it out a little more.

I forced a small chuckle.

"You didn't need to do that. I would have jumped at any chance to see you. I've really missed you, too."

She smiled.

"Thanks. Was that so hard for you to say?"

"I guess not.... Twenty-five large? You paid twenty-five grand just to see me?"

"The truth? Thirty. He said he wouldn't come to this side of town for less than thirty. And if you shot at him, he was going to tack on another fifty. So I guess I should thank you for not shooting at him."

"You're welcome," I said, wanting to burst out laughing but afraid to do so and blow the macho man image I had going. "So tell me, how the hell did you escape all the bullshit in Kentucky? That place is a den of evil. How did you get through it without taking a hit or two?"

"It wasn't easy. Reverend Cousins is evil incarnate. Every time I saw that man, I got creeped out. It creeps me out to even think of him now. Did you get the chance to meet him?"

"No, I didn't. I guess you haven't heard, huh?"

"Heard what?"

"He seems to have gone missing."

"Seriously? You're not joking?"

"Not joking. He went missing several years ago."

"Missing. Well, I'm not surprised. He was a bad man."

"Yeah. Funny thing, though. He went missing around the time you showed up in New York. Isn't that strange?"

"Do you think I had something to do with that? Do you really think that, Jake?"

"Actually, I think he might be here in the city. But I can't find him anywhere."

"If you do locate him, don't trust a thing he might tell you. He's pure evil. Did you hear about his crimes?"

"Crimes?" I said, acting stupid. "What crimes?"

"You didn't hear about him and little girls in the area? I'm surprised. It was big."

"Oh," I said, "you're talking about the rumors of pedophilia?"

"They weren't rumors, Jake. It was true. All of it."

"True? How do you know that?"

"Trust me on this. It was all true. And if he *is* up here in the city, he's probably doing it still. You really need to find him, Jake. You really do…. *Oh, my god!*"

She really should have been on stage. Those blue eyes just opened like golf balls. I played along.

"What? *What?*"

"It's all coming back to me, Jake. I think he was the one I saw that night. *Dear God!* I do believe it was Joshua Cousins, Jake! *He's the killer!*"

In that instant, I stopped thinking that she was toying with me. I believed her. I believed what she was saying.

"Are you recalling his face?"

"Yes, Jake. It was him, I'm sure of it. I'm remembering now. Did you know he studied the Ripper crimes? He knew nearly every detail of every murder. He even had a medical bag complete with knives. Jake! Joshua Cousins is the murderer. I'm certain of it. And he's after me. Oh, Jake! I'm scared. I'm really scared."

"Okay," I said, now believing her totally. "Okay, just remain calm, Maddie. He's not going to come anywhere near here. You're safe. Maddie, forgive me, but I have to ask. Did you know Junior was transporting young girls to New York to be prostitutes and porn actresses? Tell me the truth. It might be the reason Joshua Cousins is here."

"Not Junior, Jake. I heard it was Joshua who was doing that. Oh, Jake. He's here in the city. You need to find him. You need to find him quickly. He'll kill again unless you find him. He's a very sick man. I'm scared to death, Jake. I don't want to be alone tonight."

Well, damn it all. I was sucked into her once again. And it was all making sense now. I picked up my Maker's Mark and slammed it. I waved to Bobby. He nodded. I knew what was going to happen next.

I cursed my weakness.

CHAPTER 23

I woke up. Amazingly, I was clear headed. I looked at the clock: 2:48 a.m.

I rolled over. Maddie was sleeping soundly next to me. I recalled our evening. We drank and then we screwed each other's brains out. It was real. It happened. I wasn't dreaming.

Then it hit me. I was really screwed if Hank found out about this. Maddie was right. Hank had warned me to stay clear of her. I then recalled Hank's questions: *What are you going to do if she shows up in front of you? Have you thought about that?*

I had my answer now, it seemed. And the answer was I was going to fall into her web all over again. But this was different than I had anticipated. She was my lead witness. And now she had ID'd the killer. My case just got stronger. I finally held the upper hand.

My purpose was so clear. I had to find the reverend if it took every favor I had. I would put out the word again and this time I'd make it worth the trouble to report his whereabouts to me. Yeah. Just like Javier. I'd put cash in the hands of the first informant to come clean as to where I might find my Jack the Ripper.

I slipped out of bed and into my boxer shorts. I walked out into my living room and plopped down on the sofa facing my whiteboard.

There it was. Clearer than light. All the clues on the whiteboard had arrows leaving them and ending at the encircled name in the center of the board — Joshua Cousins. I only had to find him and this case would be finished.

Maybe Hank would find it in his heart to forgive my trip-up. While it was true that I hadn't yet overcome my alcoholic weakness, I had been getting better. The road to sobriety isn't always a smooth one. And Maddie Dumont made it all the more difficult. But I now had a witness who could identify the killer.

I would launch a manhunt unlike anything this city had seen in years. If I could get a lucky break. I'd have the not-so-good Rev in cuffs very soon.

I felt good. Really, really good.

I dropped Maddie off at her office. I suggested the tactic knowing that the department had a black-and-white waiting for her to appear at the front door of her condo. I was right. They weren't outside her office building.

I wasn't scheduled until swing shift, but I headed into the office anyway. I was going to prepare to put out the APB on Joshua Cousins. I had to write up a good description of him, since I had no photograph to use.

As Hagan would say, Holy Nellie doing something and Bucky doing something else, I didn't expect to see Grayson already sitting at his desk as I passed his office. He caught me.

"Jake! Glad to see you here. Drop your ass in front of my desk — NOW! ... Please."

I sheepishly obeyed.

He sat back in his chair and smiled at me. I knew instantly that I was a cooked goose.

"We aren't scheduled until swing shift, Hank. What are you doing here?"

"I had the black-and-white around the corner from your apartment call me when you two left so I could be here when you got in this morning."

Damn! I didn't think to look for them there. Someone must have spotted Maddie in Bobby's and notified Hank.

"I can explain..."

"Jake, this is when you want to choose to be real quiet and listen. Got it?"

I nodded.

"Good. We're getting off to a good start, then. So, you ignored my order to avoid her, huh? You got drunk again, too. You took her back to your apartment as well, also against my orders. You screwed her real good, too, I imagine. Gave her the full thirty seconds, I can guess."

He grinned as he said that last line. I was about to correct him, but instead I chose the silence of good judgment over shouts of valor and stupidity. Not my normal course of action, to be sure. But, being the astute reader you are, you already know that by now. Besides, he was only off by a minute or so anyway.

Still, I had no intention of giving him the satisfaction of confirming it. I sucked it up and maintained a straight face.

"Have I just about covered it, Jake?"

"Just about. But I would like to add something in my defense, if I may?"

"Please do, Jake. Oh, this is going to be good. I just know it."

"How about this, Hank? She positively ID'd the killer. Her memory returned. The killer is Joshua Cousins."

The smug smile Hank wore disappeared. He sat up in his chair.

"Jake, if you're messing with me, so help you."

"I'm not messing with you."

"Damn you!" he said. "I can see it coming now. You're going to get out of an ass chewing, aren't you?"

I wanted to laugh, but it would have just pissed him off more. So, once again, I held my sharp-witted retort and only answered with respect.

"I came in early to put out an APB for Joshua Cousins. She gave me a pretty good description of him, and I was about to type it up on the computer."

His eyes opened wide in astonishment. I corrected myself so as not to give him a heart attack right then and there.

"Correction," I said. "I'm going to dictate the description to one of the rookies."

He relaxed and nodded.

"Go do it, Jake," was all he said.

I stood up and started for the door. I was going to say something witty and graphic upon my departure. For a third time, though, as amazing as that may sound to you, I resisted the urge and left his office in silence.

Twenty minutes later we had released the APB. Sometimes, not often, we got hits on our all-points bulletins within hours. All I could do now was wait for any return. It was to be an arduous wait. Still, on the good side, and with a beaming inward smile to boot, I did manage to avoid a really nasty ass chewing.

I was ready now to call Hagan. I knew that my news was about to crash his whole day. I picked up the desk phone to dial when a uniform walked up to my desk.

"Jake. I need to show you something."

"Can it wait? I'm about to break some bad news to a friend."

"I certainly don't know what that could be, Detective. But with all due respect, I'm certain you'll want to hear this first."

I was instantly intrigued and replaced the phone in its cradle.

"This day just keeps surprising me. What do you have?"

"I really think you should see for yourself."

Now I was swallowed by intrigue.

"Show me," I said as I stood up.

I walked down the hall to an interrogation room and opened the door. What I saw reminded me of something I'd heard somewhere before, although I had no idea where that was or how long ago.

"Never was I so amazed and bewildered than when I first saw myself staring back at me from out of the depths of the abyss."

Don't ask me what that might truly mean, because I'm not that smart. But staring at the person in that room made me feel as if I was staring at myself — my younger self.

In the room was a young girl. She looked frightened as hell. It reminded me of when I was but a young kid. On a dare, I tried to shoplift a piece of candy from Old Man Johnson's dime store. I wasn't very adept as a thief and I got caught.

I ended up in a room very similar to the one that now held another frightened child. My father was called into the precinct. I thought I was going to be slaughtered. To make a long story short, Mister Johnson dropped the charges after I explained why I tried to take the candy. My ass got whipped good when I got home and I had to work off the price of the candy tenfold by sweeping Mister Johnson's floors in the store every day after school for a week. I never stole anything again. I wish the same thing would have happened to me with alcohol. But that's another story.

"She's just a kid," I said.

"You're gonna think differently after you talk with her," said the uniform who'd found her.

"You got a file?"

"Just a contact report for now. But you have got to hear what she's told me."

I read the contact report, which nearly gave me a heart attack. After I recovered, I walked into the room.

Jesus, she was a beautiful young girl. But those startled, terrified eyes stared a hole through me as if they were plasma torches. I smiled as gently as I could and sat down across from her.

"Your name is Candace Holmgren. Is that right?"

She nodded.

"Am I going to prison? she asked.

"I don't think so. Do you think you should?"

"No. I'm sorry. I was hungry. I didn't have any money for food."

"The store has dropped the charges. Officer Mullen paid for the snack out of his own pocket. He's the one who brought you in."

"I don't want to go to prison."

"Calm down Candace. You're not going to prison. But I hear you might be a runaway from down in Kentucky. Is that true?"

"Yes, sir. I'm sorry. I want to go back home. I'm sorry."

"Nothing to be sorry about, sweetie. You've done nothing wrong except take a snack that you didn't pay for. It's over now. I'm here to help you. You're safe here, I promise. But I'd like to know about this letter you had in your pocket. Can you tell me about it?"

I'll spare you all the detail of my interview and summarize it for you instead.

The letter she had in her possession was signed by Junior Luttrell. It was a reference letter from Junior attesting to her ability to become a model.

It was addressed to Elite Life Modeling Agency, here in New York.

To shorten the matter even more, Elite Life was suspected of being a front for prostitution. It had been well known to the NYPD for quite a while. We could never get enough evidence of wrongdoing on them to shut them down, but their clientele had a continued propensity to end up in our custody under charges of soliciting. No matter what we promised them, though, they wouldn't give us any evidence of unlawful activity. Someone had them frightened real good. The agency did have some successful models in their stable, I would say just enough to keep them on the legitimate side of the law. And, of course, they always denied any participation in the girls' extracurricular activities, citing as the excuse that "some girls just don't have success in them for the rigors of modeling."

Candace was eighteen years old. She ran away from an abusive home life. She had wandered into Junior's store looking for a job after hearing that Junior was always offering to help the youth of the area. In the eyes of the law, she was an adult and perfectly able to run away from anything she didn't like. I knew that I could only provide her minimal help. I was powerless to change the circumstances of her life. And that frustrated the hell out of me. I did, however, learn something very useful from her that I hoped would be helpful for other youngsters in her position another day.

The girls, most of them actually girls, exceptionally good-looking young girls, seemed to end their time in Junior's store with a wonderful reference letter to the Elite Life Agency.

But Junior, it seems, exacted a price for his humanitarian benevolence. The girls had to have sex with him before he would hand them the letter.

Bingo!

I had the department make the necessary arrangements for temporarily housing and caring for the young woman. It wasn't the Waldorf-Astoria, but it was clean, structured, and safe. It was a place where she could reset her life if she was willing to make the attempt.

Another saying came to mind: "*Good things come to those who wait.*"

Only a short time before, I was going to call Hagan and break the suspicions of Zyree's and Junior's shenanigans to him and hope that he could take it further. Now I had proof positive that Junior was involved in human trafficking and possibly more.

I called Hagan and regurgitated the whole Nazi thing as well as Candace's story.

Hagan sat in silence as I spelled it out for him.

I thought I had put him to sleep, because I could only hear breathing on the other end of the line. I waited for him to respond.

"Oh my, Jake," he said finally.

I was surprised.

"What?" I asked. "Nothing about Holy Nellie and Bucky?"

"I've given them the day off," he replied without even a hint of humor in his voice.

I was about to laugh at his response, but it seemed inappropriate at the moment.

"Hagan, I needed a connection to Kentucky. This is it. This could break my case wide open. I've got to find the Rev. I don't want to say any more about it because I'm not certain of anything. But I believe he is involved with this up to his collar."

"Jake, this is gonna break all kinds of things apart here. I don't believe Junior will survive this. Folks down here will have him tarred and feathered and hung by the neck until dead if this gets out. I'm afraid for him. I truly am."

"It's of his own making, Hagan. I say arrest him and let the chips fall where they may."

"You say she's eighteen years old. I can do little about her carnal escapade with Junior unless she says she's willin' to step forward and call it rape. You know that, Jake."

"I understand. She insists it was consensual. Given her circumstances down there, she was willing to trade her body for the letter to get out of the area. But it's the letter and who it's addressed to that has me burning mad. We suspect Elite Life to be a front for prostitution. You can bet the owners will deny any nefarious connections with this letter. And it is just a reference letter by any definition. There is nothing to act on here. But I think if you apply some pressure to Junior, he might spill the beans about Joshua's whereabouts here in New York. He's my lead suspect, Hagan. I could use some help in locating him."

"I understand, Jake. I'll go round him up right now and let you know what transpires. ...Oh, Jake. I almost forgot to tell you somethin' important. I got the funds for the cadaver dogs authorized. They'll be here day after tomorrow."

"That's great news, Hagan."

I thanked him and hung up the phone.

Things were starting to come together for me. It had been years since anything this good had happened to me. That wasn't true, of course. Lots of good things had been happening to me of late, but it *seemed* like years since the last. I was coming into the light of discovery and I felt good about this case again. Considering what I had been going through up until then, I took it as a small win.

CHAPTER 24

All I could do now was patiently wait for the next break in the case.

Of course, patience was not readily found among my strengths. I was struggling against the impulse to force conditions. It had never worked before, but that did not deter me from trying. I thought about asking Grayson's permission to go to Kentucky and stand in front of Junior's face as an intimidation factor. But I knew that would be met with a resounding NO! And considering my latest exploits with Miss Blue Eyes and my near-to-ass-reaming event, I wouldn't have blamed him.

After weeks of putting out feelers and achieving zero results for the effort, I was seeing the fruits of my efforts beginning to pay off. I had a solid suspect, and information that might help me locate him was coalescing quickly. I couldn't let up, though. I had to keep pressing every button I could find.

Just then Officer Rebecca McQuiston came to a stop in front of my desk.

"Jake, I got the information you wanted on this ticket stub."

"Great. Spill it."

"The ticket was purchased one week before departure with a credit card. The number is on the readout. The purchaser was Zyree Luttrell of Annville, Kentucky. Do you need anything else?"

I took the readout and the ticket stub from her hand and shook my head.

"Super job, Becky. Thanks. That'll be all."

She walked away and I sat back in my chair staring at the readout.

This was purely circumstantial evidence, but it indicated that Zyree had most likely sent Joshua on a scouting mission to New York to set up the framework for their pipeline of young girls just as Manfred of the Aryans had told me.

These freaks, Luttrell and Cousins, must have had this going on for quite some time now. I could only imagine just how many young lives these ass wipes had trashed over the years.

I was now even more resolved to put an end to the reverend's little games. I was eager also to see what Junior's part in all of this was.

"My, my. Isn't that something. My, my." I could hear him saying that word for word. The little freako.

But what had me really spooked was how the Rev had gone from pimp to murderer. I couldn't imagine what made him make that switch. It didn't matter, though. Soon I'd be staring him in the eyeballs and asking the questions that I hoped might bring him closer to God. And I wanted to be the one to make it a nice snug fit personally.

It's funny how in the manner of hours a lost and tattered investigation can coalesce into an indictable case. Sure, I wasn't there yet, but I could sense the rope tightening around both Joshua Cousins' and Junior's necks.

I felt good about it all.

I glanced down at my watch: 4:37 p.m. I was beat. I'd had a great day, but it was all catching up with me.

I didn't think one drink would hurt me, but I didn't want to drink alone. I stopped by Hank's office.

"Hank," I said, walking in and plopping into the chair in front of his desk.

"What?" he answered curtly, continuing writing something on a pad of paper without so much as a glance at me.

"I'd like to get a drink. But I don't want to drink alone. Join me at Bobby's, will ya? It's on me."

He stopped writing and sat back in his chair.

"No," he said. "But I will be needing a shot of shine in a while."

I grinned.

"Even better. I won't have to spend a penny more for that."

"I've got some reports to review. Go home, Jake. Go straight home, and I'll be over in about an hour."

"Sounds good."

I left his office and drove straight home.

I got into my apartment and poured myself a glass of hooch. I attempted to sip it when my cell phone rang. I recognized the number. It was Maddie.

I hesitated a few seconds and then answered.

"Jake Brewer here."

"Jakey boy. How are y'all?" said the strange male voice.

"Who is this?" I asked.

"You don't know?"

"Okay, pal. Joke's over. I know this is Maddie's phone. Put her on."

"That's not possible at the moment, Jake."

"What the hell?"

"Jake, Jake. Our boozy boy is back. He's been on the trail of one named Jack."

The rhyming gave it away.

"Goddamn you, you sick son of a bitch. If you harm a hair on her head, you can't go far enough away to escape me. Ever."

"Jake, Jake. Please don't use the Lord's name in vain."

"Joshua Cousins. So you *are* here in New York."

"I hear you've been looking for me lately. So proud to be worth your effort."

"You bastard. I'm gonna kill your ass."

"Jake, such hostility when I was calling you out of friendship. I have so enjoyed our good times together thus far. But you've been having a hard time finding me. How was Kentucky? Is my whore wife still doin' Junior?"

Joshua laughed.

"I'm glad it's him and not me," he continued. "That bitch is Looney Tunes. Hey, Jake. Do you think you can find me?"

"Listen, asshole. When I see you, that's where they're gonna find your body. I won't try to arrest you. I'm just gonna jack your ass off this planet, Jack."

"Oh, I just knew you'd be the fun type. Seriously, I'm so excited, Jake. Let's do it. Let's play hide and seek. Would you like that, Jakey boy? But you know there has to be rules and there has to be consequences."

"Piss off, ass face. Put Maddie on the phone. I mean it. She'd better not have a hair out of place either, shit-for-brains. Goddamn you!"

"You are a blasphemer, Jake Brewer. A true sinner. Matthew 12:34 describes you: 'For out of the abundance of the heart the mouth speaks.' Such is your lot. A sinful man who speaks sinfully. But never mind that, my son. I forgive you as Jesus forgave the thief next to him on the cross. Praise Jesus. Now, Jakey, boy, I want to play a game with you."

"Oh, so do I. It's called kill the asshole pervo preacher."

"Please, Jake. Close thy lips and open thy heart to the word. You should endeavor to improve your position in life. You should develop the skill set of life and not dwell in the depths of the abyss. But it is true, you know. I do have a fancy for the young things. I don't think that makes me a pervert, though, Jake. I like to think of it as having, shall we say, special tastes. Now, where was I?"

"Hell with you. I want to talk to Maddie. Now, asshole."

"In time, Jakey boy. Right now, though, here is the deal. You find her within twelve hours and I won't kill her. You fail to find her in time, and the Fifth Avenue Whore dies. I can't make it simpler than that."

"I want proof of life, shithead. Or I don't play."

There was silence for a few seconds and then I heard a voice I recognized.

"Jake!" Maddie choked out. "Save me, *please!*"

"Maddie! I'm coming, doll. Don't you worry. I'm coming for you and I'm going to kill that sick son of a bitch when I get there."

But Maddie was not on the line to hear my words. The killer was.

"Twelve hours, Jakey boy," said the killer.

The line disconnected.

I clicked off my cell phone and dropped it onto my sofa. I looked up at the ceiling and screamed a primal scream.

Someone banged on the ceiling and shouted at me to shut up.

"We're trying to watch a movie up here, Jake!"

That shout pretty much described the cold-hearted nature of this city. My Jack had made good on his threat. He had Maddie and I had twelve hours to find her, with no idea where to start looking. I was in a real pickle. My life was going to hell, and yet life itself, in all its wild diversity and stark, uncaring coolness, continued as normal around me. The asshole upstairs didn't give a shit that a woman's life was hanging on by a thread. He was only concerned that his damn movie was being interrupted by the screaming maniac cop in the apartment below him. At that moment, I hated people. I hated my life. Christ, I hated the whole world.

I sat seething and thinking until Hank walked through the door looking for his glass of shine.

I didn't ease into it. I let him have it with both barrels.

"Jack's got Maddie, Hank. And he's given me twelve hours to find her or he's gonna kill her."

He stopped in his tracks and grimaced.

"Our copycat Jack has Maddie?"

"Yes. I just got a call from Joshua Cousins. The son of a bitch."

"Jesus," Hank said, collapsing onto the sofa next to me. "And I didn't think this day could get any worse."

"Well, I'm sure it ain't going too well for Maddie right now either."

CHAPTER 25

Hank and I agreed that Joshua was holding Maddie somewhere common to all of us.

He'd want to control me. I knew that much. He'd want me to worry and fuss.

The killer, who I remained convinced was Joshua Cousins, had started the clock in the evening. I think he purposely did that to restrict my access to ways of tracking him.

Hank sent a CSI team to Maddie's condo with orders to consider it a crime scene and to collect anything and everything they thought might be relevant.

As for myself, I took a stab and called Maddie's office. Surprisingly, a young woman answered.

"Forgive the late-night call," I said. "My name is Detective Brewer, NYPD. Might I speak with your managing editor, please?"

I inwardly hoped that Maddie would answer and that Joshua Cousins had been lying.

"If you'll hold, Detective, I'll ring in and ask."

"Thanks."

I didn't wait long.

"Detective Brewer. This is Janet Massé. Ms. Dumont is unavailable at present. May I help you?"

The woman's voice held a very slight French accent, hardly noticeable to the normal ear, but to a detective, like me, it was distinctive enough for me to know that it was not Maddie's voice.

"So she really isn't there?"

"I am afraid not, no."

"You're French?"

"I transferred in from the Paris office a few months ago."

"Well, Ms. Massé, I know why she's not in her office."

"You do? Please to enlighten me."

"Not over the phone. Would you mind if I stopped by your office for a quick chat?"

"This is a terrible time, Detective. We find ourselves in the midst of a crisis at the moment. We are trying to approve the last of the articles for our next publication. Can it wait?"

"I'm afraid not. It's very serious. It's extremely important."

"Well, I suppose I may spare a few minutes. When might you be here?"

"I'm standing outside your offices right now. May I come up?"

"Certainly, Detective. I shall alert the security desk immediately."

"See you in a few minutes."

I disconnected the call and walked to the locked doors of the office building. I laid my badge against the door.

The guard hung up the phone and waved at me. He walked to the doors and unlocked them.

Walking into the *Le Chic Fashions* office reception area, I was behind a most attractive young woman. The receptionist handed her a piece of paper.

She turned and walked past me, eyes flashing brilliant green. I was stunned by her beauty as well. She was, in my book, right up there with Maddie.

The receptionist smiled at me.

"You're Detective Brewer, right?"

"Is she one of your models?" I asked, referring to the departing angel.

"No. She's just a Fifth Avenue Whore."

I was stunned by her words. And having Maddie referred to as such by the killer only enticed me to want to know more about that term. But before I could ask her to explain it, she continued.

"You're here to see Ms. Massé, correct?"

"Yes. That's right," I replied, flashing my badge at the receptionist.

She nodded.

"If you'll take a seat, sir, I'll see if Ms. Massé can see you now."

She picked up the phone, presumably to call Janet Massé's office.

I walked over to the seating area and plopped down ono one of the soft couches.

Damn, I thought. Their office furniture was better than my home furnishings. I gotta change my life.

I was surprised to see Maddie's door open and Janet Massé appear in the doorway, waving me toward her.

She was a pleasant-looking older woman, but miles away from Maddie's hot appearance.

I rose off the sofa and headed straight for her. As I reached the door, she smiled.

"Good evening, Detective. I've heard of you, of course. I'm Janet Massé. Please forgive my tattered appearance. Not the sort of look I would have liked to greet you with."

"Nonsense. You're quite lovely."

"Aren't you the charmer. Please. Come in."

I entered and made every attempt not to be Jake Brewer. I went for manners instead.

"Ms. Massé, please forgive me for being so abrupt, but could you explain to me the phrase 'Fifth Avenue Whore'?"

She frowned instantly.

"That's not a term I like, Detective. I find it quite derogatory and insulting."

"I didn't mean to insult. I was just wondering what it means."

"Have a seat, Detective."

I sat down in a chair in front of her desk as she walked around the desk and sat in Maddie's chair.

"It's a less than flattering term used by modeling agencies and magazines to describe a young model who just shows up in New York without experience, a portfolio, or an agent. They just come to town on a wing and a prayer. Eventually they sell their bodies and their souls just to feed themselves while waiting for the chance to make it as a model. Thus, they're referred to as Fifth Avenue Whores. Of course, for companies along Broadway or Park Place, the term could be changed for them."

"You mean Broadway Whores or Park Place Whores? Like that?"

"Yes. But the typical term is Fifth Avenue. It's here where the term came into being. As I said, though, it's not a term I intend to perpetuate at Le Chic, Detective. I find it quite offensive."

"So, Maddie was a Fifth Avenue Whore?"

"No. She was never a model."

"Interesting."

"Why would you call her that, Detective?"

"I'm not. I was just wondering."

"No, Maddie came into the company as an intern. She has never modeled that I know of. Not that she couldn't have and been a great one. She has it all, as models go."

"Yeah, she certainly does. But she's not here to help you now. I can imagine how overwhelmed you must be."

"I don't have time to think about it. As the new managing editor, I have my hands full with this upcoming publication. My only fear is that if I can't pull this off, I might be tossed into the streets myself."

"Excuse me, Ms. Massé. You said 'new managing editor.' I thought Maddie Dumont was the managing editor."

"Until earlier this afternoon she was. Her sudden resignation has caused us much turmoil. We're going to be burning the midnight oil all night. She's left us in a lurch."

"Just a moment. You said she resigned earlier today?" I asked, now really intrigued.

"Yes. She stopped into the office for only a very brief visit earlier and then left. No one thought much about it. But later we received an email from her with her letter of resignation attached. I can tell you, it sent shockwaves zinging through our offices."

"She resigned?"

"Yes. Would you like to see the emailed letter?"

"If you don't mind."

She reached across her desk and clicked some keys on the computer's keyboard and then motioned me over.

Sure enough, on the monitor was Maddie Dumont's letter of resignation. It looked like a standard resignation. Nothing unusual about it that I could see.

"Wow!" I muttered. "Just like that. No explanation?"

She shook her head.

"I can imagine your shock," I said.

"She had been scheduled to depart. I knew that. But it wasn't for three months. This sudden departure has left us in tatters. And the publication goes to print in seventeen hours. It's been quite a difficult time for me. I was prepared to take over, but not this quickly."

I moved back to the front of her desk and sat down in the nearest chair. I continued not being Jake Brewer for a moment. I reached deep into my memory of how to be polite.

"Please forgive me for showing up without an appointment, but something has transpired that you should know about. But before I can tell you, I must insist no one else know about this for now. Do I have your word on that?"

She took a seat at her desk immediately. Shock and concern swept over her face.

"You have it, Detective. Now what are you talking about?"

I told her about the call I had received from Joshua Cousins, or who I believed was Joshua Cousins. And then I suggested that it might be the reason for Maddie's sudden resignation letter showing up in the email.

Ms. Massé sat stunned, her mouth agape in shock and dismay.

"Oh my God," she finally uttered after I fell silent. "I'll have to take back all the unkind things I was thinking about her. Poor girl. Do you think he'll do it? Do you think he'll kill her if you can't find her?"

"I don't want to find out. I want to find her as quickly as I can and put this monster down. He's a very strange person. But I can't figure out why he keeps referring to Maddie as a Fifth Avenue Whore, like he knows her."

"It's clear to me that he doesn't know her at all. Maddie went from intern to editor to managing editor. She has never even considered modeling. So the killer must be deluded about her."

"Agreed," I said.

I had come here hoping somebody might give me some information about her that I didn't know. Something that might give me a place to start looking for her. Without it, I was standing in the middle of huge city with no place to begin. I guess in one regard, it worked out. The killer didn't know all that much about Maddie Dumont. The term could not be applied to her. So, perhaps it was just a general repugnance he had for any woman, or women in general, who frequented Fifth Avenue.

I sat back in the chair and let my eyes wander around the room, looking for anything that might give me a clue.

"I see you haven't had any time to personalize your new office. I guess that would be an understatement, though, huh?"

"Yes, Detective, it would."

"Well, I see things haven't changed all that much," I said, pointing to the décor around the office.

She nodded.

"I like the way she decorated it. I probably won't change too much. When I finally have the time to consider it, of course."

My eyes scanned the shelving again.

"She did have a flair for the knickknacks, didn't she?"

"Indeed. Detective, please forgive me, but I still have to put out a magazine in less than seventeen hours. Please don't think me calloused regarding Maddie's state of being. I'm shocked and very disturbed by Maddie's situation, of course, but a magazine still must be published regardless. Such is life. Is there anything else I can do for you, Detective?"

"Just a couple more things. Did she leave a forwarding address or phone number?"

"No. I'm sorry. Just the emailed resignation letter as you saw it."

"Did she, by chance, leave any personal items in the restroom?"

"Yes. Comb, hairbrush, toothbrush, and the like. Is that what you mean?"

"It is. Do you think I might have them?"

"I have them in plastic bags already. I'll get them."

She went into the bathroom and returned with several clear plastic bags filled with Maddie's personal items and handed them to me.

I spied the prescription of valium in one of the bags immediately, but said nothing. It was obvious that even Super Miss Blue Eyes, at times, needed a special calm-me-down cure. I guess she did sort of fit in with the rest of us weaklings after all.

"Wonderful," I said. "Thank you very much. This is great. Final question: Do you sign in when you arrive?"

"I don't, Detective. Most don't. That is, the employees don't sign in."

"Really? I noticed the guard station at the entry. I had to sign in."

"You're a visitor, Detective. Most of us go in and out the back door. It's closer to the parking garage."

"The back door? There's a back door to the building?"

"Most buildings do have them, Detective."

"I know. I know. I just didn't think about it. Of course, you have keys and such, I presume. Why wouldn't you use that door?"

"No keys, Detective. We use a passcode."

"A passcode? Sure. Why not? Let me ask you this. Is there some kind of device that records the passcode use?"

"I believe so. It's located in the security office on the first floor. May I ask how this could be important in helping you find her?"

"It's just dotting the I's and crossing the T's in an investigation. Normal for us."

I stood up.

"Well, you've been most helpful, Ms. Massé. Once again, please forgive my sudden appearance. I can't thank you enough for taking the time to meet with me, especially under the circumstances. I'll leave you to your crisis now."

I reached across her desk to shake hands with her.

She started around her desk, but I put my hand up to stop her.

"Don't want to trouble you. I'll let myself out. Thanks again. And please, mum's the word about Maddie."

She stopped. "I promise. But I hope you can find her and resolve this quickly. It's just terrible."

I nodded and left her office.

Reaching the first floor, I stepped out of the elevator and made a beeline for the security office. I spoke with the security guard and found out that the passcode was used several times throughout the day.

According to the guard, there was only one passcode for all the employees, so he couldn't tell me who it was that entered through the back door at any particular time. This was obviously just another dead end for me.

Since Maddie's departure, a new passcode had already been issued. They apparently didn't waste any time when it came to security matters.

CHAPTER 26

Crawling into my car, I called Hank immediately and defined for him what a Fifth Avenue Whore was. I also told him about the personal items. He asked me to come straight into the office and get them into the evidence locker.

By the time I got to the precinct, reporters were swarming even the back gate. As soon as they saw my car, they went wild with waving arms and flashing cameras.

Lucky for me, Hank had squad cars lined up so that I could drive between them and through the gates.

Slipping from my car, I ignored all the questions thrown at me and slid through the door.

I went straight to Hank's office.

"What happened? I thought the press lost interest days ago."

He looked up from his desk. The skin around his eyes was dark and puffy, his face more grey than pink. I suspected he was feeling more than just the normal stress of the job.

"Whoa!" I said. "Is the Captain on your ass hard?"

"That's *my* problem. This is *yours*."

He flung a folded newspaper to the front of his desk.

"He sent the *Times* a poem. You're going to love it."

I picked up the paper, unfolded it, and grimaced.

The headline read: DETECTIVE BATTLES BOOZE AND KILLER.

Then the article went on to spell out the fact that Maddie Dumont had been taken captive and I had been given twelve hours to find her or she would die.

Then they reprinted another one of his resplendent poems.

> Jake's been scurrying like a busy little bee.
> Our hero Jake is trying to find little ol' me.
> Will Jake be successful? Only time it will tell.
> But my bet is that Jake will only find Hell.
>
> A drunk detective is sure a lot of fun.
> He staggers around thinking he has me on the run.
> Will the Fifth Avenue Whore be saved in time?
> Or will her lovely head soon be all mine?
>
> Hours are ticking away, Jakey boy.

I looked up at Hank.

"Wonderful," I said.

"Yeah."

"I think he forced Maddie to quit her job earlier," I added.

"As I see it, it doesn't really matter. She won't be needing one if you can't find her."

"I'm not going to listen to that, Hank. I'm going to find her and kill him."

"Great. So where do you start looking?" asked Hank.

"I'm betting it's someplace known to me. I'm betting he'll give me hints throughout the day. He'll want to have some fun with this. Stretch out his sick fantasy as long as he can."

"Jake, I tried to cover for you, but Cap is boiling about the booze. Even if you solve this and win, I think you should plan your retirement. If you catch my drift."

I sat down in the chair and rubbed my face.

"I catch it. I appreciate your help, but we both knew this was coming. It's my own fault. I can work to get it under control, but we both know I'll fail unless I can find a motivation greater than the call of the booze."

"He was going to pull you from the case. But with the newspaper article, he said he can't. He doesn't want to take the responsibility of Jack getting pissed about not having you to play with and then kill Maddie."

"Shit," I muttered. "I don't blame him for that."

"How are you going to solve this, Jake?"

"I don't know. He could have her anywhere in the city. And it's a big damn city, as you know. But I still believe he'll have her stashed somewhere that I'm aware of. I mean, what would be the point of goading me into finding her unless he can enjoy the search?"

"You don't think he's taken her back to Kentucky, do you?"

"You mean back to his cabin in the Dan'l Boone? Jesus! He just might. I gotta call Hagan."

I did call him and recounted what had been going on up here lately. Then I begged him to send a patrol car out to Joshua's cabin. He promised me he would do that on the double and get back to me as soon as possible.

After we disconnected, I dropped the phone onto Hank's desk and sat back in the chair.

My cell phone rang. The call was from Maddie's phone.

"Hank!" I said, rotating my hand in a hurry-up motion. "Start a trace on Maddie's phone!"

He picked up his desk phone and dialed.

I answered my phone.

"Did you like that plug I gave you in the paper, Jake?" said the now unrecognizable voice. "You're a real, honest-to-goodness star. I've made you famous. Can I get a *Praise Jesus* for that?"

"You can get a bullet in the head instead. Will that work for you? Hey, you sound a little horse. You haven't come down with throat cancer have ya? Cause that would be a real shame."

He laughed horsely.

"I like your sense of humor, Jakey boy. Just a little cold, but you shouldn't be worried about me. You should be worried about the whore."

"Right now you're important to me. Because if you die, I won't be able to find her."

"Well hey, Jake. I'll drink to that. Oops! Sorry about that. You're a mite sensitive to that issue right now, I imagine."

"On the contrary. I relish it. I'm an alcoholic. I'm man enough to admit it. Are you man enough to admit you're a pervo pedophile little creepy bag of shit?"

"Sure," he answered. "Why not? We are all sinners in the eyes of the Lord and slaves to our weaknesses, Jake."

Okay. I'd tried to flat-out anger him and it hadn't worked. I decided to try something different.

"Fine. So, ass hat, are you gonna tell me where to meet and greet so we can get this sick little game over with?"

"Now, why would I do that?"

"Because you know I have no idea where to even start looking for her. You want to play a game, but it's a damn big city. There's no way I could ever find her without some hints. And I know you're dying to give me hints. So why not just cut the shit and tell me where to meet? I'll show up alone. We can face each other and let the blood flow. Best man wins."

I looked at Hank. He shrugged his shoulders and shook his head: he was having trouble tracing the phone the killer was using. He made wagging fishtail signs to tell me that the phone was mobile. It would be hard to catch up to Jack.

"That would be exciting," the killer replied. "I have to admit that. But I don't think this little Fifth

Avenue Whore would find it all that exciting. Especially in the position she's in at the moment, with all those nasty knives dangling precariously over her."

"That reminds me, ass wipe. Maddie was never a model. Fifth Avenue Whore only refers to models. So besides being an ass wipe, you're an idiot, too."

"Doesn't really matter, Jakey. She worked on Fifth Avenue and she looks like a painted whore to me. I can live with that. But she can't."

"Okay. Enough. Give me a hint or give me an address. Time to rock and roll, pervo boy."

"I hear the frustration in your voice, Jake. It must be hard to be you. Hey, are you having trouble tracing the call? Kinda hard to pin it down, with me moving around the city, huh?"

"Keep jabbering, asshole. I'll narrow it down."

"I know. Well, keep watching the time, lover boy. It's getting nearer to the head-lopping moment. Maybe you should be making plans for your retirement. I don't think this is going to end well for you."

He disconnected.

"Hank! *Anything*?"

Hank was listening on his phone.

"Damn it," he said. "Okay. Thanks."

He put the receiver back into the cradle.

"No," he said. "And he powered the phone down too. Son of a bitch ain't as stupid as I thought. He's not the Kentucky hick I pictured him to be."

"Guess he smartened up some here in the big city," I said.

"Did he give you any hints where to begin searching?"

"No. Just said she's got knives hanging over her about to drop. The sick bastard."

"Knives, you say?"

"Yeah."

"Like the knives on the sign over that sushi place on Broadway?"

I was startled.

"The one with the knives made to look like sharks' teeth?"

"That's the one, Jake."

"Jesus Christ — let's roll!"

Thirty minutes later we had the place surrounded and SWAT was preparing to make the entry. Hank was coordinating with the insertion team by walkie-talkie.

Live video cameras from the local TV news surrounded us. Flashes from still cameras lit up the area even though it was already late morning.

Hank finally gave the order. A SWAT lieutenant knocked on the front door. It was immediately answered by a cook who was there making preparations for the upcoming lunch crowd.

The team rushed past him and within seconds were everywhere throughout the restaurant, including the basement.

I almost held my breath upon their breach. I hoped to hear my radio squawk and a voice shouting that Maddie had been discovered and was safe.

But the only chatter I heard was from the voices clearing each and every room. Then I heard the final voice announce that the building had been completely cleared and there was no sign of Maddie.

Minutes later, SWAT team members filed from the restaurant one by one and milled around the area, awaiting further orders.

Hank tapped me on the shoulder.

"Number one. Don't ever show up without your vest again, or I'll bench your ass. Number two. I think we were set up."

"I'm thinking the same thing. Son of a bitch. He's a gamester. He loves to mess with people."

My cell phone rang.

Maddie's phone again.

"Funny what catches your attention driving around the city, huh, Jake?" said the killer. "That sign was just made for you."

"Yeah," I replied. "Very funny. You're a real comedian."

"Your SWAT guys sure didn't get the joke, though. They looked like they really meant business."

I realized that he was most likely staring at me right then. I spun around looking for anyone who might be on a cell phone and looking my way. Of course, no one caught my eye. I looked up at the windows overlooking the area, but at those distances I could have stared directly into his eyes and not seen him.

"Take it all in, shit-for-brains," I said. "Your time's a comin'."

He chuckled.

"Relax, Jake. I'm already gone. Lost interest soon after they walked out with their heads bent in disappointment. But with only a few more hours to go, I bet you're getting nervous. Could use a drink, I bet. I'll give you a call later."

He disconnected. Hank looked at me questioningly.

"Nothing," I said. "Just more of his bullshit."

CHAPTER 27

Hank and I returned to his office. I plopped into the chair and stared blankly ahead. I was pissed as hell, but what good was it going to do me? It would be another thing if I had the bastard in my sights, but it was *his* game. I was just a pawn for his amusement. I'd been there before. I tried not to take it personal. But seriously, who wouldn't.

"Four hours," Hank said, dropping into his chair.

"Four hours, four days, four months, Hank. Hell, four years. I could search forever and never come close to finding her. He holds all the cards. I've never felt this useless and helpless before. Maybe he's right. Maybe I should just retire after this, regardless of what the Captain might say. Go away and hide and just stay drunk forevermore until I go tits up."

"I'm sure he'd love to see that, Jake. It'll give him another victory over the NYPD. I hate to admit it, but we might not win this one. I think you should prepare yourself for that possibility. I wouldn't admit it to anyone else in the building, but this one might just kick our ass."

"He's a backwoods preacher. He knows how to mess with people's minds already. He's adept at convincing people to trust him. He's a master at using people's fears against them. It takes psychological skill to convince young girls to trust him enough to allow him to do the things he does to them."

"But we're not young girls, Jake."

"Maybe not. But are we any better off right now than they are? Is it really such a stretch to think that he might possess the skill to manipulate us as well?"

"Before this whole thing started, I would have said no. But now I'm not so certain."

"I'm going to go study my evidence board. Maybe something there will help figure this asshole out."

A phone call interrupted my retreat. It was from Hagan.

"Hey, Hagan. Tell me, please, that you found her."

"Wish I could, Jake. But the good news is the dogs are headed out to the cabin as we speak. I know you're busy. I'm gettin' busy myself. I'll call when I have somethin' more. Good luck findin' Joshua. Give him a hug for me."

He disconnected.

I shook my head at Hank.

"She's not in Kentucky."

"Would have surprised me if she was."

I walked into the squad evidence room and sat down in front of the evidence board. I stared at each piece of evidence over and over, searching for the tiniest hint of where he might have Maddie.

Time passed much too quickly. When I looked at my watch, another hour had passed. I was thinking that I should be getting another phone call.

My phone rang. It was him.

"You're an asshole, but you're a consistent asshole," I blurted out.

"Is that a compliment, Jake?"

"Only a sick mind like yours would see that as a compliment."

"Okay. Have it your way.... Ah, Jake, I hate to be the bearer of bad news, but we're down to three hours to deadline. Oops! That was insensitive, wasn't it? I really should have used another term."

He chuckled and then fell silent for a few seconds.

"Not even a chuckle, Jake?" he said. "Such a serious man. I think I liked you more when you were drunk on your ass. You certainly were a lot more fun. I even remember you sitting in your little cove at Bobby's, giggling like a schoolboy at something the whore said. I admit it, I had quite the chuckle as well. For the life of me, though, I can't quite remember your words. Oh, no matter. The moment has passed. So, Jakey, would you like to know where Maddie is hiding?... Oops. I mean, where I'm hiding her?"

"Not in the mood to play your games right now, Cousins. But tell me this. Have you been in contact with Mary Beth and Kerri Ann lately?"

"Ain't seen hide nor hair of them two little tramps."

"That's no way to talk about your own flesh and blood, Joshua."

He laughed loud and hard.

"My own flesh and blood? So you don't know? You spent all that time in Annville and you still don't know?"

Okay. Truth be told, he more than piqued my curiosity. But I wasn't about to let him in on that little secret.

"Don't know what?" I asked.

"Those two bitches ain't from my loins. You need to talk to Junior Luttrell about whose kin they are."

"You're telling me Junior's their daddy?"

"And here I thought you found out all my little secrets. I put more stock in you than you're worth, I see."

"I guess so," I said. "That little detail went undiscovered. So Junior and Mercy have been carrying on for quite some time, huh?"

"Ya think, Jakey boy?"

"You're taking it much better than I thought you would."

"Junior was doing me a favor and he didn't even know it. Keeping Mercy busy gave me all the time I needed for my little soirées."

"You *are* one of kind. I'll give you that much. I might even miss you a little after I put you down."

"How kind of you, Jake. But time's a wastin'. My blade is sharp. My hand is steady. But first from the whore, I might get me some heady."

He laughed sickly.

That succeeded in getting to me.

"Enough! I've had it with you and all your bullshit. Where's Maddie? Tell me! Tell me now! I mean it, you piece of shit! Goddamn you. *TELL ME NOW!*"

"*Jawohl, mein Herr*!" he shouted. "Wow, Jakey boy. Such a commanding voice. I'm impressed. But where the hell did that come from? I guess Mister Smooth and Swarthy has taken a break, huh. That even startled me. For a moment. I'm serious. You had me shaking in my jackboots. But...still, I'm not inclined toward making it so easy for you. I'll call you again, though. As the last hour begins. I want to hear the terror in your voice. It's so gratifying to hear you squeal, little piggy."

He disconnected the call. It's a good thing, too, because his voice was beginning to really gnaw on my nerves.

I sat fuming. Time was running out for Maddie, and this asshole was still toying with me.

Then, like a starburst, it came to me. I jumped up, dashed to Hank's office, and recited the phone call.

Twenty minutes later, we were standing in front of the building where I had met with Manfred of the Aryan Nations. The Captain wasn't willing to send the SWAT team after my last hunch had failed so miserably in the presence of cameras.

All that ended up accomplishing was to give further evidence of the NYPD's failure to protect one of New York's finer citizens.

Of course, Cap gave a kindly appearance to throwing me under the bus. But hell, what did he care? My ass was done for anyway. As soon as this case was over, I would be retired. Despite the uncertainty from Hank, I'd figured it out myself. I was a goner.

So, Hank and I were the only cops there. I wore my vest this time. No sense in pissing Hank off again. I was in enough trouble as it was.

Hank went around to the alley and the back entrance. I was positioned at the front.

I looked at my watch. The second hand ticked away, and when it landed on twelve, I stepped forward and kicked through the glass on the front door. I burst into the room and saw nothing. I dashed toward the back of the building, shouting my presence and making sure anyone who might be there knew I was a cop with a search warrant. I think I shouted loud enough for the dead to hear me.

Hank and I came together in the middle of a back room. In fact, it was the same room where Manfred and I had our discussion.

There was no basement door. But there was the large round table where we'd sat and had our chat. In the middle of the table was a piece of paper.

On it was one word written in blood: SORRY.

I presumed the blood to be Maddie's, but the room was completely void of anything but the table and four wooden chairs.

Hank grabbed the note by the corner and read the word.

He held it in front of my face.

"Bag it, Jake. It's probably another dead end, but let's do our job."

I pulled an evidence bag from my coat pocket where I always kept a few and opened it. He dropped the letter into the bag and I zipped it closed.

My cell phone rang.

"Son of a bitch," I said, answering.

"Well," said the voice. "Wasn't that a damn waste of time?"

He chuckled.

"Oh, Jakey boy. So close. It's like that old secret agent on TV used to say. Now, what was that?... Oh yeah, I remember now. 'Missed it by *that much.*' "

He chuckled again.

My teeth ground together in anger.

"God, I loved that show," he continued. "Actually, this one isn't bad, though. It was great to watch it play out from my front-row seat. You went into that building like a Nazi Stormtrooper. But you're probably tiring of the Nazi references about now, aren't ya? Oh, Jakey boy. Time is about to run out. This just has to be frustrating for you. About to literally go out of your mind, I imagine. Probably wishing for just one big drink to calm the nerves. Am I right? I can understand that. That sweet golden liquid sliding down your parched throat. Go ahead, Jake. Dip into the bottle for a bit. I won't tell on ya."

I resisted speaking. He had pushed me near to the breaking point. And he was certainly right about one thing. I wanted a drink so bad I could almost taste it right then and there. Just one thing helped me hang on: the thought of blowing holes into him. But there weren't enough bullets in the world to satisfy my need to see him riddled with hot lead from my gun.

He was right about something else, too. Time was running out and I was nowhere closer to finding him and Maddie. I felt helpless. I felt alone. I felt abandoned by the entire universe.

CHAPTER 28

I had failed.

The deadline came and went. The phone remained silent for twenty minutes after the passing of D-hour.

He stopped calling me thirty minutes before the expiration of time. I tried dialing her phone and it went straight to voice mail. I was told that meant the phone was off and no signal had gotten through.

I sat alone in my office expecting the Captain to walk in and send me packing. But no one came in. Not even Hank.

I guess no one wanted to add to my misery. I appreciated the silence. I was full of doom and gloom on my own. If a bottle of Maker's Mark had been near, it would be empty.

Ten more minutes passed. My cell phone rang.

I jumped and clicked on the call, hoping to hear Maddie's voice.

"Time's well passed, Jakey. I would have called you earlier, but I was busy. She's gone, Jake. I suppose you've already figured that out. She died horribly because you failed her.

"She screamed bloody murder as she died. Did you like that one? Bloody murder. God, do I have a keen sense of humor or what? Anyway, you failed, Jake. As in your life, you failed. I guess you feel like a beat puppy about now, huh? I thought about keeping you in the dark forever. I thought about disappearing and never giving you the satisfaction of knowing whatever happened to Miss Blue Eyes. Did I say that right?

"But I guess that wouldn't be fair to you, would it? Well, to be honest, I couldn't give a rat's ass about being fair to you. But it would give me some satisfaction to see you back in the bottle again. I hear they might retire your ass now that you've turned your precinct into a laughingstock. I think that would also give me some satisfaction. I'll keep an eye on you from time to time, Jakey. I want to watch you crumble completely. Of course, you could always rob me of such pleasures by eating a bullet, I suppose. I would hope not, though. I'd miss watching you fall to pieces.

"Jakey, I've decided to be kind and give you a parting gift. I've left some evidence for you of our former Fifth Avenue Whore. At least you'll have that to remember her by. Actually, you'll have that to remind yourself of how miserably you failed her.

"I left it in an alley. I'll leave it to you to figure out which one. Although I think you already know. Oh, one more thing. I'm not saying when, but I thought I might pay a visit to that fat-ass sheriff in Kentucky one day. Make him another lump in the Dan'l Boone. I always need something exciting to do. 'Bye, Jake."

I didn't get a single word in edgewise. It didn't really matter. I had nothing good to say to him anyway.

I knew what alley he meant. But I wasn't going to play along anymore.

I radioed any uniform who might be close to where the first murder had taken place to go see what, if anything, Cousins had left behind.

He wanted me to go, of course. He wanted to watch me walk into the alley and either find nothing or find something that would no doubt send me over the edge. I didn't want him to know that I was pretty much at the edge already.

It wasn't ten minutes later when I got a radio call that there was indeed a plastic bag filled with blonde hair and blood. There was something else, too.

"Jake, I need to call you on a phone for this."

"Okay. Standing by," I replied, full of dread.

Seconds later my phone rang. It was the uniformed officer.

"What have you got?" I asked.

"A knife and a note, Jake. I thought I'd keep that off the radio."

I was stunned but also delighted that I had a uniform with brains out on patrol.

"You did great. What says the note?"

"It reads, *'We'll play again some other day.'* It's signed in blood as *JTR*.

I had the uniform transport all the items directly to the ME's office. With the hair samples I'd found in Maddie's office, we'd either have a match or not. There was nothing more for me to do now.

I had failed before to find a killer. It wasn't my first time at falling on my face. But it was sure to be my last time. I was just waiting for the Captain's dismissal letter to hit my desk. I expected it to come that day. I was still waiting by the time I was ready to clock out.

Hank stopped by. He stood in the door, leaning up against the frame.

"I could use a drink about now. Bobby's?"

"To be honest, Hank, no. I think I'm done."

"Good to hear. Too late, I suspect. But good to hear. I hope you're serious."

"Strangely speaking, I believe so."

Amazingly, the desire for a drink had vanished. I don't know why. But any want of drink failed to make my list of things I wanted. At the top of the list, of course, was the desire to hear Maddie's voice again. But I knew that was asking too much of the universe.

"I think I'll just call it a day, Hank. All I can do now is wait for Cap's decision."

"Do you need some company?"

"Thanks, Hank, but no. I'll be okay."

"You're not just saying that and going home to eat a round, are you?"

"I won't lie. It's crossed my mind once or twice today, but no. I'm not ready to give that bastard that satisfaction just yet."

"Okay. You can lie to me, but not yourself. I'll call you if anything changes. Go home and try to get some rest. I asked Doc to put a rush on the evidence from the alley. Cross your fingers, Jake."

I walked into the door of my apartment and went straight to where four gallon jugs of shine sat. I grabbed them and emptied each one down the drain of the kitchen sink. I then went to where my other booze was stored and emptied those bottles down the drain as well. Drinking had been the root of my problems all these years and by god, it was time to turn this shit around. I felt no remorse in dumping my problems down the drain.

I then moved to my whiteboard, ready to erase everything on it. But something told me not to touch it.

I backed away and dropped onto the sofa. I sat for what seemed like a full hour staring at all the clues and points of interest. Something was missing. I was sure of it, but had no idea what it was.

My phone rang.

I immediately suspected it was Hank calling to tell me the Captain had pulled the trigger on me. It wasn't Hank though. It was Doc Harrigan.

"What's up, Doc?"

"Jake, I'm sorry about Maddie. Listen, I'm still writing up the autopsy report from the last murder. I've almost got it finished. But Hank asked me to put a super rush on the things from the alley. I've done that."

"What do you have?"

"Good news and bad news. Okay, for the good news. The blade from the alley, it's a Liston blade. *THE* Liston blade, I suspect. The bad news: the blood on it and the hair is Maddie's."

"I was afraid it would be."

"Why would he leave the knife, Jake?"

"Obviously, he's letting me know that he's finished with it. It's his parting gift — or his parting bit of mockery."

"Why not just chuck it in the river?"

"Once again, Doc, he's mocking me. I'm guessing the Teufel kit, though, *is* at the bottom of the river."

"You could be right about that."

"Hey, Doc, I could be right about the sun coming up tomorrow, but it wouldn't do me any good. I think he left the blade as his final stick into my eye."

"So, you're still making this about you?"

"I hate to say it, Doc, but it *was* about me. This has all been about me. At least partially."

"I really hate to admit this to you, Jake, but I think you're right. I just hope he's finished. I don't think I could write up another report like this with what's left of my life."

"Doc, I know you have to do what you have to do. But I really wouldn't put too much more into the report than you absolutely need to. It's my guess that he's done what he needs to do. He might want to go down in history as famous as the original Ripper. Or he might have simply killed for some other reason. And now that the reason for the killing has been accomplished, he's about to disappear for good. I'm thinking we need to concentrate on the victims, Doc. I believe they're the real clues needed to answer all the questions to find some closure."

"I have their DNA, but unless I have something to match it to…"

"I know, Doc. I know."

"Jake, you know I like giving you shit. But you're the best that ever was at your job. I'm proud to be working with you. I'm sorry this one came to the end it did."

"Thanks, Doc. It wouldn't have been any fun if you didn't give me a hard time. I appreciate working with you, too."

"This lovefest is over. Piss off."

Doc disconnected.

I chuckled sadly.

He was right. This was a terrible end to an otherwise good career. But I can say this. I worked with some of the very best in the business.

CHAPTER 29

Grayson called, waking me out of a dead and dreamless sleep in my recliner. I scrambled for my cell phone.

"Yeah. Brewer here."

"I know I told you to rest, but I need you here. And before you jump down my throat asking, yeah, Cap wants to see you."

"This is it, huh?"

"He won't tell me. He just told me to get you in here."

"Fine. I'm on my way."

Hank hung up.

Well, I thought, the Captain isn't wasting any time. Probably took this long to check with the Personnel Bureau and see what his legal options were before he could cut me loose.

I glanced at my wristwatch: 12:38 a.m.

Damn, I thought. Captain must really want me gone quickly to stick around the office at this hour. Oh well, the next thought urged, might as well get it over with.

Driving along Fifth Avenue toward the precinct at this late hour was normal for me. The traffic was lighter than usual, so it was actually a pleasant drive.

Stopped at a light, I relaxed and began to plan my retirement. It had been a long time coming and I was determined to enjoy it. It was then that I noticed the shifting shadows on the side of a building extending into an alley.

Interesting, I noted.

The light turned green. I drove through the intersection and pulled up to the curb, stopping near the alley.

As I got out, I couldn't take my eyes from the dancing shadows across the face of the building. I walked into the alley and made a turn to the right, all the time watching the shadows.

I immediately noticed the large construction lamp sitting on a trailer. Saying it was a bright light would not do it justice.

The construction crew was working near an open sewer manhole. From the looks of it, there were men down in the sewer pipe with smaller lamps.

I walked up to a guy in a city maintenance uniform. He looked like the guy in charge.

"Hey, buddy," I said, flashing my badge.

"Yeah?"

"I'm Detective Brewer, Homicide. How ya doin'?"

"We're killing it, Detective," he responded with a grin.

"Good one. Hey, I'd like to ask you a favor."

"What's that?"

"Do you think you could turn off the big light there for a few moments? I'd like to go back out on the street and see what kind of shadows your smaller lamps might cast on that building there. I mean, to see if your smaller lamps cast any kind of a shadow without that giant light."

"We got a job to do here, Detective."

"I know. It would be very quick. It's important to a murder investigation I'm conducting. Can you help me out?"

"I guess so. Yeah, sure thing."

He turned to one of his workmen.

"Dave, kill the big lamp for a bit, will ya?"

Then he yelled to his other workers.

"Guys. Keep the smaller lamps burning, but don't move around for a bit. I'm gonna kill the big lamp for a little bit."

The activity of the workers halted and the light was turned off.

I looked at the building and could see no shadow at all.

"I'll be right back, buddy."

"Okay, Detective."

I walked out of the alley and stood on the sidewalk. Then I walked back and forth in front of the alley. I saw no shadow.

I walked back to the work area and turned to gaze at the building. The smaller lamps produced no shadow at all.

"Thanks, buddy," I said to the foreman. "That should do it."

"Okay. Hit the light, Dave," he responded.

A second later, the whole alley was lit up by the giant lamp. The shadows returned.

"Get what you need, Detective?" asked the foreman.

"I did," I said, "I owe you."

I handed him my card.

"No problem," he replied. "Have a good night."

"Thanks," I said. "I will now."

Walking out of the alley, I was shocked and elated at the same time. Miss Blue Eyes had given me a swift kick in the nads. That doll had pulled one over on me, and I had been too lost in those eyes to catch it. I needed to discover why, considering their history, she would have helped the Rev. My brain couldn't stop from asking the big question: *Why was she covering for him?*

I felt like the biggest jerk in the world at the moment. But that was about to change.

I pulled my phone from my pocket and hit a number. Seconds later, Grayson answered.

"Are you on your way in, Jake?"

"Hank, time to put a bow on the Ripper case."

"No shit?"

"No shit, Hank. You are gonna smile."

"Okay."

I disconnected the call.

I got back into my car and headed to the precinct.

I floated into Hank's office and landed in the chair.

"Cap wants to see you pronto."

"Not ready to see him. Listen to what I've got."

I laid out my case for him clue by clue until I had the case buttoned up tight.

I needed only one more piece — the Rev himself.

My phone rang again.

I looked at Hank.

"Busy night all over," I said. "This is Hagan."

Hank sat back in his chair to wait.

"Good to hear from you, Hagan. How's it going?"

"Are you sittin' down, Jake?"

"I am."

"Jake! Holy Nellie's in the cradle and Bucky's in the woodshed, it's bad. Real bad. We found him. Or should I say, we found *them*."

"Found who, Hagan?"

"Reverend Cousins and I think Margaret Skimmer."

I leapt to my feet.

"It's too late to be teasing. You're serious?"

"Well, what's left of 'em both would be more accurate."

"Wait, Hagan. Hank, is there a speaker on this thing?"

Hank showed me where the button was.

"Hagan, you're on the speaker. I'm here with Hank."

"That's fine. You was right about the cabin, Jake. Them dogs got down here early and I sent 'em straight to the cabin after I had a long, hard chat with Junior. It was just s'posed to be a test. Well, heck with the test. I'll make it short and quick for now. Junior knew where Joshua was buried. 'Cause he's the one that buried 'im."

"Holy shit!" was all I could get out of my mouth.

Hagan continued.

"It didn't take them dogs but minutes to find him. But that ain't the end of it, Jake."

"Tell me."

"A few minutes later, them dogs found the body of Margaret Skimmer. Now, I ain't for sure yet about it, but I suspect we got a bunch of bodies out there. Some, Junior says, was put there by Joshua hisself. Maybe even Zyree. Junior will surely tell me more by the time I'm finished with 'im. But he says his daddy and Joshua was into some troubles regardin' underage girls. They took extreme measures to cover it all up. From the sound of it, they was literal about that.

"As I heard it said by the dog handlers, them dogs went to hollerin' like mad soon's their paws hit the dirt. It's gonna take some time to dig into all them lumps, but I think we gonna end up with quite a few bodies by the time this all's done. I have no idea how many of 'em are gonna be connected to Joshua and Zyree, but I expect there's gonna be more'n a few."

I was shocked and fought to recover my presence of mind.

"But you're sure you found Joshua Cousins?"

"Oh, yeah. We got him. Had his wallet in his back pocket. Money still in it."

"Do you have a time of death yet?"

"I'm gettin' ready to email the photos taken at the gravesite to you. The ME has only started the autopsy, but it appears he's been dead for 'bout ten years."

"Just about as long as he's been missing, then."

"Yep."

"Is there a cause of death yet, Hagan?"

"Get this, Jake. There's a knife wound in the top of his skull."

"Please tell me it was a seven-inch Liston blade."

"Can't tell you that at the moment. The ME is effortin' that as we speak. Listen, Jake. You be darn careful, 'cause whoever you got out there callin' herself Margaret Skimmer from Lemmin'berg, Ohio, well, sir, it just ain't so. I don't reckon I know who she is, mind ya, but I got a body out here buried with a driver's license in the back pocket of her jeans tells me with some certainty she ain't Margaret Skimmer.

"I gotta run, Jake. Sorry to just pop this onto ya and hang up. But we's poppin' crazy down here. Everything's poppin'. I'll email ya the report soon's I can. You be gosh dern careful, Jake. I mean it."

"I will. And thanks, Hagan."

But Hagan had already disconnected. I think he must have graduated from the Hank Grayson School of Phone Etiquette.

"Why didn't you tell him about Maddie?" asked Grayson.

"Why would I, Hank? Maddie Dumont, or whoever she truly is, is not dead. I thought I had her figured out. I really believed she was working with Cousins out here. But on the bright side, although I just lost my original suspect, I now have my *real* suspect. But that does me no good unless I can find her."

"I was afraid you were going to say that," said Hank.

"You watch. It takes time to stack dominoes, but they fall quickly. I got a feeling we're just at the beginning of the end. I'll know who Maddie is pretty soon. All shall be revealed in time. I'll tell you this, though. I'm sick of being her plaything. I'm just waiting for that one last clue and I'll have it worked out."

"Well, Jake, I hope you'll get the chance to wrap this up. But now Cap will be wanting a piece of you as well. No more delaying it."

We walked together to Captain Michael O'Shaughnessy's office. He was seated at his desk.

"You're fired!" he said upon seeing me walk in.

He sat back in his chair and blew a breath into the air.

"Good god, that felt good to say," he continued. "I've been wanting to say that for days. It's not true, as it turns out. But I'm glad to get it out my system. Sit down, the two of you."

I'm not certain, but I think my eyes were rolling around in my head from shock. *Why am I not being fired, retired, or tarred and feathered?* I wondered.

I sat down and waited for my answer.

"Jake, I know you've put your all into this case. I'm not questioning your commitment to your duty as a detective. What I am calling into question is your commitment to yourself, to your fellow officers, and to this department. There can be no double standard. I won't tolerate one. Because of your alcoholism, I was going to retire your ass. But upon reflection of your years of outstanding service to the NYPD, and with the support of the Personnel Bureau, I'm going to keep you on a while longer. There is one condition, however, to this magnanimous decision. You're going to complete a full substance abuse program, monitored by the department shrink. In other words, you're on probation until you successfully complete the program. Do you agree with this condition?"

"I do, Captain. It'll be a slam dunk, too. I've already quit drinking. Not because I feared retirement. I quit for my own reasons. But I know I've given you no reason to trust my word. I've quit before and failed. But I'm not finished with this case. It's not just still open, it's *way the hell* open."

"What are you talking about, Detective? I thought we have evidence that the witness is dead and the perp escaped. The case is busted."

"Want to hear a good story, Cap?" I asked.

He did. He sat wide-eyed and stunned as I told him all about what had transpired of late.

He questioned everything, but by the time I was done talking, I had convinced him that the case was still wide open. I just needed his trust one more time. I asked him to delay the commencement of my probation until I had wrapped this case up.

To his credit, he took several minutes to consider my request. I don't think he wanted to be made a fool of. He even asked Hank's advice. Hank agreed with me. Cap was no dummy, and not easily swayed to a different course once he had come to a decision. But the merits of my request were judged to be warranted. He agreed. And then he threw us both out of his office.

When I got back to my desk, I sat in my chair for another two hours and stared at the evidence board. Finally, with my eyelids drooping, I left the office and drove home to get some sorely needed sleep, fully expecting good things to happen when I awoke.

My cell phone went off like a siren. I looked at the clock on the nightstand: 10:13 a.m.

I pulled the phone from the nightstand and saw that it was Hagan calling.

"Here we go," I said, jumping up.

I answered.

"You've got more good news, don't you?"

"I'll tell you what I know and you can decide for yerself."

"Go for it."

"I'm gonna frustrate ya a bit," he started, "and I'm sorry for that. But I want ya to hear it the way I heard it just minutes ago."

I wished I had a glass of shine at that moment. I really could have used something to dull my receptors.

"Okay, Hagan" is all I could get past my lips.

His tone sounded ominous. I was expecting good news, but now I was in doubt. My unconscious must have known something my conscious didn't, because I felt myself sliding down into a black abyss.

"A pal of mine," he started, "Sawyer Barnett, Scott County Sheriff, come into my office just to say howdy on his way up to Lexington. We got to talkin' normal 'bout unimportant things at first. Then he tells me about all the talk goin' around about me gettin' cadaver dogs out into the Dan'l Boone. Says ever'one is hopin' to close more'n just a few files on long-ago cases.

"Then, Jake, I pull out some case files and we go talkin' 'bout all them lumps in the Dan'l Boone and who we think might be stuffed down in 'em. Then he spots a photo on the front of my desk. Now, here's we go on the wild ride, Jake."

Oh, geez, my head screamed. *What the hell is coming?*

"He asks me if Leann is in some kinda trouble. I ask Sawyer who he's talkin' 'bout. He points at your Maddie Dumont's photo and says, real calm-like, 'Her, Hagan. Leann Merrick. She in some kinda trouble?' "

It was a good thing I was seated on my bed, because my whole body went weak. I couldn't move, nor could I find words to vomit up out of me.

"You hear me, Jake?"

I wanted to answer. I tried to speak, but I couldn't give voice to a single syllable. All I could get for the effort was a small grunt.

"Yeah," Hagan said. "You got the same block in your throat I had in mine.... Made it hard for me to breathe, too."

I forced an "I..." up from the bowels of my shock. That was the best I could manage.

"Yeah, Jake, that about sums up my response as well. But there's more to it. Listen up, now. Shortly after my own heart attack, once my face stopped its scrunchin', ol' Sawyer adds, 'Too bad 'bout her sister goin' missin' like she did. It was hard on her. It was hard on the whole town. And I do believe her ma and pa wasn't ever right again neither. In fact, I think it was a contributin' factor to their car accident that kilt 'em both. I ain't sayin' it was suicide exactly, but they grew into a despondent nature that went deep. After that, Leann just slipped away, mentally and emotionally that is, for a good long while. Good thing she had family that cared for her. Lived out her younger days in Turkey Creek with her aunt and uncle. Good people. Had a bit of money. Took good care of her. Got her back into school and then the university. But personally, I don't think she was ever right in the head again. Don't think she was ever able to put it all behind her. She moved out of Turkey Creek a long while ago and I ain't heard nothin' 'bout her since. Have no idea where she's at now. I hope she's doin' okay, though, poor kid. So, Hagan, what's her photo doin' on yer desk?' "

I sat in silence, still stunned, for several seconds, then managed to rediscover my voice.

"So," I started, "Maddie's real name is Leann Merrick?"

"Oh, Jake, that ain't the half of it."

"What else?"

"We had us a good long chat with Junior. He spilt it all. The little girl that went missin' all them years ago? He said her name was Marlene Merrick. Leann is her sister. But not just her sister, Jake. They was twins."

As my brain searched the depth of its own abyss for more words, my eyes began an involuntary search for anything that contained alcohol. To my immediate chagrin, there was nothing anywhere close to me. "Oh, shit" were the only words my brain discovered.

"Yep, my thoughts exactly."

"Hagan, I see it all now. The Rev got Marlene Merrick with child. He killed her to prevent the news of it getting out. Leann, Maddie, found out about it years later, killed the Rev, and Junior helped her bury the body in exchange for her helping him pipeline the girls up to New York. I'm betting that if I dig deep enough, I'll find a connection between the magazine to the modeling agency."

"Well, there ain't got to be no diggin', Jake. Junior confirmed it all. But there's more."

"Yep," I said. "Mary Beth and Kerri Ann knew about Maddie killing their father."

"Actually, Jake, they was witness to it."

"And, Hagan, I realize now who some of the victims are up here. I think Mary Beth and Kerri Ann began extorting Maddie. She killed them and made it look like the Rev was in town doing his best to be like Jack the Ripper. I suspect the third killing was either a roommate or just someone to confuse the investigation."

"Sounds to me like you're workin' it all out, Jake."

"Might be, but Maddie's disappeared. This'll wrap up the murder investigation, but it won't close the case until I find her. She's been messing with me for a while now. I forgot how smart she is. I underestimated her. I won't do it again. Anything else, Hagan?"

"Ain't that enough?"

"For now it is. I'll have to prove my theory, but it's the best theory I have. Thanks, Hagan."

"I'll call if I have more."

"Same here. 'Bye."

I immediately called Hank and let him in on the news. We agreed to meet here at my apartment later that morning after he briefed the Captain.

CHAPTER 30

I showered and got dressed. I was feeling good and more assured that the end was now coming into focus.

I heard a sound behind me and turned around. I wished I hadn't.

Standing behind me was Maddie, holding a silenced pistol. She wasn't smiling.

"Back from the dead, I see," I puked out.

"You couldn't just stay drunk and lost, Jake? Was it too difficult for you to stay in the bottle? You were doing so well, but then you found your purpose and duty again. I'm really disappointed in you."

"Leann Merrick, you're under arrest for the murders of Reverend Joshua Cousins and Mary Beth and Kerri Ann Cousins and another person to be named later."

"Wow!" she said, smiling. "I don't know who you are, sugar, but what'd you do with my darlin' Jake?"

"Knock it off, doll. I mean it. This is official. Drop the piece."

Damnit all, she kept her smile. That beautiful, gorgeous glow remained on her face. Her lips were smooth and soft. I wanted to kiss those lips. I wanted to dive into that glow and never come up again. I instantly felt like the world's biggest asshole.

"Such a manly tone to your voice, Jakey boy. I'm always attracted to real men."

"You're under arrest. The game is over, Maddie. I'm sorry, doll, but I have to take you in for questioning."

That smile remained. There wasn't even a flicker of fear in her eyes. Not a quiver of disquiet on her face.

"Well, sweetie, I'm glad it's you that wants to arrest me and not some overdressed little Cub Scout with a big, scary gun."

I wanted to cry. I wanted to die on that very spot. I wanted to reach down into my soul and tear it to pieces. Instead, I stood still and sorrowful. She noticed that.

"Jake, dear, it's okay. Don't take it so hard. I've been expecting this for some time. Let me see that wonderful smile, baby. Come on. It's all going to be fine."

I managed just a hint of a smile. She saw it as a total grin.

"That's my big boy," she replied, making me feel so small and helpless. Like a child seeking approval for feeling vulnerable and weak.

"I can't very well be seen in public looking like this, though. May I freshen up a bit?"

She was toying with me again. That broke my heart more.

"You just don't get it, do you?"

"I get it. It changes nothing, but I get it. I do have a question, though. What gave me away?"

"The shadows, Maddie. You couldn't have seen shadows on the alley walls the night of the first murder."

"Is that it? Shadows on the alley?"

"It just doesn't work, Maddie. I was heading down Fifth Avenue earlier and saw shadows on an alley's walls. When I stopped to investigate them, I saw a work crew with a huge lamp. But after they turned it off, the shadows disappeared. It is therefore unlikely that you would have seen shadows that night to draw you into the alley. In fact, there were no shadows at all."

She nodded.

"I can see how that might be a problem. But that's all I could think of on the spur of the moment."

"But even at that, I was headed down a wrong trail. I figured you and the Rev were working together up here. That you were covering for him. I believed that. I really did. But when Hagan called with the news that Cousins' body was found, I found myself on the right trail. The trail that led me to you. Motive, means, and opportunity, Maddie. It all started to add up for me. The pieces began fitting together tightly."

"Oh, sounds very exciting, Jake. All that police talk. I think I'm getting wet."

"Motive. You killed the Rev for the sake of your sister. I suspect two of the recent bodies to be Mary Beth and Kerri Ann. They've been extorting you for some time. I guess you finally got tired of that."

"You're doing great so far, Jake."

"Means. You had the Rev's medical bag with the Liston blade. You left stab wounds in the hearts to establish the blade and aim the investigation toward the Rev, who had yet to be discovered."

"Keep going, Jake."

"Opportunity. The Cousins girls have been kept close to you for quite a while. The Valium in your office. You used it to drug them both. Then you murdered them and tried to lead me to Joshua Cousins as the murderer."

"Got it all worked out, it seems, Jake."

"Who benefitted? I guess that would be a big 'duh' there, uh?"

"Yes, I suppose so."

"Grayson had a big problem with where you were that night before running into me at Bobby's. We couldn't figure out what took you so long to get only a mile and half from the murder scene."

"I understand. The time doesn't work either, does it?"

"I was struggling with it until I figured it out."

"Oh, tell me, Jake. Please. I want to hear it."

"That first killing didn't go quite as planned. Got blood all over yourself. You had to go back home to change."

"You got me there, Jake."

"Mary Beth or Kerri Ann. I don't know which went first. But it had to be one of them. It only came to me very recently that you had to kill them. But how could you cut them up so savagely?"

"I hunted with my uncle for years. I've butchered many deer. The mess doesn't bother me in the least," she said with a smile.

"Then my next question is why? Why are you here, Maddie? Why aren't you on your way to somewhere else? You were dead. All you had to do was disappear."

"I could have, but once I found out about the discovery of Joshua's body, I had to speed things up. And, Jake, you're in love with me. I knew you'd never rest until you either found my body or figured out where I might have gotten to. So I just had to come here and make certain you couldn't do that. I can't have you messing up my future, too."

"How did you find out about the Rev?"

"A little birdie called me."

"Mercy Cousins or Junior. Yeah. It had to be one of them. I'm betting it was Mercy Cousins. She knew Junior had buried him. She called you. Does she know you killed her daughters?"

"She's crazy as a loon, Jake. She still believes Joshua killed them years ago."

"They *are* Junior's girls, right?"

"You got it."

"And the Rev didn't care?"

"Not at all. He had another agenda."

"Yeah. He knew Junior was banging Mercy, knew it for quite a while. He used the girls for his own nefarious reasons. And he knew Junior wouldn't raise a ruckus about it. After all, Junior and Zyree had dirt all over them as well. But the Rev used the girls to find other girls. Like your twin sister, Marlene."

"Yes. Like Marlene."

"But you fixed him, didn't you?"

"Damn right. Drove his favorite knife right through the top of his head."

"The Teufel bag?"

"You'll never find it. It's gone."

"Took a dive into the river, did it?"

"Nope. More lost to flames."

"Good thinking. How about Margaret Skimmer?"

"You tell me, Jake. You're pretty near killing it so far."

"Okay. She was killed by the Rev, too. He had some dealings with her that were going south. She probably threatened to expose him. It was a coincidence, really. She was a runaway. Not really known in the area. Probably heard about modeling opportunities through the pipeline. She got taken in by the Rev. Didn't like having to pay for the letter with favors to the Rev, Junior, or both. You found out he was up at the cabin with her. You went to kill him with the Cousins girls. Caught him in the act of slaying Margaret. There was a tussle. The Cousins girls helped subdue him. After all, they hated him as much as you did for what he did to them. You got your hands on his blade and bingo. You ventilated his skull. But now you had two bodies to bury. What to do? What to do?"

"You're doing great, Jake. Keep it going."

"The girls' daddy, Junior, had Mercy all over him. She couldn't let her girls go to prison as accessories to murder, so Junior dug the holes and buried the bodies. You, feeling an obligation now to Junior and his girls, agreed to help direct the runaways he sent to New York and you also agreed to get his daughters out of harm's way. But they became a problem for you. They began getting costly. You wanted out of it. They wanted more and more cash. It all had to end. So you ended them and tried to pin it on someone you knew was already dead. As for you, Margaret was dead and buried in an unmarked grave. Why not use her identity and hide your own. I mean, Leann might be found and connected to Marlene someday. And that would ultimately lead to the Rev. But Margaret was unknown. Her ID would be perfect cover. By being a runaway, she was already gone."

"And she was two years older. I'm younger now. Yea for me. So keep going, Jakey boy."

"You picked me because I'm drunk most of the time. You thought you could control me easily. Manipulate the investigation. Hell, you probably planted the letter of reference into your file. I just don't know how you did that."

"Does it really matter?"

"No, not really, I guess. But if it does, I'll get it out of you sooner or later during questioning. You knew a lot about the Rev through the girls. You learned about his habits and that he had come to New York. You studied the Ripper murders. You had about everything you needed. But I do have to add one tiny side observation to this. Although I've never seen Joshua's rhyming notes, I have to say *yours* were shit. Yeah, I just wanted to add that."

She laughed.

"They *were* terrible. I admit it. But they were still better than Joshua's."

"Is that right?"

"Take my word for it, Jake, mine are better."

"I guess I'll never know that for sure, but I do know this. As long as he was only missing, you had your suspect to hand to me. Anything and everything else about him could only have been speculated about. Never confirmed. But now? Well, the dogs are out, so to speak."

Wow! I heard you were good, but you nailed it. I had to make a quick decision about you. I cut the girls off. In hindsight, it wasn't a smart move on my part. The girls were about to call the police and turn me in. I grew desperate. They used to be such good girls. But New York got to them the way it does all Fifth Avenue Whores."

"I can imagine," I said. "They got into the party life pretty quick. You exerted some control over them for a while. Maddie was coming up in the world. She was coming into more cash all the time. She was an important person in this city. And the bribes she was taking to get certain manufacturers' clothing into the magazine was growing. You got them into all the biggest party bars. You got them all the hottest clothing, in all the hottest fashions. But then came the drugs. Then came a bit of hooking on the side to make some extra cash. But they grew older and more wasted on drugs. The big companies didn't want them seen in their fashions. Turning tricks became more difficult. Time to hit Maddie for more cash. Big cash now. After all, they had watched you plunge a knife into the head of a monster, but that dead monster was starting to pay off for them. Extortion breeds more evil. And finally, enough is enough. It would never end. The more you gave them to be quiet, the more they wanted. How did I do, doll?"

"Bingo, Jake. You figured it all out. But now it's not looking real good for you. Why did you have to dig so deep? Why couldn't you just drift through the investigation in your drunkenness? You could have just breezed through it and stayed drunk the way you have been the last few years. Hell, I could have even put some cash on you that could have sent you into a quiet and easy retirement. I'm not a bad person. Joshua Cousins was a bad person. I avenged my sister. I earned that right. As for the girls, I did my best to help them. But Joshua had already killed them a long time ago.

"And us, Jake. We could have been so happy together. Well, at least until I could complete what I had to do. But I would have let you down easy, baby. You would have been just fine. You could have lounged in the mist of your moonshine or Maker's Mark and told everyone about our wild affair for years to come. But you had to go dig deep."

"But Maddie, why me? How did you know to pick me as the investigator? How did you know I was a drunk? That's the part I still can't quite put together."

"It's not rocket science, Jake. The Cutley murder case a few months ago. Remember it?"

"Yeah."

"I followed you through the case. I studied you. And one night I followed you to Bobby's, in a great disguise, of course. I sat in the booth right next to you. I watched you get hammered. Heard you talk about your 'messed-up' life. I knew right then and there you were my guy. I could now move my plan forward."

"Had it all planned, did ya?"

"Not to a T. But I'm good under pressure. I think quickly in a pinch. I adapt, improvise, and overcome better than most. I have to in order to excel in the world of high fashion as I do. And you were perfect. At least for a while."

"Maddie. What the hell?"

"Exactly, Jake. What the hell? What the hell do I do now?"

"I don't get it."

"I know, Jake. That sloshed brain of yours was doing so well for me. Why did you have to go and sober up? I was so counting on you staying shitfaced. Now I have to take care of you and get the hell out of town before I'm really ready to. Damn you, Jake! I had you where I wanted you. I was going to kiss you passionately and leave. It was to be a great exit."

"But I screwed up your dramatic departure. You had to go to Plan B — your kidnapping and murder by Joshua and his subsequent escape. So, who played Joshua?… Wait! Don't tell me. An out-of-work actor. Am I right?"

"Partially. He was a model/voice actor. He didn't work out too well though. I was forced to go to Plan C. A voice synthesizer."

"I noticed the change in the voice. Clever. What happened to the model?"

"Turns out he wasn't as dumb as I thought he was. He figured things out. Then he got greedy. Thankfully, he wasn't a strong swimmer either."

"I see. Took an unscheduled dive into the east river, did he?"

"Yep, after a mickey, of course."

"Of course. So…a voice synthesizer, huh?"

"Isn't it just stunning what advancements have been made in electronic technology today? I found it in a store. Small little thing. Fits in your hand. I got a real kick out of hearing my own voice sound like a man's. I think it came off very lifelike, don't you?"

"I don't do technology. It sucks."

"Well, I hadn't planned to use it that way, but I'd say it worked extremely well."

"So you made a fool of me and then left me hanging with nothing to do but accept the possibility that you were dead. To top it off, you were going to leave me believing that I had failed," I said. "That was so sweet of you."

"Yes. It's true, Jake. But that fat-ass sheriff had to screw that up for me. Thanks a bunch."

"Okay, Maddie. I understand. I don't know what I can do about it. And since you were planning to dump me anyway, I guess I really don't care anymore. So, there it is. I guess you'll have to kill me. It's funny. The moment I met you, I knew you were going to be my end. So just do it, doll."

She pulled the trigger.

I don't know why I was surprised. But I was. I felt the slug bounce off one of my ribs and drive deeper into my chest. I hit the ground still conscious, then watched her disappear out my front door without another word.

I could hardly breathe. The bullet must have penetrated one of my lungs. It felt as if I was drowning. I felt really woozy, then a chilling blackness rolled in over me.

CHAPTER 31

Fuzzy light filtered through my partially closed eyes. I heard voices, but I couldn't make out what was being said.

After a time, the light began to grow brighter and my vision grew sharper until I found myself staring up at Grayson.

"Welcome back, Jake," he said softly.

"Wha…what?"

"I said welcome back."

"What happened?" I eked out.

"You died."

"What?!"

"Yeah. The doctor said you were dead for over four minutes. They brought you back and have kept you in a medically induced coma for the past three days to let you heal a bit. But you're back now. You are one lucky son of a bitch."

"What happened, Hank?"

"She shot you. Lucky for you, she's a shitty shot."

"Who?"

"I suspect it was Miss Blue Eyes, Jake. Maddie Dumont shot you."

"Oh, god. I remember now. Where is she?"

"She's gone, Jake. She's gone."

"Damn. Sorry, Hank."

"It's a real bitch, but I'm glad you're still with us."

"How? How did I survive?"

"I decided to come to your apartment early. I found you on the floor in the nick of time."

I nodded as he chuckled.

"But Maddie."

"She got away, Jake. She got clean away. I'm sorry, buddy. I know you must feel real bad about that."

"I knew it, Hank. The moment she exploded into my life, I knew she was to be the instrument of my demise."

"Well, ol' man, you weren't wrong. Just glad it was a temporary state of being. Hey, did you see a white light?"

"I saw only blackness, Hank. The same as when I'm passed out from a good drunk."

Grayson laughed.

Three weeks passed before I felt anything close to normal.

Something really drove me mad during that time — something that I had to do to satisfy myself.

After I was discharged, I went home and stayed to myself for three days thinking quite a bit about a lot of things.

Finally, having made a huge decision, I drove into the precinct to surprise everyone.

And surprise them I did.

I got a hero's welcome, but I made it a point to single out the real hero — Hank Grayson.

I walked into his office. He dropped his pen to the desk and rose to greet me with a hug. He was reluctant to take the credit due him for saving my life, but after some prodding, he just smiled and nodded.

"You're making too much of it, Jake. I'm just happy to see your sorry ass again. This place wouldn't be the same without you. And I just couldn't have it that way."

I patted him on the shoulder.

"By the way, you're fired," he said, straight-faced.

"To hell with you, Hank. I quit!"

He snickered and moved back to his chair.

"Either way, you're outa here."

"Hank. I came in today to tell you that very thing."

"You're being serious?"

"I'm done, Hank. I can't hack it anymore. I've lost my touch. I almost died. Well, I guess I did die. You know what I mean. I don't have it in me to continue. Next time I might not be so lucky. I need something quiet. I need a change in my life."

Hank leaned back in his chair.

"All joking aside, Jake, I hear you. And I don't blame you."

"I'm serious, Hank. I quit the juice, too."

"Just like that?"

"Just like that. I dumped four gallons of shine down the drain the other day along with three bottles of

Maker's Mark and a bunch of others. I haven't missed them."

"Whoa!"

"I feel so stupid, Hank. I was so taken in by those blue eyes. She was everything I had ever dreamed of. I should have known it was wrong right off. But a drunk doesn't always see things clearly."

"I don't think it's that, Jake. I think you've just seen too much, period. A lot weaker guys would have quit long before this. You hung in there and you deserve a change in your life.... So, what's next for you?"

"I don't know. I really don't. Being a cop is all I've ever known. I'm lost. I don't have a plan. I just know that I can't be here anymore, doing this."

I pulled my gold shield from my coat pocket and dropped it onto Hank's desk. He stared at it, but made no move to retrieve it.

I then noticed something missing from the shelving behind Hank's desk. I stared at the shelving. My eyes must have glazed over.

"You going bat shit on me now, Jake?" said Grayson.

"Hank, what's wrong with your shelf?"

"My shelf?"

He turned around and stared at it for a few seconds and then turned back to me.

"What the hell are you talking about?"

I didn't answer right away. I just scanned the shelving behind him again. And then it struck me.

"Hank, where's your baseball? Where's your Derek Jeter signed baseball?"

He smiled and opened his desk drawer. Reaching into it, he picked it up and brought it out for me to see.

"Right here," he said.

"Why is it in the drawer? It's usually up on the shelf."

"I broke the plastic holder the other…"

"Oh, SHIT!" I shouted, interrupting him.

"What?! *What*?!" he screamed back.

"The shelf, Hank! The shelf!"

"What about it?"

I jumped to my feet and grabbed my shield.

"I'm not finished just yet, Hank. I know where Maddie is."

"Where?" asked Grayson.

"Can't tell ya, Hank. Plausible deniability."

"What?"

"I need some more time off, Hank. Goodbye."

I charged out of his office and ran to my car yelling at the top of my lungs.

"*IT AIN'T OVER UNTIL THE FAT LADY SINGS. AND BABY, THAT CHUBBY BITCH IS JUST WARMING UP.*"

CHAPTER 32

It had taken me four weeks before I had recovered enough from the bullet wound inflicted by my Lady Fair to move around as I did. I was breathing much better, but I was far from fully recovered. Still, I had an unquenchable thirst to travel to high altitudes in lower latitudes.

I sold my car for airfare and more, and booked a one-way flight from New York to Lima, Peru.

I couldn't give a rat's ass about the culture, the people, the incredible geology, or the goddamned ruins. I was hell-bent on a mission of revenge, finally and totally. And I wasn't planning on making it back to New York. At least not alive.

Landing at Lima's international airport and clearing customs and immigration, I was met by Capitán Enrique Alvarez of the Policia Nacional del Peru.

We shook hands and his eyes glistened with joy. He remembered me very well. And why not? Five years ago I had helped get him cleared of any responsibility during an unfortunate fender bender in the city. I thought the poor sap was going to have a heart attack. He sincerely believed that if he was found guilty of negligence in the mishap, he would stand before a firing squad.

I worked on behalf of my brother officer and made the discovery that it was completely the cab driver's fault. He had lied about the cause of the accident. I busted him for fraud and got all the charges against Enrique dropped and his passport returned to him. I felt good for the undertaking. And I seemed to have made an everlasting friend for my effort.

I drove him out to JFK on the date of his departure and escorted him to the gate. I left him at the gate with a solid handshake. He made a solemn promise to take good care of me should I ever find myself in Lima, Peru.

At the time, of course, I never imagined that I'd actually be standing in the Lima International Airport, shaking Enrique's hand and taking him up on his promise.

"And what are you doing here, my friend?" he asked, a huge smile sweeping across his face, probably as shocked to see me as I was to see him. "Your mysterious phone call telling me you were coming here has had me intrigued ever since."

"Enrique, here it is plain and simple. I came here to kill someone. And that, my friend, is the pure truth of it."

His face twisted into a grimace for a few seconds and then he smiled.

"A woman, no doubt," he said with a grin.

"A woman, Enrique."

"They have a darkness about them, no?"

"This one is as dark as they come."

"She broke your heart, no? It is easy for them to break a man's heart."

"Yeah. Ain't that the truth, amigo. But this one is a real killer."

"They all are, *mi hermano querido.*"

"Me what?"

"My dear brother. They are all murderers of a sort. I have been killed by the love of a bad woman many times myself."

He laughed.

"You don't understand right now. But you will by the time my story is finished," I said.

"How about a drink, my friend? A drink and you can tell me your story."

"I don't drink anymore. But I'd be honored to buy you one or two."

"Such a change in you, amigo."

"That's true."

"Fine. I'll have a Pisco Sour as you begin your story. It is Peru's national drink."

"Well, you just go for it, then. I wouldn't want to be disrespectful of international protocol," I said, grinning.

Enrique chuckled.

"Come then, my friend."

An hour and ten minutes later, Enrique sat with his mouth agape and his original Pisco Sour sitting on the table in front of him — now warm and untouched.

"*Madre de la bebé Jesús,*" he said.

"I ain't got a clue what you just said, but I'd translate that as 'Holy shit.'"

"Something like that," he said, still staring at me, his expression one of utter astonishment.

"Jack the Ripper, you say?"

"You got it."

"And she killed you?"

"I was clinically dead for some four minutes."

"*La puta perra de Satanás.*"

"I don't know what that means either," I admitted, "but yeah, that's about it."

"Jake. Per the laws of Peru, I cannot allow you to act officially here. But by *my* laws, I'd say you have no choice but to try. I want to help you, but would be shot for allowing such a thing to take place."

"Calm yourself, Enrique. I would never ask you for that. I just need you to help me find her. Then you go. I'll finish what I came here for on my own. Hey, I've already been dead. How bad can it be after that?"

Enrique smiled and nodded.

"I owe you, my friend. I can help you find her. I can do that. Do you know where to start looking for her?"

I pulled a small piece of paper from my pocket and handed it to him. He unfolded it and read what I had written.

"Ah, Piquillacta," he said. "You believe she is there?"

"I'm willing to bet my life on it…again."

"It is a distance from here, Jake. A plane ride to Cuzco, a short drive south."

"I've got the money for any tickets we might need."

Enrique guzzled his warm Pisco Sour in one gulp. He snapped his fingers and smiled.

"Then we shall go, amigo," he said.

One hour and twenty minutes by jet from Lima to Cuzco. A twenty-minute ride south in a National Police cruiser and we arrived at the Piquillacta archaeological site.

A friendly archaeologist pointed us to the main office. I stood, trembling slightly.

Enrique noticed.

"You can prepare for these moments, amigo, but it is always a difficult thing to confront your heart."

"It is, but I don't have any choice in the matter. I've got to make this right, for a lot of people."

"You've got to make sure you obey our laws, Jake."

"I really don't want this, Enrique. I'd rather take her in my arms and kiss her to death."

"Love, Jake. It is a disease not of the heart, but of the brain."

"A Kentucky sheriff calls it dark magic."

"Amigo, whatever it is, to be sure it is dark sometimes."

"Yeah. The darkest."

"Why don't you let me arrest her? I'll find something to charge her with. I can hold her until you get the paperwork to bring her back to New York."

"I have to confront her here and now. I have to face her. I *need* to face her."

"I don't know what else to tell you, except to turn the brain off and do what you must."

"Sounds good to me, Enrique. Okay. I'm going to get this done."

"I don't believe she will go back to the U.S. with you willingly.

"I have to try. I can't let her get away with what she's done."

"But what she's done was back in the U.S. She has broken no laws here. I checked. She's clean. I am helpless to help you."

"I know. I know."

I drew in a deep breath and exhaled until my lungs were empty. I drew in another breath and glanced at Enrique.

"Is self-defense a defensible position here in Peru?"

"Oh, Jake. I thought you were joking about that."

"Just asking."

"It is, but you must make certain about it. Leave no doubt, Jake.... Oh, I wish you did not ask me that question."

"I was just asking, Enrique. Just asking."

"I think it would be better for me to remain out here. Then I will know nothing for which I can be shot."

I smiled.

"Tried that myself. Didn't work out so well for me."

Enrique snickered.

"*Si*. That is true."

"Okay," I said, drawing in another breath and exhaling hard. "Here goes nothing."

I pulled my cell phone from my pocket and hit a button on it.

I walked into her office and laid my cell phone down on her desk.

Shock distorted her face.

"*Jake!*" she said, looking up.

Shock must have distorted my face as well. She looked nothing like she did in New York. Her hair was dark brown and so were her eyes. She was dressed in a simple blue denim work shirt and blue jeans. She wore little if any makeup. I had to admit it, she looked dull and unimpressive.

"Hi ya, doll," I said, grinning. "Surprise!"

I was blocking the door. Her eyes fixed on it immediately, but she was trapped. She'd have to plow through me to get to it. She knew I wouldn't allow it. She knew she had no escape.

She relaxed, stood up, then smiled.

"Hi, Jake."

"You've changed your look," I said.

"I'm going for the down-home look now."

"Yeah, not really working all that good for me. Your brown eyes. Contacts?"

"No, Jake. I took the blue contacts out."

"Oh, my. Well, Maddie dear, I just gotta say it. You're not so hot anymore. Rather dull, in fact."

"That's the look I was going for, Jake. Don't really want to stand out here."

"Smart. Well, it works. You accomplished the look you were shooting for. You're sort of a gagger now, lady."

She chuckled.

"You're not hurting my feelings, Jake. What you think of my appearance doesn't mean shit to me. This look suits my needs now."

Okay, it was petty of me to toss those lame insults at her, I know. Hell, it was pathetic. And when given the choice to either walk the high road or the low road, I went straight to the gutter. But I was hurt. Not from the bullet, but from the hole she had blasted through my heart. I wanted her to know that. I wanted her to feel a piece of my pain. But it was stupid and trivial. I admit that. She knew it, too. And what made it worse was that she chose to walk a higher path.

"And you, Jake, you're not smelling of booze. Looks like you got a new lease on life. I'm happy for you."

"Yeah, I bet you are," I replied, still wallowing in the sewer.

"I'm serious, Jake. I'm truly pleased by your transformation."

"Yeah, well, dying sort of changes one's perspective."

"Dying? Now, Jake, although you're not so hot-looking yourself at the moment, you don't look dead, much to my regret."

"You shot me, lady."

"Yeah. I know. I was there, remember? But I guess I didn't shoot you well enough."

"Oh, you succeeded. I was clinically dead for over four minutes. But hey, I'm baaaack."

"I'll have to do it better next time."

"That's it? No 'Sorry, Jake dear. Didn't mean to pop a cap in your ass'?"

"No, Jake. I'm not sorry about that. I'm only sorry I didn't do it right."

"Well, we can discuss it more later. Ready?"

Maddie smirked.

"If you came here expecting to take me back, Jake, you should know that I've invested a lot of money here, in all the right places, to develop high connections that will prevent that from ever happening."

"Nah, doll. I didn't come here to take you back."

"I see. What then, Jake? What did you come here for?"

"I came to get an apology from you. May I remind you once again? You shot me, lady."

Maddie laughed.

"Seriously? An apology? For shooting you? You're an idiot, Jake. But you're not that big an idiot. Come on, spill it. Why are you here in Peru, Jake Brewer?"

"You took my life, doll. I'm here to take yours."

"Is that it? You came all this way just to kill me?"

"Who said anything about killing you? I said I'm here to take your life. Well, that's not exactly what I meant to say. What I meant to say was that I came here to take your happiness from you."

"Really? Take my happiness away? Oh, you are so precious. And how will you do that, Jake?"

"I visited your old office a while back. I was just trying to find some closure to this game we played. A Ms. Massé was kind enough to meet with me. A funny thing. She had been so busy with taking over your job, she hadn't had the time to personalize her new office. I got to looking around. Not a thing had changed. Everything in there was as you left it. Except for one item. A very interesting item."

Maddie frowned.

My eyes searched around her office. They found what they were seeking.

I walked to the shelving on the wall next to her desk and picked up the Incan statue that had been kept on the side shelf in her office at *Le Chic Fashions*. I rolled it in my hand.

"Damn it," she said. "So that's how you found me. I knew I should have left it behind. But I just couldn't."

"I know. You said it was the most important thing in your life. As long as you had this, you said, you'd always be happy."

"Jake. I walked away from *Le Chic Fashions* with millions. I'll give you five million just to walk away right now. Just put that down and I'll make you disgustingly rich. You can lavish in Maker's Mark for years. Would that be apology enough for shooting you?"

"Wow! That's probably more than I could spend during what's left of my sorry life. But…two things, lover. I'm not here to get rich. And I quit drinking altogether. No, actually, I came here to take your happiness, like I said."

"Jake, put that down. I'm serious."

"You're serious? Oh, I know that. But you did say that you stole this statue, right? By rights it belongs to the people of Peru."

"Jake, I'm not kidding. Put that down."

"Not gonna happen, doll. You see, my amigo outside, Enrique, he's with the national police. I think he'd appreciate the return of the artifact. I'll bring him in and ask him."

Her teeth clenched tightly. That beautiful face scrunched up into an ugly contortion of twisted flesh.

The letter opener, laying at rest on her desk, was snatched up in a flash. She lunged at me. I parried her blow, grabbed her wrist, got hold of the letter opener, and jammed it into her throat.

I let it go and stood back. I grabbed my cell phone and held it up so she could see it, although I don't think she cared at that particular moment about anything else except the letter opener in her throat.

While she gagged and sputtered and blood gushed everywhere, I clicked off the video feature.

"My get-out-of-jail-free card, doll. I Learned how to use the video feature on the plane coming down," I said. "Don't you just love technology?"

Her eyes rolled up in her head and she hit the floor with a sickly wet thud — dead.

I felt great.

EPILOGUE

I watched from my office as Hagan Duggar walked through the front door and up to the desk deputy.

"Is he in?" I heard him say.

"He is, Hagan."

"May I step back and visit with him?"

"Of course."

Hagan stepped through the gate and walked back to his former office and stuck his head in through the open door.

"I hear a chicken steak callin' me, Jake."

I chuckled and sat back from the computer keyboard.

"Hi ya, Hagan. I hear it calling me, too. Come on in and take a seat. I'll be able to go in a bit. I just gotta finish filling in these requisition forms on the computer and send them to the printer. I need to get them signed so I can hire that new deputy."

Hagan sat down and grinned. He pulled a flask from his back pocket, opened it, and took a swig. He held it out to me. I waved it off.

"That's not me anymore, Hagan."

He screwed the top back on and slid it back into his pocket.

"Just wanted to make sure. Hey, congratulations on your election win. I knew you'd be a shoe-in for sheriff."

"Well, thanks to your support."

"Heck, Jake. You're closin' more old cases than I can even remember knowin' of. You got an army of rabid followers hereabouts. You're appreciated here, Jake."

"I sure wish you would have stayed on the job, Hagan."

"Bein' mayor has its perks, Jake."

I chuckled.

"Yeah, I bet it does. Don't have to go out digging around in forest lumps anymore."

He laughed.

"No, sir. That's what you're for. Is he comin' today?"

"Yeah. I think he's on his way into the office right now."

"Things are gonna change, Jake. I'm excited for the future of these parts."

Hank Grayson walked through the front door, through the gate, and through my door.

"Welcome to Kentucky, Hank," I said. "I hope you like chicken steak."

"I do," he said, grinning, "and I hear you're hiring a new deputy today."

"I am, buddy. I got your badge right here."

THE END

ABOUT THE AUTHOR

Val Edward Simone was born in Seattle, Washington, and has been writing since 1980.

Val has published action/adventure novels; historical fiction; western novels; short stories; a collection of thoughts, musings, and observations; a collection of children's short stories; and several children's picture books. He continues to work on many other novels, short stories and screenplays.

He is also a strong advocate of early childhood development through the arts and continues to support all efforts toward helping children discover their own creativity through reading, writing, and drawing.

Val currently lives and writes in Arizona.

His websites:
Valedwardsimone.com

Connect with Val and Other Books

<u>Connect with Val Online:</u>
Instagram: @valedwardsimone
Facebook: valedwardsimone

Other Books by Val Edward Simone

Novels/Novellas
Blood Trackers: One Crazy Love Story
Blood Trackers 2: Revenge of an Angel
About Things I Lost Long Ago…scribblings from a foolish heart
The Wondrous Life of a Long-Ago Man
Comes the Devil to Crooked Creek
Captain Delightable's Magical Tales of a Minchon Warrior
A Minute of Forever
Into the Light Boldly…an odyssey of self-discovery
The Firestone…Is Mankind Ready?
The Story
Adventures at Dead River
The Art of Living Between Hell and Breakfast
5th Avenue Whore
Love Most Foul (Coming Soon)

Short Stories
Manifest Destiny
The Secret Life of Goner Andling
Love Bytes
Dragons Within
The Problem with Dragons
The Unfortunate Dragon
The Fairy Collection
Through the Waterfall
Fairy Forgotten
Emily's Wish
Kaylee's Secret
The Wizard of Sebastianville

Children's Picture Books
Felix
The Gingerbread Pony
The Littlest Bell
Mean Muley McGrudge
Otto and Kevin
Proton Gator
Sammy Sparrow Spy

Children's Coloring Book
Proton Gator & Friends Coloring Book